NICK'S CHOICE
(*In Your Arms* Series Book 1)

Charlotte S. Snead

Published by Van Rye Publishing, LLC
www.vanryepublishing.com

Library of Congress Control Number: 2019904648
ISBN-13: 978-0-9982893-6-6
ISBN-10: 0-9982893-6-1

Dedication

This book is dedicated to wives and mothers,
especially all those mothers of preschoolers I have had the privilege
of mentoring for over twenty years.
You do the toughest job in the world, and I honor you.
I believe in the next generation, because of you!

Contents

CHAPTER 1

The Marine

"AT EASE, Corporal."

Corporal Nick Costas slipped into parade rest, his hands locked tightly behind his back. His eyes didn't waver from the lieutenant's face.

The officer waved him to a chair. "Take a load off, Corporal. We need to talk."

Skepticism hovered on Nick's face—a wariness that gave the lieutenant pause. But he slowly lowered himself to the chair in front of the desk and waited.

"I guess you figured out you've been booted upstairs?"

Nick watched with the same expectant, cautious look in his chocolate brown eyes.

"I told Gunny what to do with you, but he had a few words to say. Seems he's given you a few chances, and you let him down."

Nick's head dropped, but he quickly looked up. "I'm sorry about that, Lieutenant. Gunny's a good guy."

"You're restricted to base for ninety days and demoted to E-3, is that clear?" Nick nodded. "I wanted to make it E-2, but Gunny felt it would demoralize you. He's no softie, so I was surprised. 'The kid's a good Marine. We need to give him a chance,' he told me. Gunny loves the Marines and won't tolerate anyone who makes the Corps look bad.

1

He gave me a little light reading." The lieutenant picked up Nick's military records and dropped them on his desk. "He's right. You are a good Marine. The first one I've ever met who passed IST and didn't have to go through the full PEP. How'd you manage that?"

"I prepared for enlistment for a year and a half. Studied the requirements and got myself ready."

"You did two dead-hang pull-ups, forty-eight crunches in two minutes—four more than the requirement—and ran almost two miles in thirteen point two minutes—almost a half-mile more than the requirement. You must've wanted to be a Marine pretty badly."

"Yes, sir."

"Why, Corporal?"

Nick shrugged. "I wanted to be the best. It's a good gig: three squares a day, a bed, and a roof over my head. I never had it so good."

Lieutenant Jack Anderson's eyes scanned Nick's face. He saw no hint of sarcasm. "You like the Marines?" Nick nodded. "Then why do you give us so much grief? Your first leave you were almost AWOL. You've had more quarter-decks than any man should survive. You could've run across America four times."

Nick suppressed a grin but said nothing.

Anderson flipped a page, his eyes widening as he read on. "These scores on your Core Values, Marine History, and Code of Conduct tests are perfect. You studied ahead?"

"Yes, sir."

"You dismantled the rifle blindfolded in record time and passed the swim test in full flak gear. I see why Gunny calls you good potential, but you're no use to the Corps if you can't get a handle on yourself, Costas." *Was that a tear in the kid's eyes?*

"Yes, Lieutenant, I understand. I'll try harder. I won't disappoint Gunny again."

The lieutenant rubbed his hand over his eyes. The clock above his head jerked with a click that Nick heard in the silent room.

A muscle ticked in the young Marine's jaw, and he blinked rapidly. His eyes shifted when he realized the officer was looking at him.

"Okay, kid, what do you like to do?"

Nick stared at him without comprehension.

"I asked what you like to do. What jobs do you enjoy? Other than food prep. You've had so much KP you could qualify for a sous-chef. What have you seen in the Corps that you'd like to do?"

"I heard the Marine Band at Pendleton, Lieutenant. I like those uniforms. They're slick. I'd like to wear a uniform like that."

"How old are you, Costas?"

"Eighteen."

Anderson frowned. The kid was young, though somehow he seemed older, worn down by life. He'd seen the wariness in his eyes. He was small—probably not more than five feet eight inches tall—but compact, muscular, and in perfect shape. Just eighteen years old, according to the record in front of him. Jack sighed. "It's tough to get into the president's band. Most of those guys have studied music all their lives, been to music schools—some of them are lifers. What instrument do you play?"

Nick shrugged. "None. I never had the money for an instrument, never took band in school."

Anderson flipped to a page in the records. GED—the kid had a GED. Costas dropped out of school at sixteen but had a nearly perfect score on his GED. "That pretty much lets the band out, doesn't it?"

Nick suppressed a sigh.

"So, why'd you drop out of school, Costas?"

"I ran away from my foster home. It's hard to catch the bus when you live under a bridge. You can't exactly go to school without a shower and clean clothes. I went to the school board office, got a GED prep book, went to the recruiter and got the Marine enlistment stuff, and studied."

It was Anderson's turn to nod without a word. The silence lasted until Nick shifted in his chair. The lieutenant seemed to wait, almost like he was listening to someone Nick couldn't see. "Let's revisit the band idea. Ever do any electronics, sound systems?"

Nick brightened. "I used to help with stage productions when I was in school. Ran the soundboard."

A grin split Anderson's face. He picked up his phone. "Corporal, when is the Marine Band coming to the base?" he said into the receiver. Satisfied, he hung up and looked at Nick. "You are to return to barracks. You will remain in quarters and do what Gunny requires. In two weeks, the Marine Band comes to the base. You will be assigned to help: grunt work, carry and lift, string and run wires, and be a gofer. Don't blow it, Costas. I want to see what you're made of. Don't make me sorry."

Nick sat in the chair and didn't move while Anderson moved his records to the side of his desk and turned to other paperwork.

"You are dismissed, Corporal. Your reduction in pay is retroactive to the date of the infraction. No more fights. Other Marines are not the bad guys."

Nick sprung to his feet and gave a smart salute. He let out a long-held breath.

Anderson rose, returned the salute, and added, "Just where and why did you get that knife anyway, Costas?"

"In the market, Lieutenant. I grew up in the barrio. Small Hispanic kids like me needed to level the playing field—lots of big NBA recruits in the next block."

Anderson looked at him steadily. "Were you into gangs, Costas?"

"No, just tried to save my a . . . skin, Lieutenant."

Anderson smothered a smile. It was impossible not to like this kid with the dancing eyes. Somebody had to give him a chance, and it looked like the Corps was the only one he had left. He nodded curtly and repeated, "Dismissed." They exchanged salutes, and Nick left.

Gunnery Sergeant Randy MacDowell stood up with a question in his eyes when Nick walked out of the office. He laid his hand on the boy's shoulder but turned to the secretary when she hung up the receiver. "The Lieutenant wants you in his office, Gunny. Take a seat, Corporal."

MacDowell entered the office and closed the door behind him.

Anderson stood up and exchanged a salute with MacDowell. "You're right, Gunny, something about that kid gets to me, but we don't have time to babysit him. He's gotta man up."

"I've spent a lot of time with him, Lieutenant."

"Obviously," Anderson said dryly.

"He's got scars on his back—bad ones. The guys ride him about it. Call him tiger-fighter, that kind of thing. The boys tell me this fight started when the other guy—who is a bad Marine, in my opinion—was picking on a timid kid. Costas stepped in, and the bully referred to his mother in unflattering terms and said ugly things about his heritage."

"So, where'd he get the scars?"

"Abuse in the foster care system, sir."

Anderson let out a curse, unusual for him. "Unbelievable. Don't they monitor those homes? What happened to his parents?"

"Never knew a father, and the last time he saw his mother he was five. She was hauled off to jail, and he spent months in the hospital, malnourishment and old fractures. It's in his medical history. He came into the Corps and immediately went on double rations. Apparently, he'd been living on the streets for some time, but his test scores were out the wazoo. He's a good kid at heart."

Anderson waved off his next comment. "I know you like him, Mac. I've returned him to your nursery. Put him on KP, whatever, and in two weeks assign him to help with the Marine Band when it comes. He says he's done sound in high school, and he likes the uniforms. Maybe we can find something he likes, he's good at, a niche. It's the best I can think of."

MacDowell rose and snapped off a salute. "I hope we don't both regret this, Lieutenant."

"Me, too, Mac. But something needs to lead to redemption in that kid. He's never had a break."

Gunnery Sergeant MacDowell agreed. "He's polished my boots until he wore the leather off them. Told me the Corps wasn't so bad: he had a roof over his head, three squares a day, and a bed. Sounds like the Corps is the closest thing to family he's ever known."

"Yeah, he told me that, too. God help him make the most of it. He's running out of rope here. I'll pray for him."

Mac nodded, about-faced, and left. When he entered the outer office, he said, "Come on, kid, looks like you made it by the skin of your teeth again."

Nick rose and followed. "Thanks for sticking up for me, Gunny."

"Don't make me regret it, Corporal. Let's go take those stripes off. What'd he bust you to?"

"E-3, Gunny."

"He recommended E-2. He cut you a break. He was pretty ticked off when you sent Douglas to the hospital." Nick opened his mouth. "Don't say anything, Costas," Mac said, cutting off Nick's comment. "You owe me a five-mile run and one hundred push-ups. You think we can find a mountain to climb in this God-forsaken country?"

"Kuwait isn't so bad, but I feel naked without my sidearm. Lots of hostile folks out there."

"Rules of Engagement, Corporal."

"I know, Article 91, Gunny."

"You've got the Uniform Code of Military Justice memorized, Costas, so here's another lawful order: don't screw me over again. I'm out on a limb for you. Report to KP at fifteen hundred hours, after you've given me those one hundred push-ups."

"Yes, Gunny."

Mac dropped a hand on Nick's shoulder briefly. "Let's get back. Douglas is out of the infirmary today. Steer clear of him, you hear me?"

"Yes, Gunny."

* * *

Two weeks of KP, one thousand four hundred push-ups, and five five-mile runs later, Nick reported to the sergeant major with the Marine Band brought in to entertain the troops. "Lance Corporal Costas reporting for duty, Sergeant Major." Nick smartly saluted.

The Marine Band Director, Sergeant Major Johnson, glared at him. "Where's your other stripe, Corporal? Seems you have one missing. I'm not here to run some sort of reform school. You got that? I have to take what they give me, but I've got no time for slackers, that clear?"

"Yes, Sergeant Major."

"Move those crates to the stage and run those wires to the sound pit. Move it, move it! We've got a show to put on at nineteen hundred hours. You cost me five minutes, and the other stripe is gone, you hear me?"

"Yes, Sergeant Major."

Nick hustled to back-breaking chores without complaint, rapidly moving crates by dolly to the stage and stringing wires without complaint under the careful guidance of the band's stage director, Master Sergeant Miller.

"Take a break, kid," Miller said, handing Nick a Coke. "You haven't stopped since we got here."

Nick looked at the sergeant with wary eyes and finally reached out his hand and took the Coke.

"It's not a trap, kid. Everyone's entitled to a break, even in this man's Marine Corps."

A smile edged on Nick's lips. "Thanks, Sergeant. It's hot in this country. I thought L.A. was hot, but this beats all I ever saw."

"You got that right. Let's sit a minute, and then you can help me uncrate this soundboard." Miller nodded to the crate in front of them.

Nick's eyes lit up.

"You ever run a soundboard?"

"In high school. But it was nothing like this big mother."

"Courtesy of Uncle Sam. Nothing but the best."

Nick saw that when he helped lift it out of its cushioned crate. His eyes got large as they traveled across the switches and levers. "Wow," he said, in awe.

Miller liked the chocolate-eyed kid. He appreciated quality, that's for sure. "Maybe, if we have time, I can show you a few things. Would you like that?"

Nick's eyes leaped from admiring the soundboard to Miller's face in unbelief. "Yes, Sergeant, I would," he almost whispered.

Sergeant Miller checked an urge to run his fingers across the kid's head and pull him into a bear hug. "Let's hustle then."

Nick bent his head and back to the work.

"Sergeant Miller." Nick turned and saw the hostile sergeant major, Johnson, approach. He kept at his work while the two sergeants moved off to the side. "I get furious when they shift their discipline problems to us. You see the missing stripe on his shoulder? He's obviously a loser. You let me know the minute he gives you any trouble. How's he doing?"

"He's the hardest working Marine I've ever seen, Sergeant Major. A good kid."

The older man raised his eyebrows and studied Nick. He raised his voice. "Get those crates on stage."

"Done, Sergeant Major."

"Get those wires run. We have a show in three hours."

"Done, Sergeant Major."

"How many men did they send over?" the sergeant major asked Miller.

"One—just Corporal Costas."

The sergeant major glared at Nick. "I can't stand lazy spics."

Miller straightened and looked at his superior. "I didn't hear that comment, Sergeant Major. My mother's Mexican."

The sergeant major stared at him and finally broke eye contact.

"Sorry, Sergeant, that comment was out of line."

"A bit of a racial stereotype, sir," Miller said levelly.

The sergeant major spun on his heel without a salute and left.

Miller looked at Nick. He had to have heard.

Nick shrugged. "Guess that explains a few things. Your mother really Mexican?"

Miller smiled. "One quarter. Enough to qualify?"

Nick grinned. "I'm only half Salvadoran myself, but it shows."

"Yeah, kid, it does. Come on, sit here and let me show you how this gizmo works."

Nick's fingers flew over the soundboard. They seemed to be drawn magnetically to the exact switches and dials. The kid was a natural. When the stage crew did sound checks, Nick handled them with a minimum amount of instruction.

"Corporal Adams, reporting for duty."

Miller looked up and snapped a salute at his sound technician. He slid over. "I want you to teach Corporal Costas this evening. Let him watch, and help, if he can."

"Sure, Sarge." Adams turned to Nick and stuck out his hand. Nick stood and gave him a firm shake and an appraising glance. They rehearsed the performance. Adams took a break, but the band wanted to run through one song again.

"Can you handle it, Costas?" Miller asked.

"I can, sir," Nick said calmly, a quiet glow in his brown eyes. His hand hovered over the board, and his superior watched. Nick flawlessly handled the board, but at one point he turned the sound up on the trumpet when the cheat sheet didn't indicate a solo. Miller quietly pointed it out.

Nick shrugged, grinned, and said, "I know, but he's great, isn't he?"

Miller laughed, put his hand on the kid's shoulder, and said, "That's not our call, Corporal."

"Cut, cut," Nick heard from the stage. "That's it! Who did that?" Fear leaped to Nick's eyes. "That's what was wrong. Write that in—the trumpet takes over right there. Who did that?"

Nick raised a tentative hand and shrank as the director ran down the aisle. The director grabbed Nick's hand and shook it hard. "Where'd you get a natural like this? He's one in a million. How old are you, kid?"

"Eighteen, sir."

The director shook his head. "How'd you know to cut to the trumpet?"

"I dunno. He's great, and he had this look, you know?"

The director grabbed the sheet off the table and made a few quick notes. "I've never been satisfied with this piece before. You let me know when you see anything else." He turned to the stage and jogged toward it. "All right, let's start from the top. We're keeping the trumpet bit."

Emboldened once more, Nick left the instructions and turned up the sound on the drums at another point. The assistant director looked back, grinned, and gave him a thumbs-up. Nick grinned, too, and his eyes sparkled.

Miller dropped a hand on his shoulder. "Easy, son, you've got good instincts, but don't get too cocky."

Nick carefully followed the instruction sheet for the rest of the number.

Adams returned. He watched Nick carefully and broke into a smile. "He's good, Sarge," he whispered.

When the band pulled out from the base, Nick Costas said farewell to Gunny and the Lieutenant. "Thanks for giving me a chance." He snapped off a smart salute.

MacDowell grabbed him into a fierce embrace. "Don't screw up, kid, and good luck. Keep in touch."

Lieutenant Anderson extended his hand for a firm shake. "God told me to hang in there with you. I'll leave you in His care, and my prayers will follow you, young man." He smiled. "The bus is about to pull out, Corporal. You'd better put this stripe back on."

Nick's smile lit up his entire face. "Yes, Lieutenant, right away," and he jogged to the bus and out of their lives.

MacDowell got postcards from the young man and watched him move up in the ranks and mature into a fine Marine. In four years, Nick was a staff sergeant and had completed two years of college in sound engineering. One day, a letter came. MacDowell searched for Lieutenant Anderson, now a captain, and put in a call to his duty station. Once he got him on the line and exchanged pleasantries, MacDowell said, "Remember the Hispanic kid who gave us so much grief?"

"Nick Costas. I still pray for him, and I get cards occasionally. What's up?"

"I got a letter. He's due to re-up and wants some advice. He's a staff sergeant now, so he's doing good, but he's also completed a couple of years of college and wonders if he should go on to Berkeley to finish a degree in sound engineering. I don't know what to tell him. Johnson would probably come after me if I tell him to go for it. He couldn't stand him at first, but now he says he's the finest young Marine he's ever worked with."

"Let me pray about this, Sergeant. I'll call you around fifteen hundred hours. Is that good?" When he eventually called back, the captain said, "Cut him loose, Mac. God used the Corps for a season, but He has big plans for this kid from South L.A."

"He's got nobody but us, Captain."

"He has God," Anderson quietly replied. "Give me his address, and I'll write any recommendations he needs. Send me his latest eval."

"Yes, Captain."

CHAPTER 2

The Intern

NICK'S LAST SEMESTER at Berkeley he served as an intern in a Hollywood recording studio. He met some big-name stars, but his favorite musician was a guy named John Randolph. John drank to begin the day, to get through the middle, and to finish up at night. But he could play drunk or sober, if Nick ever saw him sober. He moved around any stringed instrument like no one Nick had ever seen—and he'd seen plenty, even as a kid fresh out of the Marines. John was a master on the mandolin. His fingers knew the strings of his instrument like a skilled lover.

Before graduation, Nick was offered a job at the studio, and he went to work right away. His work was excellent. Everyone said he had natural instincts, maybe among the best in the business, but that his personal life was sketchy. One Monday morning, he showed up hungover with a shiny ring on his left hand.

"Where'd the ring come from, Nick?" John Randolph asked.

With a lopsided grin, Nick told him he'd been to Vegas, met a woman, and they got hitched.

"Just like that? What do you know about her?"

"She's gorgeous. She has this fancy place not far from here, and, phew." Nick wiped his brow with a lascivious grin. "She works for an escort service—a real professional woman."

John shook his head, patted him on the shoulder, and walked off, calling back, "Good luck with that, kid."

When Nick's wife left him a mere six weeks later, he knew where to find John. They'd finished recording for the day, so he'd be at O'Toole's drinking or playing a gig, usually both. John was as Irish as they come. He could lay on the brogue as thick as if he had just stepped off the boat, and the crowds loved him. He ran a tab at the bar and did the gigs for no charge. Nick didn't know who got the better end of the deal, Sean O'Toole or John, but the crowds Randolph drew in placed odds on O'Toole's.

"Hey, Nick, why so glum? Have a beer on me," John said as Nick walked in the door.

"Iris left me. She went to Vegas for the weekend with a paying customer."

"Told you marrying a hooker would come to a no-good end. Why'd you do it anyway?"

"She has this great kid—curly-haired Latina girl, about five years old. She never knew a father."

"What does she do with the kid when she has weekend clients?" John pulled up a stool. He was on break.

"She leaves her with her kid sister. I'd go for custody, cite moral charges, but the aunt's married to a great guy, and she wants her. She'll be fine there." Nick chugged his beer, determined to get a good start on a roaring drunk.

"Easy, man, it's laced with Irish whiskey."

"Good, I'll have another." Nick slammed the mug down and signaled to the bartender.

John took him home sometime after one in the morning and stayed with him. The musician was a good guy—maybe a drunk, but he had a heart as big as all outdoors. Nick liked him, even if he was depressed all the time. He got Nick going the next morning with a slug of the hair of the dog that bit him. He was an expert on hangovers. When Nick's eyes focused, John gave him a fatherly look. "Why'd you choose a woman like that? Didn't your mother ever teach you anything?"

"My mother was a coke-head. Last time I saw her I was five years old. Neighbors called the cops because her boyfriend was beating on me—broke my arm that time. I spent weeks in the hospital after the cops took me to the ER. They treated me for malnutrition and old fractures, with plastic surgery for burn scars." Nick refused to look at John and quickly changed the subject. "Why don't you date? Don't you need a woman? I need a woman, man."

John gave Nick his melancholy smile. "I've loved the same woman since I was twenty years old. Never be another one for me. When you've loved like that, the rest of them are merely ways to get through the night." He poured himself a beer, added a generous dollop of whiskey, and threw it back. "What you gonna do on a Saturday?"

"Iris left divorce papers and a note. She said, 'Sign them and get out by Sunday night.' Guess she has a high roller on the line."

"First, you need to freeze your accounts and call any credit cards," John advised. He helped Nick do all that before the bank closed at noon. They went to lunch, and between the two of them, they cleaned every trace of Nick out of Iris's fancy apartment. John stuck close the next few days, and then he disappeared.

The next time Nick saw him, John was different—still sad, still crazy gifted, but as sober as a judge. They came out of the studio, and Nick asked, "Where've you been and what happened to you? I've been to O'Toole's for weeks. Finally, they told me you'd quit. What's up?"

"I've exchanged masters. The bottle used to be my master, and now Jesus Christ is."

"You got religion, man? How'd that happen? Good Catholic boys like us don't mind mixing booze with candles."

John gave Nick a rueful attempt at a smile. "Doc gave me less than a year if I didn't get off the sauce—bad liver."

"Tough luck," Nick said, adding a curse. "You going to AA?"

"No, I'm a grateful believer in Jesus Christ who struggles with al-cohol addiction. I left the doctor's office and saw a sign for a Christian radio station. My wife's a Christian. Her prayers haunt me. I turned on the radio in the car, and they gave local announcements for concerts, fundraisers, and a recovery program for people with hurts, habits, and hang-ups. Seemed like God took my hand. I went to a meeting that night. I've been sober a month." He pulled a plastic chip out of his pocket and showed Nick. "I got this for one month of sobriety."

"Whatever works for you. I won't ask you to join me then," Nick said and walked away.

* * *

Nick and John worked together occasionally, and John continued on the straight and narrow. He seemed more at peace, but he was a dark Irisher. He brought his Bible to work, and instead of pulling on a beer, he took long drinks from that book and wrote in the margins. He'd close his eyes and wait to be called back in the studio. His work got even better, which Nick didn't think was possible. He'd stay late and play his instruments, spending a lot of time at the keyboards; Nick didn't even know he could play keyboards. But John's genius was the mandolin. He got sounds out of that baby like no one had ever heard before. But he was sad—really sad—and Nick didn't want to hang around him. Then John disappeared again.

After a few months, Nick asked where John was.

"He's signed a contract in Nashville. He left more than two months ago," the studio boss said.

Nick shrugged, but he thought about it and finally found out where John was and checked on openings. They advertised for a sound engi-neer. Nick was ready to ditch Hollywood, and the money was good in Nashville, so he sent in an application.

"Nick Costas!" Nick heard when he walked in the door for an inter-view. John turned to the interviewer and said, "If he's looking for a job, hire him. He may be a kid, but he's great!" John introduced him to the head honcho. "I gotta run. I'm in studio three. Drop by before you go."

Nick got the job and went by to thank John. He shoved open the door and groaned when he heard the keyboard player. He was passionless—and if anybody could wring passion out of a turnip, it was Nick's Irish friend. Nick had watched John for years, and he could make a person cry just listening to his music, without word one. The peace John had shown since he'd been sober vanished that day. He lost it. He stormed out of the studio and called the keyboard guy everything but a musician. Nick had to laugh. John was right; the guy was clueless.

"Get back in here, Randolph, we've got to get this done today!" the producer screamed.

"He's not a musician. Don't you get it? *I'm* a musician. I can't work with him," John said.

"You're a lousy backup musician, Randolph. Do what you're paid to do. I mean it. We'll take ten, but if you're not back here, consider yourself on probation."

"Music is what I am, Jeff," John said and went toward the break room. Nick followed him. He figured he'd have the Book open when he got there, and, sure enough, Nick found his Irish friend sitting and crying over words on a page. After a few minutes, John rose and went back into the studio. "Come on, Nick. Let's see what we can do with this kid."

There is no hope for this guy. Where did they get him? Out of the sanitation department? Nick wondered.

The keyboard player sat there going over the music again and again, mechanically. John lowered himself beside him on the bench, put his arm around him, and apologized. "I'm sorry, son. I threw a little tantrum there. Can you forgive me?" The guy's mouth dropped open, and John patted him on the shoulder. "We were all young once. Don't freeze up. You know the notes. It isn't the notes. It's the emotion. You gotta *feel* the music. See here, let me show you." And John scooted

16

beside the keyboard player, playing the same notes with such tenderness that tears came to the kid's eyes.

He did have emotion. Coulda fooled me. Nick stared at John Randolph. Jeff walked over to Nick, still fuming. "I hear you like this madman. You deal with him. I'm outta here." Nick was thrown into the deep end, but he was with the best in the business, and it felt like coming home. Within five minutes, John joked with the kid and encouraged him, and he loosened up until he did a credible job.

John Randolph was different now, and Nick watched him closely. Instead of John taking him out for beer, they went for coffee. And John tried to get him to go to his church. "My mom was Catholic, John. The nuns took me into parochial school, even when I was a foster kid. I hated that stuff. How could God stick me in those crummy homes and allow me to be beaten time and again? He doesn't seem too helpful or even too nice, in my opinion." Nick turned John's invitations away bitterly. He had no use for religion.

John went to church and played his music. Night after night he'd stay late in the studio, and Nick realized he was making music, writing songs. Nick stuck his head in the door one night. "It's a beautiful melody, John. Did you write it?"

John looked up from the keyboard, tears in his eyes, and nodded.

"Has it got words?"

"They're coming." Nick turned to leave and then looked back. John swiped his eyes with his sleeve. "It's for me wife. Me sweet brown Indian girl."

John looked so vulnerable that Nick forgot where he was going and sat beside him. He draped his arm over John's shoulder and said, "Tell me about her." And he did. Nick had heard John's brogue at O'Toole's when he charmed the crowds, but when he described the woman he loved, it was straight out of his heart. "You've been gone a long time, John. You've made her into a fantasy. She hangs the moon and stars, she's beautiful and kind, and she loves with passion and tenderness. No such woman exists, my friend."

John swiped his eyes with his sleeve. "She's my only love—which you wouldn't know a thing about since you're on number two already. Where'd you get this one?"

"On that cruise to the Caribbean. I did sound and got a free vacation. She was in the troupe of performers—a dancer. The ship's captain married us."

"You broke your record. Been married six months this time, right?"

Nick frowned. "You're right, though. I should take more time to get to know a woman. This isn't going so well. So, what happened with you and your true love?"

"Ah, sure, and it's been eighteen years. Cursed bottle, how could I love it more than the best woman God ever created? God gave me her love, and I destroyed it. Me son and I got into a fight one night. Exchanged blows we did, and he told me to get out—seventeen years old he was. Told me to go to hell—so I did. Played honkey-tonks across the country and ended up in Hollywood."

All the time he talked, he played. John could always do that, talk and play; music flowed out of him, an amazing musician. That night, "Brown Indian Girl" was born. It was the song that catapulted him to fame—his wife Alice's song. His love poured into the music.

"It's good, John, really good. This will make you a star. Get words to it."

"I'm no poet, Nick. I'll have to ask God for words."

"Whatever." Nick patted him on the shoulder and stood. He liked the guy, but he never heard of anyone asking God for words to a song.

John gathered up pages of musical manuscripts, stuffed them into a leather bag, and smiled his sweet, sad smile. "We'll see," he said. And three nights later he asked Nick if he could stay and hear what he had. They ordered some pizza and went into an empty room. The lyrics broke Nick's heart. John picked up his mandolin and played an accompaniment in his unique style.

Nick began to make up tracks in his head and figured how they could use John's piano and mandolin on the recording. "I know just the percussionist who could work with this music. Don't you let anyone else work with this, John. It's mine."

John looked up from the piano. "No one else will get near it, Nick. You're the best. I have a violin accompaniment, kind of a soaring descant, in my head that we'll work on."

"You've got a sure hit here," Nick told him. They cut the song, and John did all the instruments except percussion, but he insisted he wouldn't sing. "Okay, we'll get a singer. But you're a decent singer, and your emotion can carry this song."

"I won't sing it, Nick. I can't."

"Sure, sure, old man, we'll pay someone. I'll make a few calls."

They recorded the song over the next few weeks, in their downtime. Long after everyone left the studio but them, John cut each track and Nick pulled them together. It went out as a single and was an overnight sensation. Bluegrass musicians all over the country requested permission to use it, but John's success frightened him.

"Why are you scared of this?" Nick asked John one day. "This is what musicians dream about, man. You're headed for the big time."

John turned his sad, sea-green eyes on Nick and said, "They'll know me. My family will know it's me, and I don't know what to do. They already hate me. I abandoned them. They were poor. I left Alice with two teenage kids. I up and left. Disappeared. Who can forgive sin like that?"

His pain was palpable, and Nick didn't know what to say. "Maybe God will give you words again," was all he could think to reply.

"Sure, and I'm going to need a miracle, Nick."

"I've never seen one of those—except for your song. If God's in the lyric-writing business, maybe He can tell you what to say to your family."

John chuckled. "Did you know God once spoke through an ass,

19

Nick?"

"Are you calling me an ass?"

"Now would I say such a thing?" His eyes twinkled at his young friend.

"You're right, though. They'll know you. No one makes that signature sound on the mandolin. Jeff told me to tell you you've been nominated for country music song of the year."

Actual terror crossed John's face then. "I've got to call them. God, help me."

Nick put his hand on John's shoulder. He wished he knew John's Master so he could pray for him, but those things were strange, so he patted him and said, "Good luck. I hope it goes all right."

Nick asked him every day for a week if he'd talked to his family.

"I'm trying to reach me daughter." John blinked and lapsed into a thick brogue. "She's the child of me heart. I didn't hurt her like I did me Alice and me poor wee Jimmy." When Nick cornered him, he admitted he'd called his daughter's home and her shop for a week, but he'd hung up time after time.

"You've got to do this. The Awards ceremony is in a few months, and you'll be out there in front of God and everybody!"

"Ah, so you admit there is a God, Nick?"

"If there is, He'd be there for you now, wouldn't He?" Nick shot back.

* * *

The next day, John told Nick he'd talked to his daughter and her husband, and a few days later, he told him they were coming to Nashville. Nick had forgotten about their visit when he called John in to work on some tracks. "Hey, John, thanks for coming in," Nick said as he listened intently through headphones and flipped various dials. He looked up and saw John wasn't alone. "This must be your brown Indian girl." He crossed the small space with his hand out.

John put his arm around Missy's shoulder. "No, this is my daughter and her husband, Missy and Tim Raines from West Virginia. Missy looks like her mother, my brown Indian girl." John introduced his friend. "This is Nick Jo Costas, best producer in the business."

"Not the best, but the only one who puts up with you, Randolph." Nick grinned, took Tim's hand, and acknowledged Missy. "He's been a wreck waiting for you. It's all he's talked about for a week. You staying for the weekend?"

"We leave after church on Sunday," Missy replied.

"I hate to take up your time, but we have a deadline. John isn't gonna like this." Nick turned to him. "When we mixed it, the bass dominated. It comes across too loud. If I tone him down, the mandolin is too soft. I'd rather work with you on this than that piece of junk punk. He's banging my wife, I swear. Can we fix this?" Nick flipped a few switches. Music bounced off the walls, and drums dominated the melody.

John grimaced. "It's not even good percussion."

Nick shook his head. "He's showboating. Why don't you grab your instrument and we'll redo the mandolin? Fancy it up so I can overpower this piece of—" He glanced at Missy and bit off his words.

John showed Tim and Missy where to sit outside the studio so that they could watch through large windows.

Missy grinned. "Won't this be fun?" She was precious, a tiny bit of a thing, and she and her husband looked like they were eating each other with their eyes. Nick hurt to watch them. He never knew love could be like that. He was almost certain his second wife was running around on him.

John sang at the Bluebird Cafe the Friday night that Tim and Missy were in town, but Pat did sound instead of Nick. Pat told Nick that Missy sang with her father that night and was amazing. John raved about her too.

"Sure, and you're a wee bit prejudiced, wouldn't you say?" Nick teased John—he liked to imitate his brogue. But when Nick heard Missy on stage at the Country Music Awards a couple of months later, he was spellbound.

Nick met John's wife, Alice, over the weekend when John won his award. She was an older version of Missy, but serene and calm, not bubbly like their daughter. Missy was an odd mixture of her parents. She looked exactly like her mom, but she had her father's music and then some. Nick was amazed at the way John's family embraced him after seeing John's terror when he first contacted them.

"It's the story of the prodigal, Nick—only it's the prodigal father instead of the prodigal son."

"What will you do? I hear Alice refuses to move to Nashville."

"For now, I'll go back and forth, but I wrestle with it. We've been apart too many years, and leaving her gets harder each time."

"She obviously loves you. Thanks for inviting me to the whatever-you-call-it."

John smiled. "We renewed our vows. Glad you came. Did I tell you she never divorced me?"

"Only about fifty times." Nick slapped him on the back and turned to walk to the studio.

The studio bigwigs got nervous. John had become an overnight sensation, and he and his kids recorded a song his son wrote, which quickly climbed the Christian charts. So, John changed his professional name. Nick had never heard his real name, Ian O'Malley. It suited him better.

"My middle name is Sean—Irish for John—and the family lives in Randolph County, West Virginia," Ian O'Malley said. "So, I came up with John Randolph."

One day, Jeff stuck his head in the door. "Nick, John is flying home this weekend, and we need him back next week for a big album we're doing. I'm scared one day he won't come back. He's crazy. Go with him. Make sure he gets on that plane Monday morning."

"Man, did you ever think about my weekend plans?" Nick demanded.

"I thought your wife left."

Nick shrugged. "Rub it in. You're right. I might as well."

"Good, here're the tickets. See you Monday." Jeff ducked out of the room before Nick could say anything else.

On the flight, John—now Ian again—admitted he wanted to quit Nashville, but Nick tried his best to talk him out of it. "You've got Nashville in your blood. You'll dry up and die without the lights, the stage, the mic."

"I don't know. I'm not happy being apart from the family. Missy and Jimmy are both having babies, and Alice won't leave them or her job at the hospital."

"She's a nurse, isn't she?"

"We're praying mighty hard for God to open new doors, maybe right there in West Virginia."

"Can anything good come out of West Virginia?" Nick asked and leaned his head back on the seat.

CHAPTER 3

Nick Decides to Stay

S EVERAL MONTHS LATER, Nick flew to West Virginia again to attend Jimmy's debut musical performance. Ian and Alice had built a new home with a studio for recording with their children in West Virginia. Ian realized Missy would never leave her mountains, nor would his precious brown Indian girl. He was proud of his son Jimmy's talent and twisted Nick's arm to come for a week. He promised he'd get Missy to sing, and Nick arrived two days before rehearsals.

Nick worked the soundboard for the open house and once again felt the magic of Missy O'Malley when Jimmy tricked her into joining them for the performance. She sang without a flaw, and Nick suspected she had perfect pitch. He arrived at Missy's house late for breakfast the next day. She welcomed him and asked how long he would stay in West Virginia.

Nick blew on his coffee and looked over the rim of his cup at her. "Ian wants to start his own production company here. He wants to hire me to be his producer. If I were you folks, I'd pray about it, but since I don't know Ian's 'Master,' I weigh my options."

Missy patted his arm. "Jesus rarely requires blind obedience. He gave us minds to use. Weighing your options is always a good idea. Can we help?"

"Maybe. Your dad knows the only way you will record is here in

West Virginia. 'The lass dinna fit in Nashville. All she wants is her beloved mountains.' We won't pull him back there much longer either. He resists more every time. I can see why, with this family. I lost my second wife to the Nashville scene, and Alice wasn't about to move there."

Nick leaned back, crossed his legs, and continued on, saying, "I have two considerations: Jimmy's no problem—music has become a fire in him, and he'll be every bit as good as his dad. But will you help us record? You have a magical something. *And* affordable housing. Two divorces hit a man's pocketbook."

"West Virginia is cheaper than Nashville. Singing is natural as rain for me. I'll sing in Daddy's studio, if anyone wants to listen."

"Your dad's album *Recovered and Free* is flying off the shelves, and we want you on the Irish lullabies CD we're planning. We did some recording last night. Ian got you the best contracts in the business, and he was hard-nosed about your project. 'Ya made a slave out of ignorant me, lads, but you'll not do it to me children,' he said." Nick did an incredible impersonation of his friend.

Nick looked around the table. "He got a copyright on all Jimmy's songs, and an attorney presented his demands. We were over a barrel. We tried to negotiate, but your dad wouldn't take our calls. When we finally got through, he roared: 'Do ya not know I'm on a honeymoon? I've better things to do than talk to the likes of you. Ya heard me offer—take it or leave it.' And he slammed the phone down."

Alice laughed. She'd heard the other side of that conversation in person. Ian had been propped on one elbow, and she had been lying in the crook of his arm. "Your royalty checks as beginning singers wouldn't have been anything like they are now," she noted. "Every time the boss writes out the checks he cusses 'that slick Irisher.' Ian gave on two things, though: he played accompaniment on most of the tracks—mandolin, keyboards, fiddle—and he let you use his John Randolph name. We did the write-up to change to his real name."

Nick scratched his head. "How clever. Ian's fans recognize his name for our benefit. He agreed to play mandolin backup, but that was a bargaining chip, and Irish lullabies are public domain—no songwriters to pay off. This is a shrewd businessman. I might talk myself into this move after all. Do you know some fiddle place Ian talks about? He said it's every bit as good as the Bluebird Cafe, and he wants to give local talent a fair bargain, not make slaves of them."

"If we hit a good night at the Purple Fiddle, you'll see the talent in West Virginia. And you have to come to the Augusta Heritage Festival next year!" Missy was so enthusiastic that Nick had to laugh.

"I need a new start. My life is at rock bottom right now."

"I'll introduce you to Mike Green. He could relate. Your stories are quite similar."

"Mike Green, the author who writes war novels? He lives here?"

"He lives in a ski resort area about forty-five minutes away. Tim designed his home."

"And Missy decorated it," Alice added proudly.

Missy winked at Tim's father, Todd, who poured himself a fresh cup of coffee. "It pays to keep good company. Tim and I work together now. God fitted us together. Tim was my missing half."

"The best thing Tim ever did for our family was to bring this little gal into it," Todd added. "He never laughed the way he does since Missy came into his life. She's his joy, and our pride and joy as well."

Missy hugged her husband's father from behind as she rose to refresh Nick's coffee. "The joy of the Lord is our strength. You have to enter Daddy's blarney contest, Todd!"

"It's the God's truth, every word. I love you, gal," Todd confirmed.

"I love you, too, Todd." She leaned her head on his back and patted him.

"We had mass hysteria in this kitchen this morning," Missy's father-in-law said. "I never laughed so hard in my life. But be careful, Nick, these kids have no respect for their elders. If you hang around here, you'll have no secrets. Maybe these Indians read tea leaves or something."

"Nobody had to read tea leaves to read the look on your face last night," Missy said.

Todd's wife, Anne, patted her blushing husband's hand as he lowered himself to a chair beside her. "You'd better quit while you're ahead, dear. Why did you come in here anyway?"

"It's cold out there. It's a cutthroat rivalry, and I'm in the middle of it." They heard the clank of horseshoes and the shouts of laughter outside. "Do we have to leave this afternoon?"

"I have nursery tomorrow."

"I'll change the sheets and move you over here to our place, Nick," Missy said.

"I'll take you up on that. Here come the cutthroats now." Nick rose and shook hands. "Pretty fine performance last night, man." Nick clapped Jimmy on the shoulder.

"I learned from the master. No one moves around those strings like Da. The banjo's a bit rough, but the fiddle's coming, and you know the little flip on the mandolin? That sound you knew had to be Da."

"A band member once told me no one else in the world could make that sound on the mandolin," Alice said.

"He's right—it's John's signature," Nick agreed.

"If I work hard, the world might have two people who can make it," Jimmy said.

"Ah, you will, lad. I've heard you!" Ian exclaimed proudly.

"Not performance level, but it's coming. Don't teach anyone else, Da."

Ian looked thoughtful. "But I have two grandsons and three granddaughters who might take to music. Willow will have the hands for it. And the younger Todd's fingers are kind of stubby, but he can sing." Missy and Tim's son, Todd Lee, was named after Missy's father.

Nick picked up Jimmy's hand. "They're darker and minus the

freckles, but they're your hands, Ian."

Missy took her brother's other hand and brought it to her lips. "You took such good care of your hands all these years. Fess up—in your heart of hearts, you wanted Da to come home and teach you, Jimmy."

"I told myself, 'if wishes were horses, beggars would ride,' but the flame burned. Not like Mom, though. You always knew he'd come home, didn't you, Mom?"

"I always prayed he would. About ten years ago faith began to grow. When Tim brought 'Brown Indian Girl' home for me to listen to, I knew John Randolph was Ian. It was my pet name for him. If anyone else used it, they stole it. But that mandolin had to be Ian. I wondered why he hadn't come home."

"You went to Nashville seven years ago, John—sorry, Ian? Before we met in Hollywood?" Nick asked.

"Yes, but I longed to come to Hollywood after the Lord turned my life right-side out ten years ago. I prayed my wife and son would forgive me, but I was totally unprepared for the love they've given."

"We should take him out back and beat him. He seems unable to understand grace, which is freely given and freely received," Jimmy said. He drew his father into a hug.

"We never encountered more love than we see in the O'Malleys," the elder Todd said, as he rose from his chair. "Sit, warriors. Get something warm into you. Tim, you belong with the O'Malleys, with your Italian hair and skin; but your boy is all Raines—Indian."

"The Indians captured white babies and adopted them into the tribe," Anne said.

"Only to replenish what the whites killed of our people," Missy defended. "And we welcomed those who joined us. This one here, he's my love-slave." She kissed Tim and went to replenish the sweet rolls.

Everyone laughed, but Tim said, "I'll never leave the tribe."

Jimmy looked around for his wife, the other adopted member of the tribe. "Is Julie having trouble with Willow?"

"Willow won't settle with this excitement, but she needs a nap," Missy said.

Jimmy walked back to the bedroom, and Julie came out, pushing her long blonde hair off her face. "What an iron will that little one has. Fortunately, Jimmy has one to match. She's too much for me. It isn't fair. Missy got me into this and look." Julie pointed to where Missy's son Todd slept on the carpet, beside Julie's older daughter, Maryanne, who was quietly coloring.

"Am I too much for you, Mommy?" Jamie, the first of Jimmy and Julie's three children, crawled under Julie's arm.

"You are, but I love you, and I'll never let you go. You're my firstborn. What magic did you do in there?" Julie asked when Jimmy rejoined the group.

"You're a softie. You can't let her have the upper hand."

"It's the Irish lullabies that did it. Don't let him kid you," Missy said.

"I need that album *now*. I'll put a player in the nursery and keep it on constantly," Julie quipped.

"Our first order of business, Ian. We'll give that album to them and be done," Nick said. "Jimmy has so many songs in him. We'll be off and running with O'Malley Productions."

"Ah, so you'll stay here in West Virginia?" Ian smiled broadly.

"I want to be a part of this wild Irish tribe."

"God be praised! Did ya hear, Alice?"

"One prayer down, a few more to go." She smiled at him.

"I followed Ian from Hollywood. I loved to work with him. Remember the first day I came to Nashville, and you walked out? Jeff was furious." Nick chuckled.

"I'll never forget. 'Time is money,' he screamed at me. I told him music is who I am, and he said I was a lousy backup musician. I was ashamed of my behavior."

"I followed you from Hollywood because I liked to work with you.

But that day I knew for sure I really wanted to."

"For heaven's sake, why? I acted horribly that day."

"First, I respect your standards, Ian. You don't do less than perfect. Second, stars throw tantrums, and you were on your way to being one then, but I never saw a star apologize like you did. You came back, humbled yourself, asked for forgiveness, and patiently instructed the keyboard player, who had no sensitivity—zip, zero, nada. You got him to understand, and we had few retakes."

"Jeff walked out on us. He said, 'You deal with the madman,' and you've been a good friend to me ever since, Nick. You get it."

"You're a consummate professional. You're harder on yourself than anybody else. No gimmicks with mics and tracks—pure performance art. I love it. It's rare in today's music world."

"I'm glad you like the studio here, because he was a tyrant about it," Alice said. "He sent stuff back and fussed with the installers. I couldn't live with the man."

Jimmy grinned. "You had your ways, Mom."

While everyone laughed, Ian said, "Now ya see, Nick, the lad has no respect for his elders."

Nick shook his head. "Maybe not, but he loves you more than you deserve."

"Ah, no one knows better than I do. You don't know what I did to this poor lad." Tears sprung to Ian's eyes.

Jimmy walked over and draped his arm around his father. When Ian tried to say something more, Jimmy cut him off. "Julie and I decided to sell the garage," Jimmy announced. We'll build a home out here, close to the studio. I have more songs working in my spirit. I don't have time to be a mechanic anymore. Jerry will buy the business and our house. I'll teach him the business side and get out as soon as I can."

"Jimmy's business was in my backyard. Now I only see him if we chase him over here." Julie laughed.

Nick turned to Jimmy. "Can you and Missy help us with some

tracks for this lullaby album, so we can finish it and move on?"

Jimmy rubbed his hands. "Can't wait!"

"Sure, but I'll never give up my work on houses with Tim," Missy said.

"West Virginia will be good for me. I grew up in Los Angeles," Nick said. "You folks are so grounded. I couldn't believe Alice refused to move to Nashville, but it had no attraction for her, so I wouldn't dare ask you two to move there."

"For I know the plans I have for you," Missy began, and everyone joined in: "Plans to prosper you, to give you hope, and a future. Welcome, home, Nick."

CHAPTER 4

GI Barbie

THE O'MALLEYS WORKED HARD on the lullaby album, and Nick started to attend divorce care after he met the facilitator, Missy and Tim's friend, Mike Green, on a trip with them to Canaan Valley. Mike had recently come to faith, and they talked long into the night at his house, after Tim and Missy had gone to bed. Back in Elkins, where Nick stayed at Missy's house, he often spent time in the evenings with questions from his Bible readings. He was fascinated with Mike's courtship of his former wife. Nick began going to church with the O'Malley family and Mike Green. After services one Sunday, Nick asked Missy who the "GI Barbie" he had met there was.

"Barb Westfall was in uniform when she dropped the kids off with her mother this morning because she left for National Guard camp today."

"She was pretty rude. What's she got against me?" Nick inquired.

"She's had a rough time. Her husband was killed in Iraq. She found out she was pregnant after the funeral." Tears hovered in Missy's eyes as she told Nick the story.

"How tragic. Why doesn't she get a compassionate discharge? She's the surviving parent," Nick said. "I've been to Iraq three times. I may even have met her husband."

"She was in Iraq for fifteen months herself. They only had five months together before he went back for his second tour, and he was killed the first week there. We thought her pregnancy would undo her, but her baby girl brought her peace. She also has two boys. They were twelve and five when Bob died. She said she'd never have another child, so God gave her a daughter."

* * *

At the end of the next week, in a terrible rainstorm, Nick spotted a vehicle with a flat tire and pulled over. "GI Barbie" was changing a tire while inside the car her baby screamed.

"Mrs. Westfall, let me do that while you comfort the baby."

"I wasn't very nice to you a couple of weeks ago. I was upset. I had to leave the kids for two weeks. I owe you an apology." Rain ran off the hood of her jacket, and drips caught on her lashes.

"We can discuss it another time. You're soaked, get inside," Nick urged. He quickly changed the tire and threw the jack and flat into the back of her SUV with a clang. "Be sure to get it fixed, so you don't ride around on the spare. I hate those stupid donuts."

"I owe you big time. Can I take you to dinner?"

"Unnecessary, but thanks."

"If you haven't eaten, we're headed for Bob Evans. Please join us."

"I'll join you then, but no way a war widow takes *me* to dinner. Your country, including me, owes you more than we can ever repay."

Tears sprang to Barb's eyes. "That's sweet. I feel terrible for the way I acted. See you there?"

"I'm right behind you. I'd feel better knowing the spare works okay."

Nick caught the restaurant door for Barb as she struggled with the toddler, and he followed her inside. Since she was about his height, he looked almost straight into her hazel eyes that carried a weight of sorrow. He laughed. "I need a towel." His jet-black hair sparkled like diamonds as he shook his head.

When she wasn't dressed in fatigues and clunking around in boots, GI Barbie was an attractive lady, Nick thought. Her light brown, almost blonde hair hung free when not in the severe bun she wore while in uniform. They waited while the hostess found a table.

"I'm sorry. I don't know your name. I know you from church. You came from Nashville with Ian O'Malley?"

White teeth flashed against Nick's dark complexion. "Nick Costas, producer for O'Malley Productions. I asked Missy about you because everyone at church has been friendly. I was a little stunned at your reaction to me."

Barb colored. "It's an automatic response to anyone in the entertainment field. They aren't supportive of the soldiers."

"Not all entertainers. Most of Nashville stands solidly behind our troops. I traveled to Iraq three times with different groups. I barely escaped an explosive device at a Bagdad market the second time I went over."

"I feel like a heel. May I call you Nick? Please call me Barb."

Nick chuckled. "I asked Missy who 'GI Barbie' was. She told me your name. It was quite a coincidence."

Barb cocked her head. "A compliment or an insult?"

"I meant neither. Let's forget it and start over." He gave a slight bow and fell in behind her as the hostess led them to the table. "I'm Nick Costas. I attend church with Missy and Tim. I've seen you there." He stood behind her chair and waited for her to settle her toddler with a cracker and a sippy cup.

"And I'm Barbara Westfall, but everyone calls me Barb." Nick admired the efficient way she handled the child, who refused to make-up to him. "Don't feel bad, Nick. She's been clingy since I got back."

"Have you filed for a compassionate discharge?" Nick asked. He pulled her chair out, and she sat.

"I pray about it. The need is so great. I hate to abandon my team."

"You need to think about those three kids. How old are your

folks?"

"I'm the youngest of five. My dad died of black lung several years back, and Bob's parents aren't really the best choice, if anything . . ." Her voice caught.

Nick covered her hand with his. "Let's not go there. We'll enjoy our meal." He picked up his menu. "Missy and Tim pray for you. God speaks to them, and He'll give you direction, too."

Barb nodded. "I couldn't make it without God. I found out I was pregnant after Bob was killed. She's a good baby, our only girl. I always wanted a girl."

"Missy says God gives us the desire of our hearts."

"What's the desire of your heart?"

"Maybe to know God the way they do, the way you do, and to get O'Malley Productions onto a solid footing, and for Missy to know God's gifts in her life. She thinks her 'real job' is her work on houses with Tim, but she has amazing talent and an unusual something when she sings."

"Missy never realized what a blessing she is. She's humble, and she's tempered by something in her life. I know you're Ian's friend, but he abandoned them, and they were dirt poor. Missy married late, but God brought her a wonderful husband. We all adore Tim. Aren't they sweet together?"

"Yeah. I watch them. I've messed up bad—divorced twice. When I lived in their home, I realized I've never really loved anyone. I've been selfish, self-centered, and vain. They tell me God wants me, but I don't see how."

"Jesus loved you so much that He left heaven to take your place on the Cross. Let God heal your heart as only He can," Barb urged.

"They gave me *Mere Christianity*. It's an interesting read. I can't poke any holes in their lives. I have so much respect for them. I knew Ian in Hollywood and in Nashville. When he reached out to his family, he was terrified. I was astounded how they welcomed him home. Like the story of the prodigal, they killed the fatted calf and rejoiced. He's been transformed. The difference is amazing. When I first knew him, he was a drunk. He got sober, but he was depressed as only an Irishman can be. Now he sparkles. He and Jimmy are producing tons of creativity with their music. They seem to feed off each other."

"I was too much of a mess to come to the open house, but I heard it was fantastic."

Nick picked up the check and reached for little Alice Marie. She turned her face to her mother but flashed him a grin. He placed his hand on her curls and twirled a silky blonde tendril around his finger. "She is a beauty. Looks like her mother."

"That's definitely a compliment." Barb smiled, and they walked out. "I'm glad we made peace. Thanks for dinner and for forgiving my rudeness. See you Sunday. I'll pray for you to find your way home to Father's House, Nick." She offered him her hand, and he took her long slender fingers into his hand with a smile.

"Thanks. I'm flying to Nashville for a few days to wrap up some business there, so I won't be in church this Sunday. Maybe next week. Be sure you get that tire fixed."

"Thanks again."

"You bet. My pleasure." He stood beside her car and held her door while she buckled her daughter in. "Bye now," Nick said as he closed the door. He tore his eyes from her face, grinned at the child, and jogged to his bright red Porsche.

CHAPTER 5

It Isn't Religion

NICK RETURNED FROM NASHVILLE with his divorce final. When he called Missy, she told him Mike was at their house, so he went there. They touched a match to Missy's carefully laid fire. The kindling snapped into a flame and caught the bigger branches, which in turn caught the logs. They sat in front of the fireplace on the long, comfortable sectional. Nick needed a shoulder to cry on. Two marriages, two divorces, two betrayals, and he was still paying his first wife alimony, even though she was a professional escort who took her services long into the night and had kicked him out when she'd roped herself a sugar daddy. Unfortunately, her catch had a gambling problem—hence the pursuit of alimony.

Mike had entertained his ex-wife the weekend Nick was gone. "She tried her best to seduce me. It was a long weekend, but by God's grace, I behaved like a gentleman. I called Missy at 5:00 a.m. for prayer."

"You didn't sleep with your wife?" Nick asked.

"My ex-wife. We aren't married now. I'd like to marry her again, but I was unfaithful, and she hasn't forgiven me. I was at our vacation spot in the Hamptons when she walked in to surprise me. Surprised both of us, not to mention the other woman. Not a pretty picture."

"Tomcatting around, were you?"

"I'm ashamed now, of course, but I was a swinger then. Clare knew

I'd been married three times. We signed a prenup, so I got out of it clean financially, but she turned my daughters against me, and that hurt. They wouldn't see me for years. They started to come around last year, and I'm sure it was due to Missy's prayers. Watch out when that woman prays for you."

"You want to marry your ex-wife? That's heavy. Losing your daughters must have been a blow. I lost my first wife's daughter, and it about destroyed me." Nick looked up. "And I was only with her six weeks or so."

"I was bitter, but I deserved it, so what can I say? I'm glad the girls and I are working things out now. They've seen a big change in me since I came to know the Lord."

Nick was grateful when Missy and Tim arrived. The conversation was getting a little too challenging. Missy told them she'd be right back and went to get Todd at her sister-in-law's home down the lane.

"Did you two get women all figured out?" Tim asked as he hung up his jacket.

"The only thing I've figured out is I don't know how to love a woman," Nick said. "Mike has got to be a saint, not sleeping with his wife. From what I see, it seems natural for you and Jimmy to put your gals first. I've been self-centered. I guess I want a woman to revolve her life around me."

Mike laughed. "That's human nature. We all want the world to revolve around us. It's called the sin nature, and that's the original sin."

"You guys, and Ian, too, defy human nature. Beats me."

Tim dropped his hand on Nick's shoulder and sat down beside him. "We don't do it by ourselves. The Holy Spirit lives in a believer's heart and helps us to love beyond our selfish abilities." He looked over at Mike. "How're you doing?"

"I maintained the victory, but it was a struggle. It was a trap. She confessed before she left that she wanted to hurt me the way I hurt her."

Missy walked in, and Tim leaned against her shoulder. She brushed her lips on his brow and rubbed his back. "Did you make any progress, Mike?"

"I asked her forgiveness. Someday, maybe, she'll be open to trying again. But—and this may be jumping ahead of God—if she'll have me, should I marry her again even though she's not a Christian?"

"That's thorny. Scripture tells us not to be unequally yoked, but it also tells us the unbelieving spouse is sanctified by the believer," Tim said.

"Go over that more slowly." Nick frowned.

"Paul tells us not to marry a non-Christian. An unbeliever pulls a believer down. However, if you're married, and one person gets saved, God can use the believer to bring the spouse to Himself," Missy said. "The unbeliever who chooses to stay in the relationship is set apart— sanctified—by living with the believer. A believer brings the blessings of God into the household."

"Suppose the 'unbeliever' walks off? Runs around, like my ex-wives?" Nick inquired.

"Then the believer is free. Adultery breaks the covenant bond in marriage," Tim explained. "Mike's case is complex. Clare is his wife of many years and the mother of his only children. Christianity isn't about rules, it's about relationship. No one can give Mike a definitive answer. Only God can show him what to do."

"I thought Christianity was a bunch of rules: thou shalts and thou shalt nots?"

"I thought so, too," Mike replied to Nick. "And, sadly, lots of Christians do. God gets blamed for lots of stuff because His kids get wrong-headed notions."

"I learned in catechism what we were supposed to do, buddy. No two ways about it."

"Let's put it another way. When you grew up, did you know what your mom or dad expected of you?" Tim asked.

"I had foster parents, but kids in normal families would. Sure, I guess. Not that they always do it, though."

"You don't need a rule book. If you love your parents, you want to please them, and you try to do what makes them proud and happy."

"Makes sense, but how do you know what God wants?"

"Get to know your heavenly Father," Missy said.

"He doesn't appear in burning bushes anymore or speak from a cloud," Tim went on. "Mormons talk about a 'burning in the bosom,' whatever that means."

With a puzzled expression, Nick looked at them and shrugged.

"We read our Bibles," Tim said. "Jesus lived among us and taught us how to live. He lived it and demonstrated how. Often, I'm led by a Scripture that comes to mind, and guiding principles are revealed by God's Word. Read the Book of Mark, for a start, and watch Jesus in action. Jesus is God. He said, 'If you've seen me, you've seen the Father.' We get to know God when we study the life of Christ."

"And the Holy Spirit leads us," Missy said. "When Mike called us, he said he 'felt' he shouldn't sleep in the open loft. He went downstairs to the locked bedroom instead, to stay put. His simple obedience delivered him from even stronger temptation. Call it instinct, a hunch, whatever—he was right on."

"I called and asked for help," Mike said. "God speaks to us through the advice of more mature Christians, as well as good teaching and preaching."

"I've been reading the translation you gave me, Tim," Nick said. "It's easier to understand than the one the Sisters gave me. But I thought lay people aren't supposed to understand the Bible."

"A lot of Catholics are regular Bible readers and participate in Bible studies. I can get you in contact with some of them," Missy said.

Nick looked thoughtful. "No, thanks. I like your church. I want to continue there. I see something in you that I need."

* * *

With much trepidation, Mike began sending cards and emails and making calls to Clare. He found willing allies in their girls, who eagerly fostered the rekindled romance. One night, Allyson told him her mother hadn't been happy since the divorce. His daughter told him Clare seemed glad to hear from him. With that information, he invited them to come for Thanksgiving, and he at least didn't get an outright refusal.

Nick continued to attend church and divorce care. Often, he asked questions about his Bible readings. He watched Mike's courtship, Ian's life, and one young widow from afar. He began to volunteer around the church and enjoyed his work with the scouting program. The young widow's oldest son was in his group.

One weekend, Nick went up to the mountains to stay with Mike, now a good friend. As soon as he got into the house, he exclaimed about the beauty of the drive, with the rolling fall foliage exploding in vibrant colors. Red, burgundy, yellow, and orange hillsides tumbled into variegated valleys.

"All of creation points to our Heavenly Father, Nick. Jesus said if we neglect to praise Him, the rocks will cry out."

"I read in Psalms this morning that the trees of the fields will clap their hands. It sounds like something out of *The Lord of the Rings*."

"Tolkien was a mentor and friend of C.S. Lewis. Their writings are allegorical." Mike and Nick sat up late and talked about God. Mike was surprised how many questions he could answer easily. "I fought Him for so long, and now I wonder why. How foolish to turn away the only unconditional love we'll ever experience. I ran from my pain into one relationship after another."

"You're saying the love I see in the O'Malleys is God's love?" Nick asked.

"What do you think?"

Nick closed his eyes, and Mike saw tears slip under his eyelids, so he rose and went into the kitchen to leave his young friend to his thoughts. When Mike returned to the great room with cheese and crackers, Nick blew into a handkerchief. He looked up. "I lived in foster homes all my life. I had a couple of good foster parents and more not-so-good ones, but I always knew they wouldn't be forever. They'd move on, and I'd be left behind. If I messed up, I got sent back. Talk about love with conditions. I've had two wives run around on me and leave. I don't have any family. I don't want to be left behind anymore, but it's hard to trust."

"That's tough."

"No religious platitudes, Mike?"

"Nope."

"What am I supposed to do? Take some flying leap into whatever?"

"I could say, 'Taste and see that the Lord is good.' My friend, Ed, who's having Tim build a house for him, scoffed when Missy told him God had never failed her through the tough times. How could a good little Christian girl have tough times? I told him about her rape and the daughter she placed for adoption." Nick's eyes went wide, and Mike realized he didn't know about that either, so he relayed the story again.

Once again, Nick felt tears sting his eyes. "She has so much joy. I'd never guess she'd suffered like that."

"God tempers us in His refining fire. Have you seen blacksmiths work with metal? In red-hot heat, iron becomes malleable. God makes us, molds us, and changes us into what He wants us to be, like Christ Himself. All my mistakes, all my sin, has brought me to this point, to this day, where I can sit across from you and say He made all things new for me, and He'll do the same for you."

"God knows I need it. Is it too late?"

"It's never too late, until we draw our last breath."

"I want a do-over. I want a change like Ian found. I never believed the depressed drunk I knew in Hollywood could be so full of love and joy the way he is now. He's a different man. Will you help me pray?"

A big grin spread over Mike's face. He leaned forward, placed his hand on Nick's shoulder, and showed him the way home to Father's house.

CHAPTER 6

Faucet Repairs

ONE AFTERNOON, Nick was going into the studio late. They had worked on a video until after ten the night before at the O'Malley Productions studio, so he wasn't due back there until one. He stopped at Subway for a sandwich and saw a morose Barb Westfall in a corner. He dropped down across from her.

"Hey, girlie-girl. Why so glum?"

Barb looked up. "You sound like the O'Malleys, Nick." She smiled and then heaved a huge sigh. "I got my compassionate discharge, so I need a job. I have no income and no healthcare. I just came from an interview at the bank. I got the job, but it doesn't feel right."

"If you prayed and got the job, wouldn't that be an indication of God's leading? I'm new to all this, but I want to learn."

"I figured you'd made a commitment. I see you at church all the time, and you look happier."

Nick leaned back in his chair. "I'm more at peace than I've ever been in my life. I don't think God wants a loser like me, but I want to serve Him the rest of my life. I have great examples in the O'Malleys. They are honest, hard-working, fair, and they sure know how to love their women!"

Barb covered his hand with hers. "God has no 'losers' in His family. You're on the winning side now, and you're surrounded by an amazing family."

Nick looked up, surprised at his response to her touch. "Thanks. Have you talked to Jerry about a job?"

Barb's forehead knotted. She didn't recognize the name.

"He's Jimmy's old partner, who bought the garage," Nick said. "The billing is way behind. They hired a new mechanic, and business is brisk. Jimmy goes over to help, but the accountant suggested a billing clerk. Jimmy insisted on medical coverage for employees as part of the buyout package. Maybe I could take you there and introduce you."

A tray crashed on the floor. Barb jumped and looked around defensively.

Nick squeezed her hand. "You're not in Iraq. It's just a baking tray." They could hear kids laughing.

Barb relaxed and then realized she hadn't released Nick's hand. She blushed and quickly removed it.

Nick called the studio. The artists who had booked it for the afternoon had canceled. He gave Barb a thumbs-up and asked Jimmy for the number for A&J Garage, explaining her situation to him. Snapping the phone shut, Nick said, "Let's go. Jimmy said he'd call ahead for us."

* * *

Barb quickly gathered up her purse and her resume. When she stepped into the noisy garage, she felt comfortable. The familiar smells of oil, gasoline, and diesel fuel carried her back to her work in the Guard. Jerry sat at the desk in the office, glaring at piles of bills, accounts payable and receivable, and odds and ends. He looked up at her and pointed to the software.

"I can't make heads or tails out of it." He stood and extended his hand, introducing himself. "Jimmy called and said he was sending you out here. You've had some experience in transportation in the National Guard?"

"It can't be any tougher than the program I used in military transportation," Barb assured him. She opened the program. "It's fairly straightforward. With a bit of help from your accountant, I can handle this. But, I have three kids and need to make more than minimum wage."

"I start everyone off there, but with your experience, I could offer more. I have three kids, too, and Jimmy's never led me astray. My wife's a stay-at-home mom right next door. Our youngest is in pre-school, but we have a new baby on the way. If your kids are sick or something, bring them out here. It'd be fine with us."

Barb blinked back moisture. "You're like Jimmy. How kind!"

Jerry shrugged. "I'll never be as great as he is, but God's given us new hearts, and we try to love His way. It works better. Are you on board, or do you need time?"

"When can I start?"

"Yesterday." Jerry laughed as he held up the stacks. "Seriously, could you start tomorrow? I need some cash flow to make salaries."

Barb rushed out to tell Nick the good news. He stood in front of the garage, talking to a pregnant woman. Jerry put his arm around his wife, Suzie, as he extended his hand to Nick. "Thanks for bringing Barb over. She'll fit right in. Sweetheart, this is Barb Westfall. She's a friend of Jimmy's and goes to our church."

"Aren't you Alan's mom?"

The mothers knew each other from the church scouting program their kids attended, so they chatted comfortably. Jerry went back to work after he dropped a kiss on his wife's cheek. She smiled radiantly. The birds sang louder, and the sun shone brighter, but a flash of pain swept across Barb's eyes even as she smiled brightly and made her goodbyes.

Nick closed her door quietly and moved around the car. "You okay?"

"I'm pretty good most of the time. It's been over two years, but seeing them so happy, you know?"

"Yeah, I never saw love like that until I watched the O'Malleys. I've been married twice and never knew how to love a woman. I deserved every rejection I got. Earned it the hard way."

"You're divorced, Nick?"

"Twice, with hookups in between. Not a pretty picture. You know their story?" Nick looked back at Jerry and Suzie's house. "God brought them together and made them a family. Jerry rescued her and the kids from her first husband's abuse." Nick glanced across the seat and added, "I go to recovery with Suzie. She was one tough little cookie. This pregnancy has softened her up. She positively glows. Jerry's right, God taught them to love His way. Where to now?"

Barb hesitated and looked over at Nick. "Uh, do you have some time? You may be sorry you asked. Do you know anything about plumbing?"

Nick grinned. "One of my foster fathers was a plumber. I worked with him in the summer. I'm at your service, ma'am. Whatcha got?"

Barb laughed. "A man of many talents. I've got a leak under my sink, and I can't afford a plumber."

"I'll take a look, but don't you want to get the kids?"

"They're at daycare. You don't mind?"

"Nah, I like kids."

They swung by Subway to pick up Barb's car, and Nick followed her to her house by way of the daycare. He pulled his Porsche into the driveway beside her van. The small white-sided house with dark blue shutters was well-maintained, and its yard perfectly groomed. It looked like her, tidy and neat.

Barb's curly-headed blonde toddler slipped out of her car and ran to Nick. "Hi, Unca Nick," she said as she lifted her arms. Nick swung her up with a smile, and Barb watched, amazement on her lovely face.

Why did I think she looked severe? Nick wondered. *Those hazel eyes could melt ice.*

Barb's dirty-blonde hair curled softly around her heart-shaped face.

She'd cut her hair differently.

"Hey, girlie-girl, how're you doing?" Nick said. He looked over at Barb. "She must've picked 'uncle' up from Todd and Willow. I get them at the nursery a lot. You don't mind?"

Barb shook her head quickly. "I'm surprised. You only saw her at Bob Evans. She doesn't usually take to men. Robbie, this is—"

Robbie stuck out his hand. "Hello, Brother Nick. What're you doing at my house?"

"Your mom asked me to look at a leak under her sink, man. Is that okay?"

Robbie nodded curtly and led the way into the house.

"Sorry," Barb whispered behind Nick. "He gets a little protective."

"He's protecting his mother. I honor him. He's a good kid. I help with the scouts," Nick answered quietly as he shifted Alice Marie in his arms and caught the door. He placed the tot gently on the floor and steadied her until she toddled off. "But this young man I don't know." He turned to Barb's middle child. "Hi, I'm Nick Costas. What's your name?"

"My name is Alan Butler Westfall, and I'm nine years old. I go to Moorefield Academy, and I'll be in the fourth grade, and I'm Alice Marie's big brother."

Nick smothered a chuckle and held out his hand. "I'm proud to meet you, Alan Butler Westfall in the fourth grade at Moorefield Academy. I know a wonderful woman named Alice—Alice O'Malley. She goes to our church."

"My baby sister is named for her. She saved her life when she was Mommy's nurse."

Barb's eyes swam. "The cord was looped around her neck, and Alice opened her airways. I couldn't have stood losing her, too. It's one of many things the O'Malleys did for me. They got me through the horrible time after Bob died."

"Good folks, the O'Malleys. The best thing I ever did was coming to work for Ian. I found Christ in West Virginia."

Barb laughed. "It is 'Almost Heaven,' you know." She pointed. "The leak's in the kitchen."

Nick lay on his back and looked under the sink. After a bit, he scooted into the center of the kitchen, where Robbie stood over him. "I need to go to Lowe's. Look here, Robbie." Nick stood and pointed to the floor of the cabinet. "This leak's been here a while. It's rotted the cabinet floor. Should we buy some wood and replace it?"

Robbie puffed up as he leaned over to look where Nick pointed. "Well, it doesn't look nice. Is it damaged?"

"I'd say the bottom will fall out, and your mom won't be able to put her cleaning supplies there anymore."

"Oh, then I guess we'd better, uh, do whatever you think."

"I think you need to measure the cabinet floor. Does your dad have a tape measure around here?"

Robbie nodded, went down to the basement, and returned with it. Nick showed him how and where to measure and then stood with paper and pencil to jot down the dimensions Robbie called up.

Barb marveled at how Nick brought the troubled teen into the project. Soon, they left for the store.

"Thanks for helping, Mom. The sink leaked for a while, but I didn't know how to fix it. Dad would've fixed it." Robbie glanced nervously at Nick.

"I'm sorry about your dad. It hurts a lot for you, but you're lucky to have had a good dad who loved your mom and you. I never had a father."

"That's biologically impossible," the teenager replied.

Nick chuckled. "Okay, smart guy, I never knew my biological father, and my so-called 'stepfathers' only wanted what they could take from my mother. I was five when I started my journey through foster homes. Be thankful you had a dad. He taught you a lot, and you have a terrific mom."

Robbie regarded Nick carefully. "How was that? Foster homes, I mean."

"It was no walk in the park. I ran away a bunch of times, called for help even more, and got moved around to more places than I can count. I joined the Marines when I was seventeen, just to get away."

"I didn't know you'd been in the military. Were you in a war zone?"

"The first Gulf War, but it was still better than the foster care system." Nick shrugged and turned into the store. "I had a couple of tough-love sarges who straightened me out before I could become a felon. One of them got me to work with sound systems for the Marine Band. I had a knack for it, so I got out and finished college in sound technology and production. I ended up working in Hollywood, then Nashville, and now I work with O'Malley Productions."

"That's cool."

Nick drew him into a headlock as they went into the store. "Yeah, it's cool. I couldn't ask for a better gig. I'm gonna ask God if I can work for them when I get to heaven."

Robbie laughed as he straightened up. Nick wasn't such a bad guy after all. They worked side by side the rest of the afternoon, putting in a new faucet and rebuilding the cabinet floor. Nick didn't boss Robbie. He worked with his lines and showed the boy how to use the electric screwdriver to fasten the board down. When they finished, Barb invited Nick to stay for burgers.

"I'll start the grill, Mom," Robbie announced cheerfully.

Barb shook her head as the door slammed noisily after him. "You got on his good side, Nick. You were patient with him."

"I was a kid once, a thousand years ago. He's a good boy. You do a good job with him."

"Thank you, but you're not that old."

"It was another lifetime ago. I never had church to teach me I was a valuable human being, important to God."

"What about your folks?"

He shrugged, moved into himself, and shut her off.

She picked up his vibes, remembering about his foster homes, and she busied herself with the burgers. "Here, take this tray of burgers, and I'll follow with the rest. Alan, would you bring the silverware and plates, please?"

They sat down around the deck, and Robbie offered Nick a soda from the cooler.

"You grill like a pro, man. Who taught you those skills?" Nick asked.

"Jimmy O'Malley. They spent a lot of time around here after, you know . . . after."

Nick nodded and stood beside Robbie in front of the grill. "I never knew to put the salt and pepper on *after* you turn them. I always wondered why my burgers and steaks were so dry. Thanks for teaching me, Robbie. Good job!" Robbie swelled at the praise, and Nick pretended not to notice when half a burger broke off and slipped into the fire.

After a lively meal, Alan begged to get their suits on and turn on the hose. Barb readily agreed. "You guys were patient while we got the sink fixed. Cookies now, or after?" Everyone agreed to wait, although Nick complained he'd smelled them all afternoon and wouldn't be denied. "We won't cheat you. You deserve more than cookies, and I insist on paying you for all you bought at Lowe's," Barb said.

"No, ma'am, you've given enough for your country." He held up his hand to stem her protests. "It's all I'll say, Barb."

"You're a kind, good man, Nick Costas." He laughed shortly. "No, I mean that." Once again, her hand rested on his, and he tried to stem a flood of emotion.

"Come on, let's get these kids," he said, jumping up and running into the yard to grab the hose.

Alan shrieked, put his hands over his head, and laughed. He gulped at the cold water. Barb swooped up Alice Marie and took off running.

Nick tried not to hit her with the water directly, but Robbie grabbed the hose, drenched her, and then turned it on Nick, who held his hands up in a vain effort at self-protection.

In the midst of the laughter, Barb slid in the mud. She held Alice Marie to her breast, laughing until the tears streamed down her face. "Robert Daniel Westfall, you rinse me off right now!"

Robbie still laughed, but he gentled the spray and rinsed the mud off her. When she put the toddler down and straightened up, her wet T-shirt clung to her body. Nick's laughter faded as he looked away. "I'm quite soaked!" he observed. He pulled his shirt away from his torso.

Barb looked down, and her face turned scarlet as Nick fastidiously looked elsewhere. She crossed her arms. "I'll go change. Turn the hose off, kids, and put on dry clothes before we freeze. I'll get us cookies and ice cream."

When Barb came out in a loose blouse and jeans a few minutes later, she placed a beach towel around Nick, who didn't trust his voice as he admired her neat figure. His embarrassment for her was evidence of new life. The old Nick Costas would have made coarse comments or obscene gestures—probably both. After warm cookies and ice cream, Nick rose and thanked them all for the meal and the fun.

"Thank *you*. Thanks for my job, my faucet, and the cabinet repair. Let me get another towel for the car. I'm sorry I don't have any dry clothes to offer."

"This big guy will catch up to me soon. Your dad must've been a big man, Robbie."

"He was taller than Mr. O'Malley and Mr. Jimmy. I look like him."

"I saw the pictures on the mantle. I'm glad your mother has you. You're a handsome guy, but don't let it go to your head," Nick said. He looked up as Barb came out with another towel. "I'll bring these back at church. I'll let myself out the side gate, so I don't drip through your nice living room."

Barb struggled with a sleepy toddler, but she offered to walk him to his car.

"I'll go. You take care of Alice Marie," Robbie volunteered. Nick flicked the towel at him and chased him, and then he got in his Porsche. Robbie touched his arm. "Thanks, Nick. Thanks for giving Mom her laugh back. She had fun tonight. I had fun. We all had fun."

Nick waved as he backed out of the driveway. He picked up his phone from the console and saw a missed call from Mike. He punched in a return call. "Hey, Romeo, how's the love life?"

"You tell me. I hear you were at Barb Westfall's all day. You didn't answer your phone."

Nick grunted. "She needed a plumbing repair. I fixed her faucet."

"Took a long time. She's a pretty gal. Surely, you noticed."

"She deserves a lot better. I don't know how to love a woman, much less father a terrific bunch of kids whose father was a military hero, so don't even go there."

"You're a new creation. God is a Father, and He can show you how to—"

"That's enough." Nick cut him off bitterly. "I don't think I'll ever love again. We're talking about *your* love life here. Did you hear from Clare?"

"She's coming with the girls for Memorial Day. Come up this weekend. Help me strategize."

Nick laughed. "You'll have her eating out of your hand, you old love machine."

"I'd like to crank up this love machine again. It's been a long time."

"Yeah, I hear you, man," Nick replied as he shook off an image of Barb shivering in her wet T-shirt. "I think I'll go home and take a cold shower."

"Wouldn't be thinking about the lovely widow, would you, Nick?"

"You're getting on my last nerve. Did I ever tell you I got locked up for assault in my old life?"

"All right, sorry. You coming or not? Let's go to the Purple Fiddle and scope out the action."

"I'd like that. You've been a good friend to me, Mike. Did you hear my ex is getting married? The first one has run out of alimony, and now I don't have to pay the second anymore either. Thanks for helping me get the remarriage clause into the divorce. I paid my first wife for ten years!" Nick checked the traffic, moved over to the slow lane, and asked, "You think you can learn to love God's way?"

Mike took a deep breath. "I'd sure like to try." He chuckled. "I whispered to Tim that he ought to try to get a piece of that Shawnee warrior action the day I met Missy. He gave me this you-know-what eating grin and told me the same thing: 'I'd sure like to try.' May God help me love Clare like he loves Missy. He practiced restraint for seven months while she dealt with her issues. Clare has come with the girls several times, and it's all I can do. I'm ready to set a date. We get along great on the Internet and the phone. We've had a couple of wonderful laughs recently. You think I should buy a ring, in case the moment comes?"

"It never hurts to be ready, Mike. God bless, man. What I wouldn't give to love like that."

"I'll pray for you."

"If God brought me someone like Suzie, I might feel like I had something to offer. But Barb . . . She's so pure, like Missy and Alice, you know?"

"Two unwed mothers whom God made pure: one a victim of rape, and the other a teenage pregnant bride. And then there is you, Nick Costas—born-again believer in the Lord Jesus Christ, whose sins are buried in the sea of God's forgetfulness."

"Mike, I don't think you hear me," Nick answered harshly.

"God loves you, and I love you, too, you old scoundrel. 'Night, Nick."

"Bye, Mike." Nick heard a honk behind him. He was much too

slow for the traffic. He pressed his foot on the gas and surged his Porsche forward.

* * *

Alice Marie was asleep, and Alan was in the tub when Barb sank on the couch beside Robbie. "Whatcha watching?"

"Nothing much." He glanced at her, tossed the remote on the couch, and asked, "Mom, would you ever think of marrying again?"

"What brought that on? I don't know if I could ever love again. I loved your dad very much. I always will."

"I remember you guys together, but Nick's a good guy. He'd never try to take Dad away. He told me you were blessed to have me 'cause I look so much like him. He looked at the photos in here, and he talked about Dad. Most people avoid the subject, you know?"

"He's a nice guy, Robbie, but he's just a good friend."

"It was good to hear you laugh, Mom. He's a great guy. He treats me like a man. He's had a tough life. He hasn't had much love in his life, like we have."

"What did you guys talk about?"

"Mostly about his foster homes. He told me I was lucky to have a dad. When he took his shirt off to wring it out, I saw these awful scars on his back. He must've seen me stare, because he turned around real fast and said, 'I told you foster homes were no picnic.' One of the scars had a jagged edge and a hole, so I asked him about it." Robbie shuddered and looked at his mother. "He got beat with a belt. The metal side was down, and it went in and tore. He never had stitches, because the foster family didn't want to lose its income. It must've gotten infected. How does God let that happen to some kids?" Robbie's voice broke, and Barb took him into her arms as her own heart broke for a little lost boy named Nick. "He said he didn't know how to love, but he was real kind to me, and I was kinda mean to him at first."

"He understood, honey. He said you did your job, to protect your mother, and he honored you."

"He got taken away from his mother when he was five, Mom. Five! That sucks."

"Yes, it does, Robbie. It does suck. We should pray for Nick."

"Yeah, and maybe God can let us teach him how to love." Tears swam in Barb's eyes, but as she blinked them back, a sudden memory of the jolt she'd felt when her hand had touched Nick swept over her. Perhaps she *could* learn to love again, she thought.

CHAPTER 7

Nick Meets His Match

T HE PHONE RANG in Missy's quiet office. She frowned, but when she saw the caller ID, she picked it up immediately.

"Missy? This is Barb Westfall. Have you got a minute?"

"Sure, Barb, what's up?" Missy never refused to set aside time for her friend.

"I need to talk. Could we do lunch some day this week?"

"Wednesday okay? I can bring a salad into the office. Are you all right until Wednesday?"

"I've tons to do here. I'm catching up the backlog, and quarterlies are due." Barb liked working at the garage for Jerry, Jimmy O'Malley's old partner. With Barb's background in military transportation, the job was a perfect fit.

Tim's architecture firm and Missy's interiors company shared a building, so he was usually around. But he wasn't there when Barb arrived for lunch and found Missy setting up grilled chicken salads. "Looks yum. Where's Tim?"

"Business lunch." Missy called out to Tammy, her office manager, and sat. "What's up?"

Barb threaded her napkin through her fingers, not meeting Missy's eyes. After they blessed the food, she nibbled at her salad. "This dressing is delicious. Tart but sweet." Missy waited. Barb swallowed and cleared her throat. "It's, uh, about Nick. You know him pretty well, don't you?"

"I met him in Nashville before he came to work with Daddy, and he lived with us before he moved into his apartment. Yeah, he's a good friend. Why?"

"I wondered. I mean, I know he's had a hard time in life. He told Robbie about his foster homes."

"He doesn't talk about that much. He must like Robbie a lot."

"He talked with him about losing his dad—told Robbie he was lucky to have had a dad like Bob." Barb looked down and carefully folded her napkin. "I wondered, you know, if you thought he would ever . . . uh, marry again?"

Missy studied her friend. "He's twice burned. He said he never would. He paid alimony to two wives. Both ran around on him. Mike— you know our friend Mike Green, who lives in Canaan Valley? Anyway, he's furious with Nick's attorney. Nick's going to divorce care with Mike, and Mike is big on new beginnings. Nick came to Christ a couple of months ago, and he sometimes attends recovery with Daddy and Jimmy. He never was an alcoholic, but he had relationship problems. He didn't choose wisely, and his wives ran all over him. Daddy says he takes all the blame. Why do you ask? You like him?"

Barb's face colored. "Robbie thinks we are called to help him. He wants me to marry Nick. He thinks we can teach him the love of a family—love he's never experienced. I loved Bob so much. I never thought I'd marry again."

"That's a poor reason to marry—noble, but poor. You can't build a marriage on pity. You have to love someone, be attracted to him."

"Oh, I didn't mean . . . I mean, I am . . . *attracted* to Nick. He's been kind to us, a good friend. He repairs my car and my plumbing, and the kids adore him. But, I'm running out of excuses to call him. A couple of times our hands touched, and I felt this jolt, like electricity. I've never felt anything like it. Bobby and I knew each other all our lives, and we were so comfortable. We were always together. It was good between us—the sex, you know. But I never felt this . . . jolt. I was shocked. I don't want to chase after Nick because I feel lust, like a needy widow, but when Robbie said that, I began to think . . ."

"I remember when I first felt that 'jolt.' It's kind of breathtaking, isn't it? I was afraid of passion. Did you know I was raped when I was seventeen?"

"No! God bless you. How awful!"

"Do you remember Tiffany? She visited here. She's my birth daughter. When Tim came along, I was afraid of love. Mom made me go to recovery. It took months and a lot of love before I was able to come to Tim with the passion God intends in marriage."

"Wow, you'd never know. Anyone can see the sparks fly now!"

Missy laughed. "God restored all that the enemy stole. Anyway, that's why I don't want you to even think of marrying Nick simply because he needs you. You have to love someone to build a marriage."

"I think I do, or I could, but he keeps me at arm's length. Robbie and I are out of excuses to get him to the house. The other night, I brought out popcorn. We were all watching a movie, and I sat next to Nick on the couch. He took a handful but jumped up and went to the fridge for sodas, and then he sat down in the chair. He seems to push me away, and I don't know how to break through."

"It took Daddy ten years after he came to Christ to call Mom."

Barb groaned. "Don't tell me that, Missy. I can't wait ten years! I wonder what's wrong with me. I think if he doesn't kiss me, I'll die."

Missy patted Barb's hand. "We'll pray for God to give you and Nick direction. If this relationship is His will, and your family would be healing to Nick—he adores your kids—then He will bring it to pass. God," Missy began, in her usual way of including God in her conversations, "we need some help here, sir. Please intervene on behalf of Barb and Nick. If you're drawing them together, then turn Nick's heart and give him faith and courage to believe. You gave him a new life. Now, give Barb faith and patience to wait upon You. If it's not Your will, then make that clear to Barb, and release her from this attraction."

Barb murmured her agreement, and the women joined, "Amen."

"Thanks, I feel better. I'll wait on the Lord—as long as it is not too long!" Barb grinned. "You'd better pray for Robbie, too. He's crazy about Nick, and I'm afraid for Alice Marie because she's so attached to him. By the way, are you guys coming to her birthday party?"

"Yes, we'll be there. I can't believe she's two! Todd and Willow have picked out her gift already."

"Alice is off Saturday, and she'll keep her. But I need to borrow Tim's truck to get Alice Marie's new bed home. I've got to get her crib out of my bedroom. Guess I've lost my computer room."

"Consider it done. We'll help."

* * *

When Saturday came, Nick was at the studio. Missy saw Barb pull into her parents' driveway to leave Alice Marie with them. Missy glanced at Tim. "Don't you have a conference call, Tim? I wonder if Nick could take Barb."

"I can read you like a book, matchmaker, but, as a matter of fact, I do."

"I'd take her, but I can't help her put the bed together. Let's see if he can go."

Missy and Tim had previously enlisted her mother and father in prayer support for Barb and Nick, so Ian caught on immediately. He told Nick he wanted to call it a day, and Missy asked to speak to Nick.

"Your dad's done for the day. I can take her," Nick offered. "Let's go, Barb." They walked up to Tim and Missy's to fetch the truck.

When they got to Barb's house, the boys were at softball practice. She helped Nick carry the bed parts in. She carried in the side rails, but the door slammed on her hand. She cried out.

Nick rushed from Alice Marie's new bedroom. "I told you I'd get that. Are you hurt?" Barb was cradling the hand, which was already turning blue. "Can't you wait a minute? Here, let me see." Barb blinked back tears, both at the pain and at Nick's harsh words. He guided her into the kitchen, wrapped some ice in a towel, and tenderly placed the pack on her hand. His gentle concern took the sting from his angry words. Barb sniffed, and Nick reached for a tissue on the counter and tenderly wiped her tears. "Here. Is that better?" He indicated her hand.

"Thanks. I wanted to help. I hate having you do everything."

"Why can't you accept a little help?"

"I have no one else. My dad's gone. I need to get along by myself. You were kind to help me with this, but . . ."

"Do you think we ought to take you to the ER?" Nick lifted the ice pack and winced as he looked at her hand.

Barb gingerly opened and closed her hand. "I don't think it's broken. I've got to get ready for the party."

"Would you please stay out of my way, then? I'll get this bed together and see what else I can do to help in here. Don't hurt yourself again!"

"Yes, sir. I'll set the table with paper plates and plasticware. Is that too much?"

Nick's eyes twinkled, and he touched her cheek, "I'll allow it. Call me if you need anything." When he heard a loud crash a moment later, he came on a run.

Barb, still favoring her injured hand, sat on the kitchen floor, covered with plastic containers. "I tried to reach the tablecloth I hid up there, and everything crashed down." Nick scowled, but Barb was tickled when he joined in her laughter, gave her a hand, and pulled her to her feet.

"Have you got everything now?" he asked, taking a step toward the cabinet just as she did. He looked at her, startled, as they collided. He steadied her, feeling the all-too-familiar lurch of his heart when they touched. When she looked up, their lips only a few inches apart, the

61

urge to kiss her overwhelmed him. His mouth brushed hers, but he was surprised to feel her response. Their lips met, and her arms stole around his neck. The kiss deepened far more than the light one he intended. He broke away.

"I'm sorry. That never should have happened." He stepped back. "Do you need anything else?"

Disappointed at his rejection, Barb blushed and shook her head.

"I'll get back to bed. Uh, Alice Marie's bed. It's coming together nicely." Nick abruptly turned and left.

Barb sat down heavily at the table. Tears stung her eyes. *It was a nice kiss. I wanted that kiss.* She walked down the hall to the new bedroom. "It's almost together, Nick."

He looked at her briefly, but his eyes quickly shifted away. "She should have this bar installed, so she won't fall out."

"Thanks. Do you need anything?"

"Nope, I'm good, thanks. How's your hand?"

"What? Oh, it's better. I'll have a nasty bruise, but it feels better."

"That's good." Nick still didn't meet her eyes.

Sighing, she turned away and went to finish the cake. When she heard things moving around, she was too humiliated to go back. "I'll be darned if I'll offer to help again," she muttered to herself, throwing the knife into the sink with a clatter.

Nick stuck his head around the corner. "You okay?"

"Fine, thank you. I've been taking perfectly good care of myself for years now!"

"Pardon me," Nick said, with a hint of sarcasm. "You wanna come see if this is all right?"

"I'm sure it's fine."

"Oh, come on, Barb, please?"

She stomped down the hall and stared. Alice's bed was complete, with Cinderella sheets and a Cinderella comforter. Nick had even hung Cinderella curtains.

"Oh, Nick, you shouldn't have done all this!"

"I had to give her something for her birthday. Do you like it?"

"Oh, yes! How can I stay mad at you when you do this?"

"I'd like to know why you're mad to begin with. Come see if this is okay." Nick led her to her own bedroom, where he'd replaced the crib with the computer desk he'd moved from the new bedroom. "The computer's all hooked up. Where do you want the crib? By the way, you want me to get a wireless router in here? Robbie will need his own computer for high school next year, and it'd be much easier."

"This is beyond okay. I didn't expect you to do all this. I don't know how to thank you."

"Just tell me why you're angry. I didn't mean for that to happen, in there, in the kitchen. I'm sorry."

"Don't be sorry. I wanted it. I guess more than you." She turned her back to him, so he wouldn't see her tears.

"No, not more than me, Barb. It's . . . I'm no good for you."

"Don't you think I should be the judge of that?"

"You don't know me, Barb. If you did, you'd run like the wind. Trust me on this." Nick gathered up his tools and tossed them into his toolbox.

Barb couldn't have answered over the harsh clatter even if she'd found the words. She was relieved when her boys rushed in. "Is Mr. Tim here?" Robbie called.

"No. Nick used Tim's truck to bring the bed home. Go wash up; folks will be here soon."

"Wow, Nick, that looks great!" Robbie enthused.

Nick drew him into a headlock and simultaneously tousled Alan's hair. "Hey, Alan! How're you doing, buddy? It doesn't look too shabby, but it would've been easier with your help. Your mom slammed her hand in the door."

Robbie eased out of his grasp and turned to his mom. "Let me see, Mom."

"I'm fine. Look, Nick put my computer desk in my bedroom where the crib was. Wasn't that nice? Now, go shower, both of you. People will be here any minute. And don't leave wet towels all over the floor."

Missy and Tim opened the door. "You need a hand before the troops arrive?" Missy asked. "It looks nice. You're all set. Should I make the Kool-Aid? Let me see the new bed. Do you need help, Nick? Tim's here."

Smiling at her friend's typical barrage of words, Barb reached into the refrigerator and pointed them down the hall. "Go see what Nick's done. It looks darling!"

A flurry of activity ushered the rest of the crowd through the house: Missy's mom and dad, Alice and Ian O'Malley; her brother, Jimmy, and his wife, Missy's best friend, Julie; and all the children.

"Mike stopped by, Barb, and he's here with us, too. Is that okay?" Julie asked.

"Of course! The more the merrier. Hey, Mike."

"I told them I shouldn't crash your party. You don't know me well."

"You do divorce care at the church, don't you? And you're friends with the O'Malleys and most welcome in my home."

"I know this guy, too. Hi, Nick." Mike and Nick shook hands.

Robbie came into the kitchen, his head still wet from the shower. "Help me with the grill, Nick?" he asked. The two of them headed for the deck.

"Robbie's crazy about Nick. Nick's been so good for him," Barb said. Jimmy and Mike exchanged glances while Missy and Barb scurried around the table and placed last-minute odds and ends. "Everybody grab some lemonade, and let's go outside."

Barb swooped Alice Marie up in her arms. "Hi, birthday girl." She turned to Missy's mother. "Did she have a nap?" Alice said she had. "Good, she'll last through supper and her presents. Missy, grab the tray of ketchup and mustard. Julie, I have lettuce and tomato in the fridge, but we can get them when the burgers are done."

Mike followed Nick out onto the deck and watched the interaction between him and Robbie. Obviously, they were close. They bantered with genuine affection. Alan played catch with Jamie and Jimmy. Jimmy and Julie's daughters, Maryanne and Willow, sat in a corner with Alice Marie and played with their dolls.

Alice's mouth curved into her quiet smile. "Those are my special girls, Mike."

Ian dropped his hand on her shoulder. "Every baby you help deliver is your 'special child,' nurse," he teased.

She reached her hand up to pat his and leaned into him. "Every child in this yard is extra-special to me, Ian."

He dropped a kiss on her cheek. "I know, love. Come on, Tim. Let's toss a few to those boys."

After burgers, the party moved into the house, where Alice Marie ripped paper off packages, bestowed kisses, and nicely shared her new gifts. "Good girl, baby," Barb said. "You have another gift down the hall, from Uncle Nick. Let's go see." She took Alice Marie by the hand and steered her to her new bedroom.

Nick had all the reward he needed as Alice Marie's eyes widened and her precious little mouth formed an "O." She flung a smile at him. "Thank you, Unca Nick!"

"Nick hung those curtains for you," Barb informed her.

The birthday girl jumped up and down, holding her hands up to Nick, who laughed, gathering her in his arms. "I love you, Unca Nick!" She planted a big kiss on his cheek.

"I love you, too, girlie-girl. Happy birthday!"

Tim whispered to Missy, "She won't come to me or Jimmy. I thought she was afraid of men."

"She is," Missy whispered back, "but she sure loves Nick."

The party drifted back to the front of the house, but the little girls stayed in the new bedroom. "We should've painted the room before you moved her," Nick said. "Maybe next weekend?"

Tim glanced at Mike, who glanced at Jimmy. Ian smothered a grin and turned so Nick wouldn't see. When the girls began to quarrel, parents moved in to take their tired children home. Todd, who was left out of the girls' play, cuddled in his mother's lap. Julie and Alice had cleaned up, so Barb was left with nothing to do when the door closed. She gathered up one of the new books and settled the younger kids on the couch to read.

Nick stuck his head back in the door. "Ten o'clock in the morning next Saturday. I'll bring the paint."

"Can I miss practice, Mom?" Robbie asked. "I wanna help."

"We'll make it three o'clock, Robbie. How's that?" Nick offered.

"Thanks, Nick. See you then."

"See you Wednesday night at scouts, man!" Nick corrected as he ducked out the door.

"So, Mom, how's it going with you and Nick?"

"Robbie!"

"Well, have you kissed him yet?"

"Shh!" she cautioned, and she glanced toward the little ones.

Robbie grinned. "I want to hear all. We need to get this show on the road. I'll be in high school next year." Barb blushed. "That good, huh?"

"Robert Daniel Westfall, that is enough!" After the two younger children were in bed, Barb sat down beside Robbie on the couch. "This isn't easy for Nick, Robbie. He told me today he isn't good enough for me."

"That's not true! We all like him. He's awesome. You like him, don't you?"

"Yes, Robbie, I really do, but we need to give him time, and we need to pray for him. He's had a lot of hard blows in life."

"Man, this is a bummer. Let's start now." He bowed his head. "Jesus, we lift Nick up to you. You knew him when he was a little boy, so You know how tough he had it. I think You brought him to us to show him the love of a family, Lord. Help us to do that, and help him to let us in. God, help Mom to love him so we can have a family. Thank You. Amen."

Tears rolled down Barb's cheeks as she choked, "Amen."

Robbie put his arms around her. "We'll just keep trying." He patted her awkwardly.

"When did you grow up, Robbie? Dad would be so proud."

"I grew up a lot when I saw the scars on Nick's back, and he told me I was lucky to have a Dad." Robbie was thoughtful. "I never realized how much love we had. I was mad at God because He took Dad away, you know?" Barb studied her son's earnest face. "I couldn't believe anyone would do that to a kid, and Nick turned out good. I mean, he's so nice and all. He told me he didn't know how to love, but Jesus said you know people by their fruits, and he's been really nice to us."

"Yes, he has," Barb agreed. "He's a good man."

* * *

In his solitary apartment, Nick railed at God for his attraction to Barb. *Why are You doing this to me, God? She deserves better. Why did You bring her into my life? I don't want to love her.*

Nick picked up his Bible and read: "Every good and perfect thing comes down from the Father." He impatiently flipped to another page and saw: "Give thanks to the Lord, for He is good, and His mercy endures forever."

He flung it aside. "Crap. Who says God talks to you through His Word?" Nick swore if God laughed, he heard Him. And the thought, *Do you think I'm not talking to you, Nick?* popped into his head. "God, all I have to give that precious woman is diseases!" He thought he could have that checked out, to confirm it. Then he'd know for sure he wasn't good for her.

While Nick argued with God, Mike and Ian sat in the O'Malleys'

67

living room and prayed for him. "He's crazy about Barb," Ian said. "That whole family loves him. Did you see the little girl leap into his arms? And Robbie likes him. He remembers his dad clearly, so it seems to me he'd be the toughest to win over."

"Nick's had a hard life on the streets of L.A. He thinks he hasn't anything to offer a sweet woman like Barb."

"He's not the only one with scars, Mike. Come on, let's agree together for him."

The two men bowed their heads. "Lord, speak to Nick through Your Word. Remind him that he's washed, clean, and that You make all things new."

Jimmy slipped into the room and sat beside them. He bowed his head and added his prayers. "God, if this relationship is ordained by You, give them courage and faith to see it through."

"Amen, Lord. Even as Alice prayed me home and continues to love me as You complete Your work in me," Ian added.

Jimmy prayed for Mike's ex-wife, Clare, as well. "Nick tells me she'll be in for the Fourth, Mike?"

Mike nodded. "Thanks, Jimmy. I need all those prayers and then some, but I sense some openness in her. We've been communicating regularly since last Thanksgiving."

"God gives you grace when you need it, Mike."

"And He promises not to tempt us more than we are able to bear. I'm headed over to the apartment." Missy and Tim built two apartments behind their house for their constant stream of company, and Mike had his own key. "I'm sure Missy and Tim have prayed, too, and Nick has met his match when Missy starts to pray."

CHAPTER 8

In Your Arms

IAN WOKE UP CONFUSED from his dream. He was running, searching, lost. He felt someone in his bed. Looking across, he saw his life-love, his brown Indian girl. His heart constricted as his breath caught in his throat. The bedroom of their new home was bright, washed with the full moon flooding through the sliding glass doors from the deck.

Alice loved a full moon and kept the drapes open to fall asleep in its light. Ian propped himself up on his elbow. "Thank You, God," he whispered, staring down at her. "How I love this woman. I'll never understand her love, but I thank You for it." Seeing her stir, he fell silent, but her dark eyes fluttered open, drowning him into those deep pools. Tears blurred Ian's vision. Alice reached up to brush them away.

"What is it, my love?"

Stretching out beside her, he gathered her in his arms. "Ah, *asthore*, I had the dream of 'Brown Indian Girl.' I was lost and alone, searching for you."

She snuggled up to him. "I'm here now, Ian. I'll never be apart from you again. I'll fly to Nashville with you, if you need me."

"Why, Alice? Why do you love me? Why didn't you marry a better man after all I did to you and the children?"

She traced the scratchy stubble of his chin with her gentle fingers.

"No one was you, Ian. I have always only loved you."

"I don't understand."

"It's God's gift, and I was helpless in its grip." She looked thoughtful and turned in his arms. "I loved Pops. He was a wonderful father, and he took care of his family, but he was not . . . he had no joy. He was a stern man, a good man, and I knew he loved me. But you gave me laughter. You taught me to play, to dance. I drank from the fountain of your music and poetry. I love you, Ian."

Ian turned on his back. "Missy looks like you, but she is full of laughter, and music springs out of her like one of our mountain streams—Jimmy, too. Maybe I *have* given them something."

"Jimmy's happier than I have ever seen him, and Missy has your music, your laughter, your mischief."

Ian smiled. "I told her once she has a wee bit of leprechaun. She smells like you. I love the scent of you—it is dark, warm, pulsing."

Alice gave a short, bitter snort. She had such a forgiving and generous nature that the harsh sound didn't seem to come from her. "That's a nicer description than what I got as a child: 'You stink like a dirty Injun!' I heard that often."

"*Aroon*, you smell of the deep dark woods, of God's creation."

"And I love the Irish of you, your lilt, your affectionate names, and your dancing sea-green eyes. How could I love anyone else after you?"

Ian nuzzled her neck. "When I am in your arms, I feel God's love." He pulled her back into his embrace and began drinking in the scent of her. Their soft murmurings turned into cries of delight as they stripped off each other's nightclothes.

* * *

Ian noticed Nick appeared healthy when he came in late from a doctor's appointment the next morning. "I'm working on a new song, for Alice's birthday," Ian announced.

"Do you need my input?"

"Nope. It's a surprise."

Jimmy and Ian had prayed earlier that the new song, "In Your Arms," would minister to Nick. Since Alice's birthday party was set for after church, Ian had to perfect it by Sunday. Jimmy had called the pastor earlier, arranging for a special; they had a deadline. Despite Alice's complaints about Ian's trips to Jimmy and Julie's house every evening, he wouldn't let her accompany him. Julie and Missy, aware of the secret, were trying to keep her occupied with distractions every night. One night they went to Walmart, another night they watched a Hallmark movie, but, by the end of the week, she was annoyed.

On Thursday night, Missy sharply interrupted her mother's complaints. "Give it up, Mom! He's got a surprise for you. It'll be worth it, believe me. Now, get off his case, or you will so regret it."

"You aren't supposed to tell," Julie protested. "No, Willow, cut that out! Todd, just bop her."

"Don't tell him that, Julie!" Missy laughed at her sister-in-law's frustration with her strong-willed little girl. "If you have a better way to get Mom off Dad's case, feel free."

"It'll be worth it, Alice. You'll see," Julie confirmed.

Chagrinned, Alice hugged the two younger women. "You two are diversionary tactics?"

They laughed. "Let's get the kids in the tubs and ready for bed."

"Where is Jamie?"

"Mom, would you not ask any questions, please?" Missy begged her.

Alice shrugged. "I assume this will all be over after my birthday?" They nodded. "Come on, kids, let's get a bath. Maryanne, run into the bedroom and get some jammies for the little ones, please."

* * *

On Sunday, Ian walked to the front of the church after a short worship, and the pastor introduced him as the testimony for Recovery Sunday.

"Not all of you were here when I walked out on my family twenty-two years ago," Ian began, "but my precious wife never let me go. I'd been sober for ten years, but I couldn't face my family. I had failed them for many years. The best day of their lives was the day I left. I spent ten miserable years in degradation. A doctor's diagnosis brought me up short: sober up or die of liver disease. God led me to a recovery program in California, and three years later I moved to Nashville. My music career began to prosper, but I couldn't bring myself to contact my family. I watched their lives from afar, reading the papers from home, but I longed for my beloved wife.

"In 2003, I wrote 'Brown Indian Girl.' I used to call my wife that, and I'm sure you see why." The congregation laughed. Alice and Missy could not deny their Native American heritage. "That song brought me home. The love of God, seen in my family's forgiveness and welcome, has brought more healing than years of recovery, so I asked Pastor if I could sing this song as a gift to my wife on her birthday."

Missy, Jimmy, and Jamie moved to the front of the church. Jamie took up a violin and began the lovely melody, and Ian sang:

In your arms, I feel God's love,
and the sins of the past slip away.
Bitter memories fade,
and joy comes to my heart each day.
God whispers His love. He restores and renews, and I am reborn,
when I am in your arms.
We never deserve what His love gives.
I never earn back what I have lost.
But grace, grace, God's grace, lives in you, surrounds me with your arms.
In your arms, I feel God's love,
and the present becomes more than I dreamed it could be,
when I am in your arms.

As the instruments faded, Ian looked across the congregation. "Thank you, brown Indian girl, for your love and faithfulness, such a type of God's own love for me. I am eternally grateful for your prayers that never let go of this wandering husband."

Alice, not given to emotional displays, sat quietly, the tears slipping down her cheeks. Mike placed his arm around her shoulder. His ex-wife, Clare, who came in from New York for the party, had tears in her eyes as well. When Ian got back to his seat, he drew Alice to her feet and embraced her as the congregation applauded.

"Not every husband has the talent to create such a beautiful testimony," the pastor began, "but when Ian brought me his song, I saw a sermon in it. Would you turn in your Bibles to 1 Peter 3? Most of us men can attest, we are who we are in Christ today because of the selfless love of our wives. Ian had it right: natural, human love, the love of a man for a woman and a woman for a man, is a type of God's love. God uses love to bring us closer to Himself, to teach us of His ways, to teach us forgiveness and patience."

He continued, drawing from Ephesians 5 and 1 Corinthians 13, and then he concluded by asking those who wanted to seek a better love to kneel at the altar. Mike's girls, who were sitting behind him with Missy and Tim, poked him as he sat with his head down. They pointed to Clare, who was making her way toward the front of the church. This time, Alice slipped her arm around *him* as his elegant ex-wife, in her stylish designer clothes, humbled herself before God.

* * *

"**M**ike, I *can't* go out there to their house. I made a fool of myself today," Clare protested as they got in the car.

"Every one of us in there today has been where you were at one time or another. I'm so proud of you, honey. It takes a lot of courage."

"No, Mike, you've shown courage. You refused to be what you used to be. I see that now. You demonstrated the new creation they explained to me when I prayed. I've seen it in you. You loved me when I was horrible to you. I am so sorry, so terribly sorry." She began to sob. Mike pulled onto a side road and took her in his arms, soothing her, brushing her hair back out of her face. "Look at me. I'm a mess. Where are our girls? Can we just go to your house?"

Mike put his finger under her chin and brought her face up. Looking into her eyes, he smiled. "You've never looked more beautiful than you do right now, Clare. The girls are at the O'Malleys' house. They went with Missy and Tim to set out lunch. You can freshen up there. Alice cried a lot herself today."

"Wasn't that a beautiful song? She deserves it, Mike. She must be a strong woman. I've been awful to you."

"I've been awful to you, too. You have a lot to forgive."

"But you've asked my forgiveness for months now, and all I've done is been hateful. I was wrong, and I'm sorry."

"I can think of a way you can make it up to me." Mike reached into his pocket, bringing out a small black box. "Marry me again, Clare. I promise I'll do better this time, God being my helper." Clare began to cry again. "Is it too soon? I will wait, sweetheart. I failed you miserably, but I promise I've never loved another."

Sniffing, she held out her ring finger. He slipped the beautiful diamond on her hand. Crushing her to him, Mike gave her the pent-up kiss he'd been holding for so long. "I hope you won't make me wait too long. I don't have the patience God gave Tim," he whispered huskily.

Clare laughed and cried at the same time. "We don't need a fancy wedding," she suggested. "We've been married before. I promise to do better this time, too, but I don't know God as well as you and the girls do."

After kissing her once again, Mike straightened up and backed up his car to return to the main road.

"How long have you been carrying this around?" Clare held her hand out, looking at the exquisite solitaire.

"Not long. Nick told me to be ready, 'just in case,' when you came in for the Fourth." He glanced across the seat at her, grinning. "You are beautiful, Clare. Here we are."

"Is that their home? It's not very pretentious, is it?"

"Missy and Tim live in the original farmhouse, the one we passed. Ian and Alice live up ahead. He has his studio adjoining the house. They aren't pretentious people, any of them. The other house, farther down the lane, is Jimmy and Julie's."

"Your house is grander than any of these, but I guess you are wealthier than they are."

"Maybe when I built the house but not now. They've hit it big-time. Ian's 'Brown Indian Girl' made platinum last year, and both Missy and Jimmy are up for songs of the year and musicians of the year for the Dove Awards. They're like the Apostle Paul—content, and they give tons away."

"I have a lot to learn about Christianity, but we're surrounded by good teachers, aren't we?" Clare opened her pocketbook and dug out a mirror. "I look awful!"

Mike opened her door, drew her into his arms, and whispered something that made her blush.

"Come on in, guys! You're holding up the party! Hi, Mom—that wasn't so bad, now, was it?" their daughter, Allyson, teased. "What took you so long?" Wordlessly, Clare held up her left hand. "Megan, come quick!" Allyson's sister stuck her head out the door. "Mom's got a ring! Our prayers are answered!" The girls ran down the stairs and threw their arms around their parents, squealing and jumping up and down.

"What kind of a chance did I have, with all you guys ganging up on me?" Mike inquired.

"Mom, we knew how unhappy you've been without Dad. You were too stubborn to admit it."

Clare rolled her eyes, and Mike laughed, tightening his arm around her. Alice descended the stairs. "This is more of a cause for celebration than my too many birthdays!"

"It was Ian's birthday gift that caused all this. Mike had told me he'd never marry me again until I became a Christian. And now I am." Clare looked up the stairs, where Ian stood, beaming. "Thank you, Ian."

"Definitely my pleasure. It was God's anointing and my joy. Food's ready." He waved his hand to invite them inside.

"Mike, aren't you glad you were prepared?" Nick grinned at his friend.

Mike pulled him into a hug, whispering, "You're next, buddy."

"I should be so lucky," he replied. But he looked sober and thoughtful, and his eyes flickered over to where Barb sat on the couch, smiling at the happy couple.

All the gifts were opened, and children were sleeping on pallets all over the floor when Nick quietly offered his hand to Barb. They slipped out the back door. "Let's go for a walk," he offered. Wordlessly, she took his hand. They walked silently along the stream behind the houses.

"It was quite a day in God's house, wasn't it?" Nick ventured. Barb didn't trust herself to speak. She was moved by Ian's song—happy for Mike and Clare but sad for her own hopelessness. She turned aside so Nick wouldn't see her tears.

"What is this?" he asked, turning her face with gentle fingers.

"It was a beautiful song, and I'm happy for Mike and Clare—that's all."

Nick leaned her up against a tree. "But, you're sad."

"I'll be okay. Happy tears." She swiped her eyes with her sleeve.

Nick took a deep breath. "I hope not, Barb. I hope you won't be okay without me." She looked up at him, startled. "I've argued with God this week. I told Him He made a mistake to give me this love for you. It wasn't fair. I even went to the doctor to be tested for all the bad things I could bring you that I'd never bring you, but it turns out I have a clean bill of health. Barb, I'm no prize. But God help me, I do love you, as I've never loved anyone my whole life." Holding her face in his hands, Nick kissed her tenderly, and once again he was astounded at her response.

Barb linked her arms tightly around his neck. "I love you, too, Nick Costas, and you love me, and my kids, far better than you know."

"Help me, Barb, because in your arms I feel God's love."

Barb rested her face on his shoulder. "I will love you. I promise you that, and God will complete the work He has begun in you. Nick?" She held him close as he sobbed in her arms.

"I don't deserve you. I never will." He choked.

"Who among us ever deserves the love of God? It's grace—God's unmerited favor. He set *His* love upon you, and then He set my love upon you."

Nick took her hand. "We'd better get back to the house. I don't trust myself alone with you. Didn't you know that?"

Surprised, she stopped and looked at him with amazement. "All this time, I thought it was me!"

He chuckled, putting his arm around her and drawing her close. "Oh, it was you, Barb. It was you!" He nibbled her ear.

She laughed, touching his cheek. "Then I guess we'd better get married soon."

He grinned. "How about tomorrow? Today? As soon as we can get the license." Swinging their linked hands, they walked together and laughed. When they came back inside, all eyes turned to look at them. Barb's face turned a brilliant red.

"See, Missy, that's how ordinary people blush." Tim laughed.

"Ian O'Malley, you have worked your magic on all of us today," Nick said with a shrug.

"Well, praise the Lord, and who wants more ice cream?" Alice responded. Ian grabbed her and kissed her soundly. "Now, you stop that, you wild Irishman!" she protested.

"And that's how Indian women blush," Tim said, reaching for

Missy, who took off running, climbing over the back of the couch.

Laughing, she cried, "Don't you dare, Timothy Lee Raines!" Her brother grabbed her by the waist to hold her for Tim. "That's not fair, Jimmy!" Tim laughed and contented himself with a hug, at least until later.

After everyone had gone home, Tim carried a sleeping Todd up the road. "Missy?" he asked in a mischievous tone, "Could I get you pregnant tonight?"

"No, you nut. I'm already pregnant!"

"Shucks."

"But, you never let that stop you before, Timothy."

"Well then, let's put this boy in his bed."

Missy opened the door for him and walked ahead to their room.

A few weeks later, two couples—Mike and Clare, Nick and Barb— walked to the front of the church, and they said their vows before a handful of loved ones. They knew their marriages would face challenges, but all things were possible with God.

CHAPTER 9

Nick's Sleepover

A FTER THE SIMPLE WEDDING ceremony after Sunday service, all the couples celebrated at a private room in the old historic inn in Elkins, where Ian insisted on hosting a luncheon. Mike and Clare were flying to New York in the evening and taking off for two weeks in Italy the next day. Nick and Barb were not going anywhere for a honeymoon. Ian had offered them tickets to Costa Rica, but after Nick had prayed, he felt Barb's kids had enough loss in their lives, and he wanted to change their routine as little as possible. He took Barb's hand, picked up Cinderella, and said, "Come on, boys, I have new poles in the car. Let's head up the mountain a bit."

Alice insisted they wait long enough for a box of leftovers for a picnic supper, but soon they took off in a flurry of goodbyes. As she and Ian waved after the departing new Suburban, Ian said, "I hope he's not getting their relationship off to a bad start, putting the kids first."

"Barb cried when she told me what they had decided about a honeymoon," Missy said. "She couldn't believe how sensitive he is to the children—how committed to them. He won her heart even more. He said he was marrying her and that included the kids."

"I can't believe he traded his Porsche for a Suburban," Ian said. "He loved that car! It's the only thing he fought for in the divorce settlement. He arrived in West Virginia with a couple of suitcases and his sports car."

Tim suggested they pray for the new family, and the O'Malleys joined hands around the table.

* * *

Nick, having loaded his family into his new Suburban and fastened Cinderella in her car seat, said, "Let's stop by the house to change into some fishing clothes." After a brief stop, they headed up the highway to the mountains and stopped beside a clear stream.

"What's the ice chest for, Nick?" Robbie asked.

"All those trout you're going to catch," he said with a grin.

"Did you bring some bait?" Alan asked.

Nick assured them he had and pulled onto a wide place on the side of the road. They unloaded the car. He helped the boys get set up and sat leaning against a tree with a sleepy toddler in his arms.

Barb shook out a blanket and set up a picnic spot. Soon, she slipped the sleeping child out of Nick's arms, and he placed Barb into the circle of his warmth. She sat between his knees, leaning back against him. He nuzzled her hair and kissed the side of her neck. She smiled and shivered.

Suddenly, Nick thrust Barb aside and moved quickly to where Alan floundered in the stream. Before the boy could panic, Nick said, "That must be some monster of a fish to pull you off balance like that!" He pulled out a knife and cut the tangled lines loose from a tree. "I don't know how good eating it will be, but it's a huge catch. I've never had tree-fish before. Do you cook it with the bark on?"

Alan giggled and stood quietly while Nick put a new hook and sinker on the end of his line and showed him how to cast low to the water. Nick watched Alan cast several times, patted his shoulder, and said, "Good job."

By this time, Robbie was reeling in a nice medium-size trout. Nick admired it, asked him if he wanted to take it home or release it, and helped him string it on a line and put it in the water. "We'll behead it and ice it later, when we're finished," Nick promised. "Let's catch a few more, and Mom will have enough to cook tomorrow."

Cheering them on from the bank, Barb said, "Those who catch must gut and clean. I'll cook."

"I'm new at this mountain living thing," Nick complained with a grimace.

"I thought you were a big Marine, Nick? You need a kid to clean your fish?" Robbie teased.

"You don't see a pole in my hand. That's *your* fish!" Nick grinned. "Oh, what have you got, Alan?" Nick helped Alan pull in a trout larger than his brother's.

Robbie waded out of the river, returning with a pole. "Let's see you top a couple of kids." He handed Nick the pole.

Nick good-naturedly set his hook and sinker and baited his line. The sun warmed his bare arms, and he looked up at Barb on the bank. "Doing okay?"

She nodded with a smile and leaned down to pick up the waking toddler. The little girl wanted to be in the middle of the activity, but Barb convinced her to move to a rocky area where they could sit and watch, entertaining her by showing her the minnows swimming in schools in the shallow water.

Each of the boys caught another fish, and Nick caught one himself. By this time, the boys were rubbing their stomachs and asking what kind of food they had. Barb rose and began setting out their light supper.

Nick feasted on the vision of his bride's long legs, smiling when she caught him. He raised his eyebrows, and she blushed. He laughed and waded out of the water. He tousled Alan's hair and said, "You dried up just fine. I was proud of what a good sport you were there, kid." Alan grinned at him while Robbie pulled the stringer of fish out of the water. Nick threw Robbie his knife and pointed to a large flat rock in the middle of the stream. "I'll gut and clean mine and one of Alan's, Robbie. You can gut your own and your brother's other one."

"Deal," Robbie agreed, as he flipped open the knife.

After the men washed up, they all sat cross-legged on the blanket while Barb served up the plates. Alice Marie reclaimed her spot on Nick's lap, and he brushed his lips in her hair. "Having fun, Cinderella?"

"I want to fish, too, Unca Nick," she said.

"I saw a Cinderella fishing pole in Walmart, just your size. Next time, how about we have a pole for you?"

The child contented herself with eating fried chicken, but soon asked, "When?"

"Maybe we can take her to the lake tomorrow, Nick," Robbie suggested. "There's a dock she could sit on."

"We aren't going back to work for a couple of days. Let's see how the weather holds out," Barb said.

Nick rolled his eyes. "Fishing two days in a row?"

"Please, Unca Nick? Please get me a Cinderella pole?" The toddler threw herself against him, almost knocking him backward.

He laughed and circled his arm around her. "All right, baby. Tomorrow we'll go fishing again, unless it rains. I can always pray for rain."

Barb chuckled and began to clean up. "We have leftover cake at home."

After they put the trout in the refrigerator and enjoyed another piece of wedding cake, an awkward silence fell on the group. Robbie stood, yawning and stretching significantly. "Guess we'll turn in early tonight, huh, Alan? It's been a busy day, and if we're going to have another fishing day tomorrow, we'd better get some rest. Who wants the first shower?"

Alan looked up, blushed, and agreed. "Yeah, good idea, Robbie. We should do that." He didn't look at his mother or Nick.

Barb hurried her little girl to the bathtub while Nick gathered the dishes, and Alan headed for the shower in her bedroom. Robbie helped Nick in the kitchen. "This was a great day, Nick. Thanks."

"We got some nice trout," Nick said.

Robbie looked up as Alan came into the room. He put his arm around his brother's shoulder and leaned down to whisper in his ear. Alan nodded. "Why don't you read while I shower, and we'll turn in early?" the older boy said and headed off.

Barb called out. "Nick, you are in demand back here." He walked back to the Cinderella bedroom and found the toddler in her pajamas, her hair freshly shampooed.

"Sing to me," she begged. "The Cinderella song." He grinned and held out his arms. She jumped into them, and he swayed as he sang. She giggled. "Mommy said you're going to sleep over."

Holding her back, Nick asked her if she remembered the promises he and Mommy made that morning after church. "Pastor said, 'I now pronounce you man and wife.' So, you know what that means?" Her large blue eyes studied him. "That means Mommy and I are married now, and I'll live here."

"Forever and ever?"

He smiled. "If you'll let me."

A grin split her precious little face, and she patted his cheek. "I'll like that, Unca Nick! You'll be here in the morning, when I wake up?"

"Yep," he said. "So, you'd better go to sleep now." He tucked her in bed and kissed her forehead. "Night-night. Did you and Mommy pray?"

When she said they hadn't, he knelt beside her bed and heard her pray, blessing at least twenty people before she added, "And everybody in the whole wide world."

"I guess that covers it," he said as he stood. "I love you, Pumpkin."

"I love you, too."

Nick fumbled for the light switch, blinded by the tears that sprung to his eyes. He turned and saw Barb coming out of Alan's bedroom.

"He wants to tell you goodnight."

Nick sat on the edge of the boy's bed. "You did good today. That was a mighty fine fish you caught, and the other one wasn't bad, either.

We'll eat well tomorrow."

"Thanks for today. I had fun." Alan reached out, and Nick took him into his arms. "I'm glad you and Mom got married," the youngster said.

"Thanks. Me, too. But I've never had a family before, and I'm not sure I know what to do."

"Just be you, and don't ever leave us."

"Leaving is not an option, Alan." Nick started to add, "Until death do us part," but he remembered death had parted them from one parent already and stopped himself. "I plan on sticking around here even when you're long gone." Alan's arms tightened around his neck, and Nick hugged him, patting his back. "'Night, kid."

"'Night, Nick."

The living room was dark when Nick walked to the front of the house to tell Robbie goodnight. Barb had done a nice job converting the formal dining area into a bedroom for the teenage boy. Nick was surprised to find the boy's room dark.

"Robbie?"

"Hmm?" Robbie feigned a sleepiness.

"It's early for bed, isn't it?"

"Uh, we had a busy day. I'm kinda tired. Thought I'd turn in early. Alan has his light off?"

Nick knew Robbie couldn't see him grin in the darkness. "Yeah, he does. You're a good kid, Robbie. 'Night."

"'Night, Nick. See you in the morning. Close the door, will you?"

Nick gently pulled the door shut and shook his head as he walked toward the hall. He stood at the door to Barb's bedroom, watching as she came out of the bathroom in a soft gown. She smiled up at him. "Come on in. This is where you sleep, remember?"

He stepped into her bedroom. He had been in there before, the day he set up her computer for her. And yesterday a furniture delivery had brought the new bedroom set they'd picked out together. He noticed the bed was covered with new linens and turned down. Closing the door behind him, he said, "How much sleep do you intend to get, Mrs. Costas?" and walked toward her.

Barb's breath caught as she saw the intensity in his dark eyes. She stepped into his arms.

"Your hair smells delicious. It's so soft. You're so soft." He breathed in the scent of lavender. "I, on the other hand, am not." He moved against her, and she giggled. He backed her against the bed. "I'm glad I took my shower when we got home," he said as he lifted her onto the bed.

* * *

Early the next morning, Nick felt Barb crawl up the bed and snuggle beside him. He grinned and threw his arm around her, drawing her closer. "Do you intend to give me not a moment's rest all night, woman? What are you doing with clothes on?"

She giggled. "It's 8:00 a.m. The boys have taken off on their bikes, and I think you should put your pajama bottoms on before my daughter finds you. She'll be in here first thing when she wakes up." Barb dangled his pants in front of him.

"Hmm," he grumbled, "I like it better when you're taking them off." He noticed she had slipped on some shorts and a T-shirt. He was decently covered when a blonde head peeked around the door.

"Unca Nick, you *did* stay!"

He held his arms out, and she dove into the bed, bouncing up and down. He groaned and looked up at Barb. "Is she always like this in the morning?"

Laughing, she said, "Pretty much. Hungry? I'll fix breakfast." She turned to her daughter. "Need to go potty, sweetie?" She held out her hand and led Alice Marie down the hall while Nick went into the bathroom off the bedroom.

About an hour later, the boys arrived, breathless and sweaty. "We rode all the way to the lake," Robbie said.

"That's over five miles! When did you leave?" his mother asked.

"About six. Anything to eat? We had cereal, but I'm starved."

Nick walked into the room and opened the refrigerator door, pulling out bacon and eggs. "I'd say you deserve a hearty breakfast after biking ten miles," he asserted.

The family sat around the table until Alice Marie asked when they were going to get her Cinderella pole. Everyone pitched in with clean-up, and soon they were on their way. After they bought her pole, they drove to the lake. Nick helped bait the poles for the two little ones and lowered himself beside Barb.

"Can she catch anything with that pole?" Barb asked.

"Sure she can," he answered. And, within minutes, the little girl was jumping up and down and screaming.

Robbie grabbed the pole just as she tossed it in the air. "Hold onto it, sis. You let that one get away."

Eyes wide, the toddler turned around. "I catched one, Mommy!"

Amused, Barb said, "You got one on the line, but you have to hold on to it, baby. Robbie or Nick will help you reel in the next one."

Nick helped Alan and the toddler reel in a couple of perch, and Robbie threw his and theirs all back.

"Not fishing, Nick?" Robbie asked. "What's the matter? A little tired today?" He grinned.

"You know too much for your own good, kid," Nick said. "You'd better not let your mother hear you."

Robbie went over to where his mother was gathering up folding chairs. "Mom, can I borrow your phone?" She dug it out of her purse and handed it to him. Walking off, Robbie spoke into the phone. He then returned to the group. "Nick, can I talk to you a minute?"

The two of them walked off, and Robbie put his hand on Nick's arm. "Nick, I know what you're doing here, and I promise you if I live to be a hundred, I'll never forget our first day—and night—as a family. But it's not fair to you and Mom. I called Julie. Alan and I spend the night with Jamie all the time, and I asked her if we could tonight to give you some privacy."

Nick started to answer, but Robbie held up his hand. "She told us to come on over. It's a good idea, Nick. We'll have fun. I can pick up a new Xbox game Jamie's been wanting, and we'll have a great time. Please."

"You are something else, kid," Nick said affectionately.

"So are you, Nick. I couldn't believe you didn't want to take a trip and leave us kids at home."

"You guys have lost too much already. I couldn't take your mother away from you."

"I think you're giving us our mother back, Nick. But now you look like you could use a nap." He gave Nick a wide smirk and walked over to his mother. "Hey, Mom, Jamie wants us to come over. Do you think we could stop by the game store and pick up that new game he's been wanting?"

Barb glanced over at Nick, knowing his intention of keeping the family together.

He shrugged. "It's fine with me, if that's what they want to do."

On the way home, Robbie told Alan that Julie invited them to spend the night, so they ought to take some pajamas and a toothbrush. They stopped by a fast food place and picked up a meal on the way home. Then, after they grabbed a few things, Nick took the boys to Julie's house. She greeted them with a big smile and waved Nick off.

Barb welcomed Nick back home at the door. "So, what happened to your well-laid plans, Nick?" she asked.

"It seems your son is determined to give us a honeymoon of sorts," he said. "Did you notice how he contrived to get the house settled early last night?"

"Do you think . . .?"

"Yeah, Barb, I think. He's thirteen years old. He's a male."

She blushed. "So, he's thinking about . . . about what we were doing?"

Nick laughed and put his arm around her. "He was. And he's a great kid. He encouraged me to take a nap—said I looked tired." He chuckled. "I *am* tired, but I've never felt more alive in my whole life. Where's the baby?"

"She's asleep. Do you want to take a nap?"

"No, but I want to go to bed. With you."

She blushed. "In the middle of the day?"

"It's as good a time as any. I figure with three kids we'd better take what we can get."

"Well, I guess."

Nick led her into the bedroom. She didn't protest too much. Once again, he kept his T-shirt on. Later, she tentatively touched his back.

"Nick, I know about your scars. Robbie told me. You can't keep your shirt on our whole life."

His face hardened. "It isn't pretty. Heather told me I was revolting, and she didn't want anything more to do with me after she saw them."

Barb's eyes got wide. "She was your wife—the one in Nashville?"

He turned away. "Yeah. She found the drummer a whole lot prettier."

"Oh, Nick."

"It's okay. He can have her. All she wanted was a free ride to Nashville and some idiot to pay for her boob job. That's me—the idiot."

"Nick, I married you, scars and all. I won't find you repulsive. It's a part of who you are."

Nick stood. "I think I hear Cinderella." He walked across the hall, and Barb heard them quietly murmuring. She snuggled down in bed, closing her eyes for just a minute, vaguely hearing them in the bathroom and her daughter's excited cries as Nick took her into the backyard. Soon, the chains on the swing creaked, and excited laughter filled the warm summer breeze. Barb drifted off.

* * *

Nick looked up. Barb stood in the kitchen doorway, her hair sleep-tossed. "Hey, did you have a good nap? We're having some tea." Alice Marie held out a tiny teacup, and he took it from her, pretending to drink, with one pinkie sticking out. "Is this the way ladies drink tea?" he asked.

"How about we get some real tea, baby?" Barb went into the kitchen and returned after a moment with some tepid tea that she poured into the plastic teapot.

"Thank you, Mommy. Now I can give Unca Nick some real tea!"

Barb perched on one of the tiny chairs and extended a plastic cup. "May Mommy please have some tea, too?" Soberly, the child carefully poured from her teapot.

Nick sat cross-legged on the patio beside the small table. After several cups, he rose. "If you ladies will excuse me, I need to go tee-tee some tea." Leaving them laughing, Nick went into the house. After using the bathroom, he looked longingly at the unmade bed. He stretched out and found himself floating in the smell of Barb.

When Nick woke, the sun was casting long shadows in the room. He walked into the living room. "Sorry. I guess I fell asleep," he said. He grinned at his bride. "For some reason, I didn't get much sleep last night."

Barb blushed. "We were just getting ready to fix supper. I'll save the trout for tomorrow night, when the boys are here. They'll be fine for one more day. Would soup and sandwich be okay tonight?"

"Fine with me. Looks like you've been coloring. What do you have?" Nick sat beside Alice Marie and praised her coloring—mostly scribbles across the page.

After their makeshift meal, they curled up on the couch and watched a movie. Barb decided that since Nick and her daughter had played in the sandbox, the child needed a bath. She hustled her to the tub.

After Nick cleaned up the dishes, he headed to the shower. He had his eyes closed, his face tilted up, enjoying the hot water, so he didn't see Barb slip into the bathroom a few minutes later. He heard the door slide open and felt her arms come around his waist. She leaned her head on his scarred back. He froze.

Barb's fingers caressed each scar, and her lips trailed behind. "I love you, Nick." He shuddered. She turned him around and brought his fingers to her lips. Taking one in her hand, she used it to trace the stretch marks on her breasts and tummy. "I was nervous you wouldn't like *my* scars, but you don't seem to mind."

Nick groaned and leaned his forehead against hers. They stood, with hot water running over them. Barb pulled back when she tasted his salty tears dripping on her face. She put her hands on his cheeks and pulled him closer. "Don't hide from me, Nick, okay?"

He nodded wordlessly. Finally, he pulled back. "You're quite a gal. You know that?"

"You're quite a guy, marrying a woman with three kids."

"Where's Cinderella?"

"She's in her bed. I told her if she was a good girl and let Mommy take a shower, I'd read her three books."

"Looks like I got the better end of this deal," Nick said, as he reached for a towel.

Barb took the towel from him and carefully, slowly dried Nick's back.

He took the towel and carefully, slowly dried her front, lingering over each breast.

"Uh, I need to keep my promise," Barb stammered.

He grinned. "I like the sound of that."

"To read three books."

"I know. I can wait."

In Cinderella's bedroom, Nick held the little girl in his arms while Barb read. He tucked the child in bed, and she murmured, "I like having you live at our house, Unca Nick."

"Thank you, baby. Can I stay?"

She nodded sleepily. "Forever and ever."

Nick went through the house, locking the doors, and then he returned to his and Barb's bedroom, feeling a contentment he'd never experienced warm him. Barb was sitting against the headboard. She looked at him and smiled. "Come here," she commanded. He walked over to the bed. She scooted over and patted beside her. He sat. She tugged at his shirt, and he ducked out of it. She spread her fingers against the dark curls on his chest. "I wanted to do this last night. I want to touch every inch of you."

Nick slid his hand under her gown. "Be my guest, Mrs. Costas."

CHAPTER 10

Learning to Love

ROBBIE STALKED OUT of the living room and slammed the door to his room, and Nick walked out of the house. Later, as Robbie was going to the bathroom, he passed by his mom and Nick's room, noticing Nick wasn't there. Hesitating, he walked back and looked at the driveway, then in the garage. Finally, he went into the kitchen.

"Mom, where's Nick?"

"Isn't he in our room?"

"No, and his car isn't here."

"I'm sure he'll be home soon," Barb reassured him. But when midnight came and went, she began to fret.

Robbie came to her door. "You don't think he left us, do you, Mom?"

Barb patted the bed beside her. "No, I don't. Let's pray, shall we?"

Robbie returned to his room and finally slept, but Barb kept vigil. About two o'clock, she heard a door quietly shut and walked out into the kitchen. "Where were you? I've been worried," she said.

"Out." Nick walked over to her and took her in his arms. "I haven't been drinking or with anyone else, if that's what you're thinking. Just driving around."

"Why did you leave?" They went into the family room. Sinking down on the couch, Nick put his head in his hands. Looking up, he confessed, "I can't stand it when he mouths off at you like that. I'm not his father, and I have no right to correct him. But you're my wife, and I wanted to smack him. So, I left."

Barb considered him carefully. "I'm glad you didn't smack him, but I could've used you to stand up for me. You can't take off whenever things get tough."

"It's all I know to do—run away—but I came back."

Barb sat down beside him, resting her head on his back as he leaned forward. "Oh, God, help us here." After sitting in silence, she said, "Robbie asked if I thought you'd left us."

"Whatever gave him that idea?"

"You disappeared without a word. It was strange for both of us."

Nick dropped his head in his hands again, and his shoulders slumped. "I'm sorry, Barb. I didn't know what to do. What should I do?"

"Let's go to bed. We'll talk in the morning."

"You haven't been to sleep?" Nick was surprised.

"How could I sleep when I didn't know where you were?"

"I'm so sorry, baby. I made a mess of things, didn't I?" They walked into the bedroom, and Barb went into the bathroom. When she came out, Nick wasn't there. She walked down the hall, crossing the family room into Robbie's dining room turned bedroom. She found Nick kneeling beside Robbie's bed. Touching him gently on the shoulder, she motioned him back to their room. "It feels crappy thinking you've been abandoned. I don't want him to feel that, ever. I love Robbie."

"I know you do, sweetheart. We'll get through this." Barb put her arms around him, drawing him into her embrace. "Just don't leave me, Nick."

"Where could I go? Heaven is in your arms, remember?" Nick drew her down into the bed, and they lay tangled in each other's arms. After he felt her fall asleep, he slipped quietly into the bathroom to get ready for bed.

* * *

The alarm went off a few hours later, and after Barb hit the snooze twice, she got up and hurried around to get dressed, skipping breakfast. "Can you get the kids fed and to daycare? I'm late for work." She grabbed a banana.

"I will, and I'll take Robbie to the studio today."

"I'm sorry we didn't talk. I love you, Nick."

"I love you, too. I'm sorry I made such a mess of things last night." Barb's arms circled his waist, and he dropped a kiss into her freshly shampooed hair, drinking in her lavender scent.

"I'll see you tonight, okay?" she said.

"You bet. I'll be here."

After feeding them breakfast, Nick took the two younger children to daycare and returned home. Looking down at Robbie sprawled across his bed, Nick felt a wave of tenderness explode inside his chest. He'd expected to feel fierce anger—instead, he fought tears. Sitting down on the edge of the bed, Nick touched Robbie's back and wept.

Robbie rolled over and opened his eyes. A look of alarm swept across his face. "You aren't going to leave us, are you, Nick?"

Through his tears, Nick laughed. "No, you little turd. You aren't getting rid of me that easy. Get up. Let's go to breakfast. Want to?"

Visible relief leaped into Robbie's eyes. He threw the covers back and jumped out of bed. "Sure! Where're the kids?"

"At daycare. I thought maybe you'd like to go to the studio with me today, but we're late, so get a move on."

"Really? You'd let me go—today?"

"If you get your butt moving, kid."

Robbie ran to the bathroom, hollering back that he had showered last night and he'd be ready soon. On the drive to Bob Evans, Robbie stole glances at Nick.

Nick recognized that look. The kid was waiting for the other shoe to drop. Nick mentally pleaded with God for the right words. After they ordered, Nick said, "Robbie, about last night . . . your mom told me you thought I was leaving you guys."

"I messed up pretty bad. I thought I'd ruined Mom's chance to be happy, by driving you away. I haven't seen her happy in years. She worried about Dad when he was deployed, and then he died, and she cried all the time. She tried not to let us see it, but I heard her at night. The day you helped her with the sink, she really laughed. I'd forgotten how nice her laugh sounds."

"It wasn't your dad's fault he got killed, you know. He didn't want to leave you guys."

"I know," Robbie mumbled. "But it feels the same. He's gone anyway."

"Robbie, I was wrong last night, and I'm sorry. I don't know how to do this family thing. You need to teach me. I was mad, and I didn't know what to do. I'm not your dad, but I really love your mom. She's my wife, and when you talked to her like that, I wanted to punch your lights out. A judge ordered me to attend anger management in my former life. I didn't want to hurt you, so I left. Now, I realize I hurt you by doing that. I remember how it felt whenever I did something really stupid and my foster parents called to have me sent away." Nick shook his head as if shaking away bad memories. "I promise you, kid, I'm not going anywhere. I'll never leave you. I couldn't leave you—not now. I love you, you little turd."

The waitress, sensing a break in the intense conversation she'd been observing, moved to set down their plates. "More coffee, sir?"

Nick nodded. When she returned with the pot, Robbie turned over his cup. "Could I have a cup, too, please?" he asked. The waitress looked at Nick, and he winked.

Robbie sipped from the cup and tried not to grimace. Nick slid him the sugar, after removing three bags and stirring them into his own cup. Robbie put three bags in his, but when he took another taste, he still struggled. Nick casually reached over for the creamers and stirred two into his coffee. Robbie selected two as well, and when he drank this time, he smiled.

"For a smart guy, you can be pretty dumb," Robbie said, looking at Nick.

"I told you it was dumb to run away last night. It's a pattern from my old days. Whenever things got too tough, I ran—been running all my life, but I'm trying, Robbie. Can you be patient with me?"

"Yeah, sure. But I've been thinking, listening to you, and I figured out something. I've been pretty mean to Mom since you guys got married."

Nick watched him intently.

"I wanted you guys to get married, you know. I told her she should marry you."

Sensing the boy's need for a response, Nick said, "Your Mom told me, but it didn't feel like it."

"I wasn't jealous, if that's what you think. It's a relief. I don't have to look after her anymore. But, I wonder if I've been acting like that to see if you would protect her from me. Does that make sense?"

Astonishment leaped into Nick's eyes. "Yeah, Robbie, it does make sense, but I don't want to hurt you, man."

Robbie looked at him with something akin to adoration. "You'd never hurt me, Nick. I know that."

Nick's heart seized. He realized, for the first time in his life, what people meant about "a broken heart," and he recalled a Scripture about a "broken and contrite heart." He'd have to look that one up later.

"Look at the time. Mr. O'Malley's going to be after my hide. Let's get out of here before I get fired."

"He'd never fire you. I heard him tell Mr. Mike that O'Malley Productions exists because of Nick Costas." Nick was paying the bill, but he looked over at Robbie and raised his eyebrows. "It's true. Honest. I heard him tell Mr. Mike."

Draping his arm across shoulders that were almost the height of his own, Nick walked into brilliant sunshine with the lad who'd become dear to him. "Tim and Missy have a girl working for them who is going to school. I wonder if we can get you into that program. Want me to look into it?"

"Awesome! I hate sitting in classes all day. I would love to work, too"

When they walked into the studio, Nick glanced around. Nothing had started up yet. Hearing Ian, he went into the kitchen, pointing Robbie to the sound booth.

Ian was talking on the phone. He held up his finger to Nick, asking him to wait a moment. "Thanks, Tim. It's what we do in God's family. . . . No problem. We'll drop back ten and punt. Jimmy and I need to work on some riffs. You've got her kids in your office? . . . Yeah, I know what you mean. Listen, you can't get anything done with them there. Let's split them up, one with Julie and one at your house. Don't you have a cleaning lady there today? Jimmy can come get them." Ian flipped his phone closed.

"You're late, but Missy won't be here at all. Jerry called about four this morning, Tim said, and she's at the hospital with Jerry and Suzie. She'll stay with them until their baby comes."

"Tim's trying to work with her kids in there?"

Ian laughed at Nick's incredulous look. "Yeah, and he's going crazy—said he'd rather have two Willows and Todds there, and he has to get some corrected blueprints delivered today."

Jimmy already had his keys in hand when he walked into the kitchen. "I heard, Da, I'm on my way. Poor Tim—those kids are holy terrors. I'll be right back."

Ian's phone rang again. "Hi sweetie, Tim just called. Better late than never, Nick just got here. . . . Already done. Jimmy's on his way, and we'll bring one to Julie and one to Mae, up at your house. How's Suzie doing? . . . That far? Maybe you can come in later then. . . . Oh, I forgot you've been up all night. Scratch that." He laughed. "We'll play it by ear." He glanced over at Nick. "I don't know. He walked in with his arm draped around Robbie like he'd been a family man for a hundred years. I told Tim it is what we do in God's family. If you can't be flexible, you can't be obedient. . . . Love you, too."

Nick poured himself a cup of coffee. "I just drank the sweetest coffee in God's creation. Robbie and I ate breakfast at Bob Evans." He gulped a huge swallow and set his cup down, heaving a satisfied sigh.

"Why did you put so much sugar in it, you dummy?" Ian wondered. Nick explained that Robbie had ordered a cup and couldn't stomach it, so he'd doctored his own until the boy could drink his. "How does it feel to be a role model, Nick?"

Nick looked up, surprised, and then he grinned. "It's pretty swell. Scary as h . . . heck, but swell. If Missy won't be here, I'll put him to work copying those CDs for the Roundaleers."

Ian told Robbie to make two hundred copies, and then he went into the practice room. Robbie looked at Nick's cup of black coffee questioningly.

"One cup's enough for a boy your age, don't you think?"

Robbie shrugged and turned to the equipment.

Nick watched him for the first few copies and then patted him on the shoulder. "Okay, you're doing good—real good. While you're doing that, I'll create their labels on the computer. I can teach you how to do that, too." They worked side by side. After a while, Nick rolled his shoulders. "Let's take a break, buddy. How about we see if Alice has a Coke for you?"

"Miss Alice only has juice. She says Coke's not good for you." Robbie walked into the kitchen with utmost confidence, opening the refrigerator and pulling out flavored water. "If you want to call the school, the counselor's name is Mr. Simpson. I think he's Suzie's uncle or something."

"Call the school? Oh, right, about working here in the studio." Nick rummaged around for a phone book. But Robbie called out the number from memory and hung close by. He wanted to hear.

"Mr. Simpson, this is Nick Costas. I married Barb Westfall this summer, and I'm calling about Robbie. . . . No problems. Why? . . . I see." Nick glanced over, and Robbie dropped his head. He explained that Robbie worked with him at O'Malley Productions and asked if Robbie could be released during school on some kind of work release.

"Well, Mr. . . . Costa, is it?"

Nick corrected his name but asked the counselor to call him by his first name anyway.

"Costas," Mr. Simpson amended. "And Nick, as in jolly old Saint Nick?"

Nick chuckled. "Hardly a saint, and hardly jolly, but yes, Nick."

"The boy needs a stepfather, but I'm surprised. Barbara was so crazy about Bob. Uh, but this is good. I mean, I'm happy for her and certainly glad you've taken the boy under your wing." He explained that the vocational program didn't begin until high school. "But I'll tell you what: we're having a team meeting in a bit, and I'll ask the other teachers. Robbie's certainly bright enough to catch up his work. It'd be good for him if he could work an afternoon or two with you. He'd have to understand no more 'Ds.' The first 'D' he gets, we'll pull this privilege. Could I have your number? I assume Barbara is all right with this?"

Nick assured him she would be and that Robbie had been working with him all summer.

"I wish all stepfathers took such an interest," Mr. Simpson replied. "I'll see what I can do."

Nick hung up. *I'm a stepfather? How did that happen? God help me.* He stared into space.

"What'd he say?"

"The vocational program starts in high school, but he's going to try to allow you to come over one afternoon a week. No more 'Ds,' Robbie. This would be a special privilege, and you have to maintain your grades and be on good behavior, understand?"

"I can do that. It's easy to make good grades. I don't know why I messed up so bad last year. Life pretty much sucked last year."

Nick pulled him into his arms. "Yeah, kid, I'm sure it did. Let's make this a better year. Deal?" Nick felt Robbie hug him back, fiercely, and he made no move to break away.

Jimmy came in and quietly moved into the practice room, where he met Ian. "What's going on in there, Da? God's making that street punk into an old softie."

"Yeah, and He's going to make us into beggars if we don't get this next album to market."

When Robbie finally eased away, Nick said, "Let's get back to work. Those folks are coming to collect their CDs today, and we promised they'd be ready." They walked into the sound booth, working side by side until two hundred CDs were stacked and labeled. Nick reached for some cases, and they put the CDs inside.

"I'll be back, Robbie. I'm going to check in with my boss." Nick slipped into the practice room, listening to the O'Malleys going over chords, trying out keys, correcting one another, and suggesting new sounds. Ian's perfection with his craft always amazed Nick, and Jimmy had the same stubborn refusal to settle for less than perfect. "Are you guys going to work through lunch? It's almost one."

In the same smooth movement, Jimmy and Ian set their instruments in the stands. "We got a late start," Ian informed him. "We've decided to do that new song in B-flat."

"Let's eat, Da." Jimmy smiled at Nick and moved to the door. "He can live on music, but I need to eat."

Nick laughed. "I've got a teenager in there. Did you know they eat nonstop? Bottomless pits." He pointed at Robbie, who was already heading for the kitchen. Nick set him to spreading mayo while he sliced tomato, and Ian got out the lunchmeat. "I don't figure Alice will have any unwholesome chips, will she?"

Jimmy rummaged around and found some hearty wheat chips, which were pretty good, they decided.

Missy bounded in the back door. "Oh, goodie, make one for me. I'm starved. It's a boy! A big, strapping boy for Jerry to go hunting with. Isn't God good?" Missy tiptoed up for her father's kiss.

Ian put his arms around her, chuckling. "How you chatter! You look like your quiet mother, but you certainly aren't like her. You have her huge, generous heart, though, girlie-girl, and I love you."

"I love you, too. You have a huge heart, too, you know." Seeing his skeptical look, she said, "Oh, yes, you do. You're a slave-driver, but you have a big heart." She took an enormous bite of her sandwich, and then she put her hand over her mouth. "Uh-oh, have you blessth thish?"

All the men laughed, and Jimmy put his arm around her while he thanked God for his precious sister and the food before them.

"You guys laugh so much," Robbie observed. "Isn't there some Scripture about a merry heart? I'll ask Mom tonight. She knows everything in the Bible."

"It's in Proverbs. 'A merry heart doeth good like a medicine,'" Missy quoted. "And that's the truth, too. Thank you for rescuing Tim today, guys. He was pretty stressed about that deadline." She stuck her plate in the sink and wiped her hands down the side of her jeans, exactly the way Alice did.

"Let's go to work, shall we?" Walking into the studio, Jimmy explained the key change.

"Sounds good to me," she said.

"Do they ever get mad at each other?" Robbie asked.

Nick laughed. "You've never seen a good fight until you see the O'Malleys go at it. They all want to do it 100 percent right, and they are passionate about it. The first time I saw them I thought they'd never work together again, and the next thing I knew they were laughing and hugging."

"Really? Then it's okay if we get mad at each other?"

"Yeah, buddy, it's okay. As long as we don't stay mad, and we forgive each other when we mess up."

"That's cool."

Nick put an arm around Robbie's shoulder. "Yeah, that's way cool!"

CHAPTER 11

Stepdad

NICK SAW ALICE coming in at around 3:30 p.m. She set her purse on the counter, firmly holding Suzie's oldest daughter by the hand. *Only a mother and grandmother could be patient with that kid. What a saint she is!*

"Say hello to Mr. Nick, Lula, and let's sit down and get ourselves calm. Miss Alice will read you some stories." The child began to whine. She stomped her feet. "Okay, no stories. We'll take a nap." The child cringed as if she expected a slap, but Alice put her arm around her and drew her close. "Which is it, Lula? Stories or nap?" They walked over to the bookshelf stacked with children's books, and the child took ten minutes selecting three. Alice herded her to the couch, hugging her the whole way. They sat down and began to read.

Nick took two mugs of coffee into the studio. "Your wife is a saint, O'Malley. Of course, I knew that already. She took you back."

Ian muttered his agreement. "I'm humbled every day. What's she doing this time?"

"Reading to Lula. She has her eating out of her hand."

Ian poked his head out of the door, watched Alice and Lula, and smiled. Alice glanced up, caught his eye, and waved. The little girl giggled as Alice changed her voice for the different characters. When they closed the first book and reached for the second, Lula said, "I like it when you read, Miz Alice. It's funny!"

"I love to read to good little girls and boys. The library has story time two mornings a week in the summer. If you're a good girl and sit quietly, you can hear nice stories there. Now, what shall we read next? Oh, Todd's Mommy's favorite, *Winnie the Pooh*. Can you turn the pages for me?"

When Nick and Missy walked out of the studio, Lula was fast asleep on the couch.

"You've ruined my evening, Mom. She'll be up all night, and I get to take care of her," Missy complained.

"She was a grouch. If she hadn't slept, she never would settle later. Some kids get over-wound, and they can't get to sleep at night. You can keep a good-natured child like Todd up, but a wired child will only get more wired. Do you want me to keep her? Where's Betty?"

Alice stood to receive Ian's hug when he and Jimmy followed Missy in. "How did it go today?" she asked as she pecked him on the cheek. He gathered her into his arms and kissed her soundly. "Stop that," she scolded.

"I canna stop, my love. I canna keep my eyes nor my hands off your beautiful self."

"It's all right, Mom. We're used to him by now." Jimmy laughed. "But, Da, Robbie's here. You'll steal his innocence."

"Ah, go on with ya. Nothing is more innocent than a man lovin' his wife, now, is there?"

"I'm going home! I feel a sudden urge to see Jules. Did you tell Nick we're knocking off?" Jimmy asked.

"I'm sorry, Daddy. I really am pooped," Missy apologized.

"Ah, darlin' girl, you helped to birth a man-child into this world. That's a good day's work."

"Anyway, we'd better get out of here. Mom has early shift tomorrow, and obviously Daddy's going to keep her up tonight," Missy said.

"Now, there's what I mean, not letting folks have their privacy," her father fussed. "Look what you've done to your poor mother."

Alice's face showed the deep tan color she and Missy shared when embarrassed. "It wasn't *her* laying that big smacker on me, Ian O'Malley. You started all this," Alice teased.

He started toward her again. "Why don't all you youngsters get out of my house?" he shouted. The door slammed behind Jimmy, but Missy sank into the couch and laughed until the tears ran down her cheeks.

"Because you work us like a slave-driver, one day, I'll collapse like this and never be able to go home."

"Ah, and your fine man will come a-lookin' for ya, sweep you into his arms, and carry you home to his bed!"

"Ian O'Malley, what has gotten into you this evening?" Alice scolded again as Nick joined them in the living room, and Robbie looked back and forth between them.

"Do ya really not know, lassie?" Eyes twinkling, Ian looked at her until she blushed again. "Sure, and it's your beautiful self, your fine, sweet body, and—"

"Oh, for heaven's sake!"

"Out, out with ya all!" Ian roared. "What does it take for a man to be alone with the love of his life?"

Nick chuckled, and Missy grabbed Robbie's hand. "You don't have to tell me twice. Come on, Robbie. Let's get away from Mom's wild Irishman. She can deal with him."

Robbie followed Missy down the stairs. "Are you mad at your dad?"

She looked at him, surprised. "Oh, no, we're having fun. Honest. It's the way this crazy family is."

"Oh," he whispered, looking up at Nick for confirmation.

"They carry on like that all the time. Ian's like Tigger, in the Pooh stories: he's blustery. You haven't seen them when they are really mad. Come on, your mom's waiting for us."

* * *

When Nick walked into the house, Robbie was relieved to see him walk calmly over to his mother and kiss her on her cheek. She smiled at him and touched his face. "I missed you today, Mrs. Costas," Nick said gently.

"Hi, guys, I missed you, too. I made lasagna. You're late, but I heard you started late. Is everything okay, Robbie?"

"Yeah, swell. I had a lot of fun at the studio. Mr. O'Malley's loud!"

"Robbie, don't you have something to say to your mother?" Nick asked.

"Oh, yeah. I'm sorry, Mom, for acting like such a turd last night."

Barb's eyes widened, but Nick quickly said, "Uh-oh, my mistake. That's my word, not his, Barb. Sorry."

She took a deep breath, and then said, "I guess that is . . . an accurate description of your behavior last night, son, but I forgive you."

"Me and Nick talked, Mom, and he isn't ever going to leave us."

Barb turned to Nick. "That's a good thing." Her heart was in her eyes as she whispered, "Thanks."

"Let's set the table, Robbie," Nick suggested. Without a word of complaint, the boy helped Nick while his mother called the others in to dinner.

After supper, Barb steered the kids toward bed. Nick leaned on the doorframe as she bathed Alice Marie. He filled her in on his day and listened to hers. Nick gathered the giggling girl in a towel, ran her into her Cinderella room, and helped her into a fancy nightgown. He sang "I'll Dance with Cinderella" and waltzed her around the room. With her tiny arms around his neck and her laughter in his ears, Nick felt his heart would burst.

Barb leaned against the doorframe this time, and she caught the tears glistening in Nick's eyes. "I didn't know you sang so well."

He shrugged. "Not me. You should hear the family I work with."

"They're incredible, but seriously, you aren't too shabby yourself."

"Kiss Mommy night-night, Cinderella. It's time to go to sleep." Alice Marie lifted her arms up to her mother as Nick laid her in the bed.

"'Night, Mommy. 'Night, Daddy," she said. Barb caught the sharp intake of Nick's breath.

"Goodnight, precious girl," Barb whispered, kissing her gently.

Nick crossed the hall to Alan's room. He knelt beside the bed and snuggled with the boy. "You ready for prayers, big guy? What do we need to talk to Jesus about tonight?" Wordlessly, Alan lifted a skinned elbow. Nick dropped a kiss on it and asked Jesus to make it well. Satisfied, the child reached up for Nick and kissed his cheek. Nick patted him as he tucked the covers around him.

"Goodnight, son," Barb said from the hall. Alan reached his arms out to her, and she quickly crossed the room and gathered him up for a kiss. "You go to sleep now, okay?"

Barb found Nick in the family room with his Bible. She sat on the couch beside him and drew her long luscious legs up to her chest. After glancing admiringly at them, Nick said, "Could you wear those shorts all winter long?" She blushed and put her feet primly on the floor. He laughed, pulled her toward him, and covered her mouth with his. "I love you. How can I thank you for giving me this wonderful family? You have great kids. You've done a wonderful job with them."

"Tell me about your day with Robbie."

"He's a good kid, honey. He'll be fine. He's growing up, becoming his own man, but he'll get through this."

"It's been a rough year."

"I know. I talked to Mr. Simpson today, from the school." Answering her unspoken question, Nick explained the call. "I realized today that I'm a stepfather."

"I kind of came as a package deal."

"That's a good thing. I've never had a family, and I like it, a lot. Mr. Simpson asked me if I plan to adopt the kids."

Barb regarded him carefully and wondered how in the world she could tell Bob's family. His parents wouldn't come to the wedding.

"I said I'd pray about it, but I thought not—they are Westfalls, and they have a proud heritage. He'll call me about Robbie's behavior, but any decision needs to be run by you since you are his parent. He suggested looking into a custodial guardianship. What do you think of that?"

"It's a lot of responsibility. Do you want to?"

"I love these kids. I fell in love with them when I was falling in love with you. Remember the day Alice Marie ran to me and called me 'Unca Nick?' I was already in over my head. I didn't want to leave your kids!"

Barb leaned against him, and his arm draped over her shoulder. She turned to face him. "I didn't know how I could do this alone. But I also didn't know how much I needed help. You're so good with them. They all love you, and I love you."

Nick pulled her into his arms, whispered in her ear, and kissed her gently until her responses prompted him to go deeper. Behind them, they heard Robbie clear his throat. "Mr. O'Malley isn't the only one taking my innocence today," he said. Barb jumped back.

"Okay, you little eavesdropper, why aren't you in the shower?" Nick called out.

"Because I've been done for twenty minutes. I'll leave you two alone to your, uh, whatever. But could I weigh in?"

"It depends. Just what did you overhear?"

"About the custodial parent thing, and how you love us, and all." Nick patted the chair beside the couch and indicated for Robbie to continue. "It'd be good. I mean, I trust Nick, Mom. And if anything should, you know . . . happen to you, I'd want to stay with him. Your Mom is too old, and I love Grandma and Grandpa Westfall and all, but I'd want Nick to take care of us. If you don't do something legal, maybe he couldn't keep us, not being related to us and all."

"Wow, that's a mouthful, and a lot of heavy thinking," Nick responded. He reached for the boy's hand. "I'm honored. I promised you I'd never take your dad away, and I mean it. But I do love you, even if you are a turd sometimes."

Robbie laughed. "And I forgive you, coward, even though you did run away."

Barb started to say something, but Nick waved her back and stood. "Come here, kid." For the second time that day, Robbie clung to Nick like a drowning man clings to a life raft. "I'll do better, but you gotta help me." Robbie nodded into his chest. Nick began to pray, for himself to be what he should be for the kids, for the kids to always love and honor their father, for them to be patient with him as he struggled to get "the family thing" down, and for God's love to reign in their home.

"Amen. 'Night, Mom. 'Night, Nick. See you guys in the morning."

"'Night, son," Barb choked out. She looked up at Nick. "I thought we were going to discuss how to handle this."

Nick looked upset. "Did I do something wrong? Tell me what to do."

"Tell me what you did. Everything, not just bits and pieces—because this is abundantly exceeding all I could ask or pray for."

"First, help me find two Scriptures. The first one is about two are better than one. Pastor used it when he preached on Alice's birthday. You'd think I could remember that long."

Barb flipped in her King James. "That's an easy one. Right here."

They leaned over Ecclesiastes 4:9 together, reading: "Two are better than one; because they have a good reward for their labour."

"What's the next?" she asked.

"Something about a humble and contrite heart."

"That's easy, too." Before Barb even turned to Isaiah 57:15, she recited: "For thus saith the high and lofty One that inhabiteth eternity, whose name is Holy; I dwell in the high and holy place, with him also that is of a contrite and humble spirit, to revive the spirit of the humble, and to revive the heart of the contrite ones." She pointed to the text.

"How do you remember all this stuff? My Bible doesn't read like that, but it's what I was trying to find."

"I've been in church all my life. We had sword drills and memorization. You can't know all this in a year. God's doing such a quick work in you. You actually *live* 'this stuff.' One of the things that attracted me most about you was your contrite heart. You seek forgiveness. You've been God with skin onto my son today. Tell me how you worked this miracle."

"It was totally God. I didn't know what to say." Beginning with breakfast, Nick went through the day they shared.

"One more thing: what's this about 'losing his innocence?' What did Ian do?"

Nick laughed and described the scene at the O'Malleys' house. Launching into his best Ian imitation, Nick described the conversation. "Robbie was a bit taken aback with his bluster, but Missy told him it was just her Dad's way."

"Ian's right, Nick. And do you know what I'm going to do?"

"What?"

"I'll be a wife loving my husband. I'm going to take you back to our bedroom, lock the door, and make love to you all night long."

Nick stood and gave her his hand. "Now, would that be a threat or a promise?"

"Both!" she responded. She led him down the hall, flipping the lights off as she went.

* * *

The next morning, Nick hummed as he scrambled the eggs. "Morning, Robbie. Or, as Ian would say: 'Top of the mornin' to ya, laddie. You sleep well?"

"Yeah. How'd you do that? You sound just like him!"

"I've worked with him for twelve years."

"I thought you just started."

"Nope. We worked together in Hollywood and in Nashville, years before I knew the rest of the O'Malleys. Good morning, squirt," Nick said to Alan. He took Alice Marie into his arms when she reached out to him, and he settled her in her high chair. "How are you this morning, Cinderella? Who's ready for eggs?"

"Mmm, me, for one," Barb said. She pulled her chair up to the table. "Robbie, would you say the blessing?"

When he finished, he said, "Mom, Nick's eyes are different."

She looked at her husband carefully. "Same warm milk-chocolate eyes to me. How?"

"They aren't sad anymore!"

Sure enough, Nick's eyes twinkled at Barb as he smiled a private smile for her and reached for her hand. "That's because I love your mother, and I love being a stepfather to you kids."

"Robbie, Nonna called today, and she and Gramps want to take you kids up to Pittsburgh this weekend. If you can handle the zoo on Friday, they'll take you to Kennywood on Saturday." Barb caught Nick's eye.

"Alice Marie will be sad at night. I'll sleep beside her," Robbie said.

Nick called Barb during a break later that day.

"Hi, honey, I was going to call you," she informed him. "Can you get away for lunch? We could meet at the house. Robbie's gone fishing with his coach," she invited suggestively.

"And the other kids are at daycare, right? I could definitely make some time for lunch. But I called to ask about this weekend. Will we have it together, or do you have a million and one things to do?"

"I thought we could go up to the mountains, maybe stay with Mike and Clare."

"I'm definitely not staying with anyone. I'll get reservations. See you about noon?"

As the group broke for lunch, Nick said he was meeting Barb. "Sounds good. Where're you headed?" Jimmy asked.

"Home."

Jimmy grinned at him. "Oh, well, have a nice 'lunch' then, big guy." After Nick left, Jimmy rummaged around to prepare food for everyone. He made three sandwiches and wrapped one up. He looked over at his father. "Nick might want to eat something when he gets back."

Ian laughed. "My thoughts exactly! They seem mighty happy and like they're doing well with three children under their newlywed feet." When Nick came back, Ian pointed to the plate: "Jimmy thought you might be hungry when you got back."

"Thanks, Jimmy." Nick picked up the sandwich without comment.

CHAPTER 12

Newlyweds

THE NEXT EVENING, Barb carried in about six plastic bags, and Robbie came in behind her with an equal number. Alice Marie squeezed her tiny body between her mother's legs and ran to Nick, who swept her up in his arms. He grabbed Alan, spun him around, and drew him in for a quick hug. "How's it going, man?"

The boy looked at him shyly. "Good, Nick." Nick held out his fist, and Alan hit it with his own, grinning.

"Anything else in the car, Barb?"

"No. Preheat the oven to three-fifty, would you?"

Nick set the temperature while Barb washed her hands and began mixing the ingredients for meatloaf.

"Thanks for boiling the potatoes, Nick. Robbie, would you set the table?"

Robbie looked like he might balk, so Nick joked with him. "If I knew where the forks were, I'd help you."

"They're in this drawer," Alan responded seriously.

"Thanks." Nick winked at Robbie. "Let's clear this stuff off. Cinderella, where do your coloring books go? Not here!" He carefully placed the books and crayons in her arms, and she ran to the bookshelf in the living room. "How was practice today, Robbie? Are you playing goalie this weekend?"

"They have an off weekend, remember? And Nonna called about a trip to Pittsburg," Barb piped up. "They're going to pick the kids up Friday."

Nick raised his eyes in question. "Just the kids?" he asked.

"You think it's a good idea?"

"Sure. Could you get Alice in the tub?"

Dressed in her Cinderella nightgown, the child returned to the kitchen. Barb put a salad on the table. After Nick settled the little girl in her chair, he brought the mashed potatoes and beans to the table. "Looks good, smells good. Let's eat," Robbie said. Nick reached out his hands, catching those of a boy on either side. They all bowed for the blessing.

When the little ones were down, and Robbie was watching TV, Nick asked Barb their plans for the weekend.

"I plan to run away with this good-looking, black-haired, chocolate-eyed man whom I happen to love very much," she replied, her eyes twinkling. "Let's call Mike and Clare and see if we can stay with them."

"If I have you alone for the weekend, we won't stay with them. I told you, I'll make reservations."

"But that's so expensive! Mike invited us to come anytime."

"Please, I want to do this for you. And for me, of course."

"Don't you want to see them?"

"We can see them and stay by ourselves, if you're sure you want to let the children go off with their grandparents."

"Nonna wants them badly. I thought it'd be a peace offering to her, and since you got Robbie a cell phone, he'll call us. He said he'd put Alice in his bed if she gets lonely."

"He's a good kid. You've done a fine job with him."

* * *

When Ian heard Nick and Barb's plans, he called Jerry, who let Barb leave at noon, and he shoved Nick out the door. "You haven't had a moment by yourselves since the wedding!" he exclaimed.

Leaving early, the couple reached Canaan Valley before dark. When Barb walked into the house Nick rented, she looked around in amazement. "This is beautiful! How much did this cost?"

Nick put his finger to her lips. "It isn't enough for you, sweetheart. Someday I'll show you a real weekend of luxury. Did you see the hot tub? How do you feel?"

"Really stupid. Thanks for stopping at the pharmacy. We have a weekend alone, and I have to stop for Midol!"

"I'm learning that the way to a woman's heart is words, and we can talk without interruption."

Barb put her arms around his neck and looked into his eyes. "I like it when you love me *without* words. This is such a bummer!"

Nick groaned. "That's not fair! Let's get ready for dinner, before I need a cold shower."

"I'm sorry. You're being so nice to me," Barb said as they drove to the restaurant for dinner.

"It's a natural part of being a woman." Nick's mouth watered as they approached the restaurant. He put his hand at the small of her back and guided her up the rustic stairs.

After they ate, they walked the dusty road along the ridge, seeing countless deer, and a mother bear with two cubs in the distance. With his arm around her waist and her head on his shoulder, they sat on a log and watched the sun's orange rays streak across the horizon. Wordlessly, they walked back to the new Suburban.

"Mike said come by about ten tomorrow, and we'll go up to Spruce Knob for a picnic," Barb said.

"What shall we bring?"

"Clare said it's her treat. Gosh, I hope she isn't in some designer outfit. She makes me so nervous."

"She can't hold a candle to you."

"She pays more for one outfit than I spend on clothes in a year."

"She's too skinny. You are perfect. It isn't clothes. It's what's under them." His brown eyes twinkled.

The next morning, Clare was relaxed and dressed in simple jeans and a T-shirt. She and Mike glowed and couldn't keep their hands off one another.

In the back seat, Barb leaned into Nick, who put his arm around her. "She looks good, doesn't she?" Barb whispered.

"Not as good as you, but she looks happy." Nick nibbled her ear.

When they stopped, the men set up lounge chairs while the ladies put a cloth and plates on the table. After lunch, they hiked, but when Nick saw the lake, he suggested they take a swim.

"No way! It's a mountain spring-fed lake, and it's freezing," Mike said.

"What do I expect from a couple of old farts?" Nick teased.

"You'll be sorry!" Mike warned him.

Holding onto Barb to balance himself, Nick slipped off his rugged sandals. He ran to the lake, dove in, and came up grinning, the water shining like diamonds on his raven hair.

Barb walked out on the dock and sat down, swinging her feet. Nick swam easily over to her, crossing his arms on the wooden walkway. He crooked his finger for her to lean closer and whispered in her ear. She nodded. Placing his hands on her legs, he pulled her into the water, beside him. She came out sputtering and shrieking. "I can't believe you did that! Why did you do that?"

He brought her face close to his and whispered again.

Barb laughed. "I'm an ice cube. Get me out of here."

Nick handily swung himself onto the dock and reached down for her.

Clare, laughing, walked toward them with a huge towel that she wrapped around Barb, holding her tightly. "That was mean, Nick Costas! What, misery loves company?"

He shook the water out of his hair and tenderly held the towel around a shivering Barb.

"Just get away from me!" she said playfully.

He pulled the towel closer and took her into his arms.

Mike walked down the walkway, holding out another towel. "We have another one. Why don't you take off that wet shirt and hang it out to dry?"

Barb watched Nick close-up, and she quickly put her arm around him. "Come on, I'll keep you warm." She brought him under her towel, and they leaned back, looking into the sun. He kissed her hair.

Later, at their house, Clare signaled Barb into the kitchen and asked about Nick's scars.

"They're from beatings he had in foster homes," Barb informed her. "He doesn't like people to see. When I saw them the first time, I wept and kissed each one. He cried and held onto me for the longest time."

"Dear God. You're kidding?"

"He had it tough growing up in South L.A. Sometimes he didn't eat for days, and he was always running to avoid the next beating. He shuts down on me, too, but he's getting better."

Clare sat down heavily, wiping her tears with the back of her hand. "Mike and I were poor little rich kids, shuttled to private schools and our parents' museum-mansions. We had plenty to eat and a warm bed. How could people do that to a kid? We'll pray for you, Barb. I knew he was a street kid, but I had no idea."

"What are you gals doing in there? Did you go to China to pick the tea?" Mike hollered.

Nick walked into the kitchen. "Do you want hot tea or cold, sweetie?" Barb asked him. "I'm going for hot."

Nick reached for a glass and some ice. "Are you okay? I didn't mess you up?"

Her eyes twinkled. "I'm fine, but your scheme didn't work."

"Mike wants hot, and so do I," Clare announced. She quickly set the cups and the teapot on a tray. Barb admired the tea set.

"We bring something home every time we go to New York," Mike told her. "Clare goes for a week or so each month and sometimes for special occasions. I go, too, since I can't let her out of my sight."

Clare shocked Barb by dropping into Mike's lap and kissing him soundly. "We were married for thirteen years. You'd think he'd be used to me by now."

"We've never been married like this before."

She traced his jawline with her elegantly manicured finger and agreed softly.

After a bit, Nick carried cups and his glass into the kitchen. Mike gathered the rest up. "I'll get it. Thanks for joining us today. I hope the 'old farts' weren't too dull for you."

Nick cut a glance over to him. "Obviously, the old man enjoys much the same things as I do."

Barb elbowed her husband. "It was a lovely picnic. Thanks so much," she said.

Clare and Mike stood on the porch and waved.

* * *

The next morning, Nick was anxious to leave. "I'm worried. Did you call Robbie's cell?" When Barb did, it went to voicemail. "We need to be there when they get home."

"They're being spoiled shamelessly," Barb assured him. However, she packed up quickly, and they left, not saying much on the drive. "You're worse than I am. When did you get to be such a parent?"

"I never had anyone to worry about before. Making up for lost time, I guess." Taking her hand, Nick brought it to his lips, marveling at the softness of her skin. "I love you and those kids."

"I know," she whispered.

They'd hardly unpacked the car when the Westfalls pulled in the driveway.

"Won't you come in?" Barb invited them. But they never shut off the engine. Robbie rolled his eyes and started into the house. "Tell your grandparents thank you, Robbie," she admonished him.

"Thanks," he said, picking up Alice Marie. She snuggled into her big brother without looking back. The door slammed behind them.

The house was quiet that afternoon. Nick and Alan settled into a game of UNO. Alice slipped into Nick's lap, and he cuddled her.

"Are you all right, Cinderella? Were you up too late?"

"I don't want to leave you, Daddy."

"You aren't going anywhere, sweetie." Nick's eyes sought Barb's. She shrugged. When the little ones were in bed, he leaned on the doorway to Robbie's room. "Things didn't go so hot?"

"It pretty much sucked. They pumped us for information—asked stuff about you." Robbie pulled up his pajama leg, revealing a deep bruise and scrapes. "Remember when I slid into third base at the Lewis County game? Nonna asked me if you did this. I told them you'd never hurt me and that she could call the coach."

His brow furrowed as he went on. "She said they knew stuff about you, like how old you are and that you'd been court-ordered to anger management, and she said that she and Gramps would take care of us. I said we are fine—even better since you married Mom. Then she said, 'Don't worry, Robbie, this happens to young widows sometimes, but I never expected it from Barbara, with Bob hardly cold in the grave.' They need to get a life. Dad's been dead for three years now. It's like they've built a shrine to him or something. What does she mean about Mom?"

"I couldn't say. But your dad is their son. I'm beginning to know what that feels like. I don't know what I'd do if anything happened to you kids. I *was* court-ordered into anger management, Robbie. It was a long time ago, when I got into a bar fight in Las Vegas. That's a good reason never to drink—my judgment was impaired. It wasn't the swiftest thing I've ever done."

Robbie's eyes glistened. He walked over to Nick and opened his arms. "You're the best stepdad ever, and the best thing that's happened to us in years."

Nick held him until the boy broke away. "See you in the morning, big guy."

"Love you, Nick."

"I'm grateful God fixed my life, and even more blessed He gave me this family. I love you, too, Robbie. I hope you know that."

"Yeah, I do."

Nick stopped by both of the other kids' bedrooms to drop a kiss on each sleeping face. He clicked the lamp off beside Alan's bed, gently pulling a book out of his hands and laying it on the table.

"Is Robbie all right, Nick? Did he tell you what happened? They didn't seem to have fun," Barb said when he came into their room.

"They didn't. We need to pray for the Westfalls. Life has just . . . stopped for them. What can we do to help? They go to church anywhere?"

"No. She said Bob and I would get over this 'foxhole religion' we got messed up in when we were in Iraq. Bob tried to get them to come to church. They came twice, for the kids' programs. Why am I so tired?"

"It was strained today. Being emotionally drained can do that to you. Let's turn in." Barb glanced toward Robbie's room. "He'll be okay, Barb. He gave me a huge hug."

"What would we do without you? You've been wonderful for him. He's come out of a dark place."

"It's hard to believe God gave me you and these amazing kids. I have a family. It's a miracle." Nick held her until she went to sleep.

CHAPTER 13

Culture Shock

NICK WAS READING his Bible in the family room the next night when he heard a tentative footstep. "Is that my Cinderella?" Hearing a giggle, he added, "I hear Cinderella at my house. Are you there?"

"I'm here, Daddy."

"Come in here." The tot came running down the hall, her bare feet pattering against the wood floor. She threw herself in Nick's lap and tightened her arms about his neck, sniffing. "Why is Cinderella up at this hour? It's past midnight, and your carriage has turned into a pumpkin."

"I had a bad dream, Daddy."

Burying his face in her golden curls, Nick breathed in the little girl's essence of sweet shampoo. "You had a bad dream?" he asked incredulously. "Princesses can't have bad dreams after the ball! Do you know what princesses do when they have bad dreams?" Alice Marie shook her head no into his chest. Tightening his arms around her, he said, "They call for the king, who waves his scepter and issues a royal edict." In a deep voice, Nick proclaimed, "The royal edict hereby decrees that the princess shall have no bad dreams in the castle! And nothing can stand before the royal decree, sweetie. So, all the bad dreams run away."

"Okay, Daddy." She snuggled closer.

Smiling at the two of them, Barb tiptoed back to the bedroom. She heard him sing softly.

"I'll dance with Cinderella . . ." When Nick felt Alice's little body slump, he carried the child and placed her on her bed, sitting in silence until she wouldn't wake again. He went into his bedroom and slipped in beside Barb. Later, after he had fallen asleep, he felt her move closer to him.

"Nick?" she whispered.

"Mmm?"

"Are you awake?"

He chuckled but didn't open his eyes. "I am now. What's up?" He felt her snuggle against him.

"I can't sleep."

"Worried about something? And Cinderella had a bad dream. What's going on in this house?"

"Nick." She reached out and touched him tentatively, rubbing her fingers lightly across the dark curls on his chest. "I, uh . . . I want you."

His eyes popped open. He propped himself on his elbow and stared down at her. "Isn't it like . . ." He glanced at the clock. "Two o'clock in the morning?"

"Do you mind?"

He laughed. "Let's see. Let me think on that: 'do I mind?' Every husband should be so lucky! Did you close the door? Did you premeditate this seduction?"

"I closed the door and chickened out. I tried to go to sleep," Barb faltered, her eyes cast down, her dark lashes fluttering against her cheek.

Nick's right hand slowly worked the button on her pajama top as faint color crept up her cheeks. "After that bold request, are you going to turn shy on me?" He moved down to the second button. "Are you sure you want me? Look at me. I want to see your eyes."

Barb brought her hands up to his face and looked at him. Her eyes glistened, and the teardrop clinging to her lashes undid him. "Don't tease me, just love me."

"It will be my pleasure, Mrs. Costas," he whispered as he gathered her into his arms.

* * *

The next morning, as Barb was making pancakes, Nick dropped a kiss on her cheek and patted her on the backside. He circled the table to tousle Alan's hair. "Hey, squirt." Alan smiled a syrupy grin. Nick sat down, watching Barb move around the stove.

"Nick, quit looking at me."

He chuckled. "How do you know I'm looking at you?"

She turned to face him, her face flaming. "I can feel it."

"I can't help it. I can't get used to having such beauty in my kitchen."

"You're hanging around Ian O'Malley too much."

"He and I are both right—and both very fortunate husbands. Where's Cinderella?"

"I let her sleep. I heard you with her last night."

"I can take her in later. Go on to work." He turned to Alan. "You want to stay home a while?"

Alan nodded eagerly.

"Have you heard Robbie?"

"He's in the shower."

"He usually showers at night."

"He was talking to a girl last night. They talked for a long time."

"Who?'

"Angela somebody."

"Oh, Angela Hicks. She's a nice girl."

"And he's a nice boy, so let's keep it that way and keep our eyes on them," Barb said as she leaned down to give Nick a kiss. He put a finger in her T-shirt, taking a quick peek. She slapped his hand, glancing over at Alan. "Cut that out!" she whispered sternly.

He laughed. "Yes, ma'am, but only I know the truth about you."

She rolled her eyes. "Honestly, I may live to regret that."

His eyes sparkling with hidden laughter, Nick pleaded, "Oh, please, please, don't ever regret that! You're leaving mighty early, aren't you?"

"I have a lot to do today. See you later. Love you, honey. Love you, Alan."

* * *

The next afternoon, Barb found Nick sitting on the floor in Robbie's room, putting together a desk for his computer. She leaned against the doorframe and held up an oval object about ten inches long. It looked like a nightstick. "What's this, Nick?"

In a smooth, cat-like move, Nick's legs unfolded, and he moved swiftly toward her, taking the object from her hand. "Where did you get this?" he asked coldly, slipping it into his pocket.

"I was unpacking your boxes."

Nick had already moved away from her, both physically and emotionally. "Did I ask you to mess with my stuff?"

"You do so much for us. I wanted to help."

"I moved it to the back of the closet so it wouldn't be in the way." He skirted past her in the narrow doorway without touching her and strode to the bedroom.

Following, she stood in the doorway, puzzled. "What is it?"

"Nothing," he said harshly.

"What is it?"

"Where're the kids?"

"The little ones are out back in the playhouse. Robbie's off riding his bike somewhere." In a swift movement she never saw, a long, narrow, lethal blade flew out of the curious object. Horror crossed her face.

"How could you bring a switchblade into my house? What if my kids had found it?"

"No one would have found it if you hadn't been sneaking around messing with my stuff. Is it any more dangerous than Bob's gun collection?"

"That's locked in a safe. This was in a cardboard box! What if they found the trigger?"

Nick snorted a short, harsh laugh. "The cops never found the trigger to this little baby."

"Did you ever use it? Why would you have a thing like that?"

"Look at me. It's a stretch to say I am five foot eight. In South L.A. some big dudes roam the street, high on coke or whatever. Yeah, I needed it."

Barb regarded him, shrinking as she took a backward step.

"Once I came up on this guy, who must've been seven foot five—an NBA recruit," Nick continued in a cold voice. "He was breaking a window in a small grocery. The owner was a little Korean who worked his butt off to bring his family to this country. I told the guy to stop. He swung around and pointed a gun at me. He was obviously high, totally out of control."

Barb sucked in her breath. "What did you do? He had a gun!"

In the same unseen movement, Nick's blade flashed out and flew across the room, landing quivering in the wall. "Let's just say, he never played ball."

She gasped. "Did you hurt him? Did you go to jail?"

"No. He begged me to free his hand; it was fastened to the storefront. He cried, and he begged me not to call the cops. He sniveled like the coward he was. He had two possessions, so he knew he'd go to prison for armed robbery. I pulled the blade out and called 911. Told him he'd better get that hand to an ER and left before anyone got there. He didn't know me, and he couldn't rat with what he had hanging over him." Nick walked quickly over to the wall, pulling the blade out and leaving a thin, two-inch hole. "I'll fix that."

"That could kill my babies in a minute. Why don't you lock it up, if you must have it in my house at all?"

Barb watched Nick move far into himself—into that dark place where he disappeared. "Well, let's see, Barb. It was packed away, in the back of the closet, and it locks into itself so well that no cop ever opened it. I've been rather busy, fixing *your* fence, replacing *your* water heater, putting together *your* kids' playhouse, setting up a wireless network to provide *your* kid computer access. I've been a bit busy in your house," he said harshly, his voice quiet, but cold.

Tears sprung to Barb's eyes. "I'm sorry. I know you wouldn't hurt those babies for anything!"

"Yeah, well, what am I supposed to do? I feel like leaving right now, but you tell me I can't do that. So tell me, what should I do here?" He sank on the bed, jerking his fingers through his black, wavy hair. "This is my bed, isn't it? May I sit on this? Don't cry, Barb. Tears aren't fighting fair. Just tell me what to do."

She flashed back to the day they'd spent looking for the bed Nick had insisted on choosing before they married. They went from store to store, finally choosing this bedroom set. The store had delivered it on the Saturday before they married. She swiped her eyes, sniffing back her tears, remembering their laughter as they'd anticipated their joy. She took tentative steps toward him. "Forgive me, Nick? Could you just forgive me?"

Nick averted his eyes. Hearing Robbie come in and call out, he stood. "I'll see if Robbie wants to go with me to Lowe's. We can buy a lockbox of some kind." He walked to the living room, saying with false enthusiasm, "Hey, man, wanna go to Lowe's? I need to get a couple of things."

Robbie looked at his mom who was sniffing back tears and following Nick hesitantly down the hall. He shifted his eyes to Nick's hardened face.

"Uh, sure, let's go. See you later, Mom." She sent him a weak smile and waved him off. After they belted and backed up, Robbie asked, "Are you and Mom okay? Is something wrong?"

Nick glanced over at him and visibly softened. "Yeah, we're okay, kid. A little culture shock, I guess."

"But, you still love her, right?"

Nick's hand reached out to ruffle Robbie's hair. "Yeah, I still love her. You can fight with someone you love, right? You fight with her, and you love her."

"Yeah, that's true. It was just so . . . like, *cold* in there. I never saw Mom and Dad fight. Dad never got mad at Mom, that I saw."

Nick was silent for a long time. "Your dad and I are different people—different personalities. But I love your mom. We'll get through this."

Robbie fell silent. They pulled into the parking lot, but before they got out of the truck, he laid his hand on Nick's arm. "I was ten and Alan was six when my dad left for the last time, but I remember them together. They loved each other, but it's different with you. She sparkles. Maybe I was too young. Sometimes when she looks at you, she melts. She really, really loves you, Nick."

"I know, Robbie. Thanks. We'll be all right, I promise. And I'm not going anywhere, okay?"

Robbie grinned and pulled up the door handle. When they turned into the driveway at home, they got out together and lifted the safe. Barb watched, holding the door for them. They wrestled the heavy object down the hall, and Robbie helped Nick bolt it to the floor at the back of the closet. Nick crouched, locking and unlocking the safe until he could do it with his eyes closed.

"Thanks, Robbie. I appreciate your help."

"What's it for, Nick?" The teen felt he must have said something wrong, because he watched Nick's eyes harden as he closed up and moved into himself.

"Would you mind getting that little package of putty on the back seat and bringing it to me, please?"

The boy went out and returned, handing it to Nick wordlessly. As he went out the door, he put his finger on a thin slit on the wall. "What happened?"

"I'll fix it," Nick said shortly. "Thanks."

Knowing he was dismissed, Robbie went out to the family room where his mother stood, obviously listening. "Is he okay?" she asked.

"What happened, Mom?"

Tears glistening in her eyes, she said, "I hurt him, son. I said some horrible things. I asked him to forgive me, but I don't know . . . your dad and I never fought like this. I don't know what to do. He is passionate about everything—most things."

Robbie put his arm around his mom's shoulders. She noticed his eyes were level with hers now and wondered when that had happened. "It'll be okay. He loves you, a lot. He and Dad have different personalities. He'll come around."

Barb looked at her son, realizing he'd grown in body and in spirit. "Where did you get such wisdom?" She patted his hand and smiled.

"A lot of it comes from Nick. He's a great stepdad." Compassion, fear, and a whole mix of emotions prompted him to put his arms around his mother, and she responded to his uncharacteristic behavior by bursting into tears, something he'd never seen her do. "Mom, he does love you, and he's not going anywhere. Remember, God told us we'd have to teach him the love of a family?"

"I know, Robbie. Did you see the computer desk he put together in your room?"

"No. Wow, did he get the wireless router hooked up?" Robbie rushed to his room. "Man, this is cool! It's not one of those kinky fake wood things. It's nice."

A little girl's scream ripped through the air. Before Barb could get out of the kitchen, Nick burst through the sliding door in their bedroom, leaped off the deck, and had Alice Marie in his arms, cradling her to his chest as he walked back toward the house.

"Shh, baby," he crooned. Nestling her in his arms, he carried her to the deck. She wrapped her arms in a chokehold around his neck.

"She got stung!" Alan cried. "She got stung, Mom."

Barb tried to take Alice Marie, but she clung fiercely to Nick, turning away from her mother. "I'll get the sting stuff," Barb said, spinning into the kitchen.

Nick called after her, "Get some tweezers, too. The stinger might still be in there." Alice Marie's crescendo of wails tore his heart, and he leaned over her, whispering softly.

"I'll get the tweezers, Mom," Robbie shouted.

"In my bathroom, first drawer on the left," she hollered at his retreating figure. "Here, baby." Barb knelt beside her daughter, who shrank into Nick, screaming hysterical refusals of help and shaking her head in a violent no.

Nick held her closely and whispered softly, "Let Mommy put the medicine on you, Cinderella. It'll take the sting away."

"You do it, Daddy." She sniffed. He looked up at Barb, who shrugged and handed him the dropper.

"Here, you have to let Daddy see, okay?" Nick coaxed her. Alice Marie held out her little arm. Nick saw three red welts, two with stingers. He quickly dropped the sting relief on them and held out his hand for the tweezers Robbie thrust at him. "Now, Daddy has to get those little splinters out. You see those? They'll hurt you, and I'm going to take them out."

"Will it hurt?"

"Maybe a little, but I'll hold you real tight, like this." Nick threw his leg around her, squeezing, and she giggled through her tears. Trapped in his grasp, she was unaware that his "hug" was really a lockdown so she couldn't jerk while he extracted the stingers. "There now, all better." Nick eased his leg-hold on her. "Call Alice, Barb. Should we take her to the hospital? What if her throat closes up?"

Barb spun around and grabbed the phone in the kitchen. She returned with children's Benadryl in her hand. "She said to give her this.

I've drawn out the right dosage, but an allergic reaction, shock, or something would be already beginning." When Alice Marie refused to lift her face for her mother, she wordlessly handed the dropper to Nick.

The toddler lifted her face to him and obediently swallowed the medicine. She sank into his chest, her fist knotted in his T-shirt. He stood and walked to the glider. He sang, gently swinging back and forth.

Soon, Missy came out onto the deck. "Is she okay?"

Nick nodded. Barb walked abruptly into the kitchen, and Missy followed.

"Isn't that precious?" Missy gushed, looking back at Nick and the little girl on the glider.

Barb fought back tears. "She wouldn't have anything to do with me. She wanted him."

Missy hugged her friend. "It's good, Barb. Little girls feel safer in a man's strong arms. When I was little, I ran to Daddy and begged him to make the bad go away. I'm glad she has Nick."

Barb sniffed. "Me, too. I'm glad we all have Nick. She calls him Daddy, but this is the first time he referred to himself that way. He said, 'You have to let Daddy see.' We had a huge fight this afternoon. I was so hateful to him. God forgive me."

"He will, sweetie, and so will Nick. He's made such a change in Robbie. He loves you and this family like crazy."

Tim stuck his head in the door. "We have the boys. Jimmy and the kids are meeting us to go fishing. Is it all right if they come?" Barb went into the garage to find their poles.

Nick stood at the door, a quieted toddler in his arms. "Robbie, my wallet is on the dresser. Go get some money for bait and snacks."

"We'll get this," Missy said. Catching his hard stare, she added, "Next time, you can treat." His face relaxed, and she sent the boys to Tim's truck. Nick carried Alice Marie back to the Cinderella bedroom.

"See how he is?" Barb cried again, and Missy put her arms around her.

Tim slammed the tailgate and walked over to them. "What's up?"

"I said mean things to him. He's hurt and angry, and he should be. I was awful."

Smiling, Tim patted her shoulder. "He'll get over this. You women know how to soften up a guy—one sure way works every time. We're taking the boys, and Alice Marie has taken Benadryl. So, go use your feminine wiles."

Missy's coal-black eyes flamed with merriment. "So, Tim, do we soften men up emotionally, or . . . physically?"

"Listen to my wife talking dirty. Both, obviously! Let's get out of the way." He turned her toward their truck and swatted her bottom. Laughing, they walked together, his arm holding her close to his side.

Barb chuckled and waved them off. She turned and saw Nick empty-handed. "Where is she?"

"She's asleep." He moved past her.

"Where are you going?"

"I'm getting some twenty-foot wasp and hornet spray from the garage. I'll kill those suckers so dead they'll never get my Cinderella again."

"Need any help?"

"Stay out of the way. I don't want you stung, too."

Barb walked back to the bedroom, watching through the glass door as Nick bobbed and weaved, waving his arms above his head, running up and back, spraying a huge nest until it dripped. He came in, boasting, "I got them!" and went into the bathroom. Standing at the sink, he scrubbed the residue off his hands and arms.

Barb sat on the bed, watching Nick draw his T-shirt over his head. His strong muscles rippled across his back. She walked to the bedroom door and closed it softly. Nick felt her shirt hit his back. He turned around and saw her stepping out of her shorts beside the bed. He dried his hands, dropped the towel on the floor, and walked toward her. He took her face in his hands and kissed her, at first gently and then more deeply. She groaned, and he lifted her onto the bed.

* * *

When Barb woke up, she covered herself with the sheet and sat up. She pulled her knees to her chest and looked down at Nick. She brushed a stray lock of his dark, wavy hair. He lifted heavy lids, caressing her with his eyes. Reaching a hand behind her neck, he drew her down and kissed her. She broke away but snuggled beside him, splaying her hand in the dark curls on his chest.

"I was jealous of you this afternoon. She wouldn't let me help. I was the only one her whole life, but she wanted you." Nick studied her face, his brow furrowed. Answering his unspoken question, Barb added, "Missy told me when she was little she ran to her father and that little girls feel safer with a man's arms around them. My dad worked hard in the mines, so Mom always took care of us. Missy said it's a good thing Alice Marie has you. It is, Nick. It's good we all have you. Robbie's a different boy, and Alan gains confidence daily. I really am sorry. I was mean, and it wasn't true. You'd never hurt my . . . the kids. Please forgive me."

"It hurt. I love these kids." He reached up and tangled his fingers in her curls.

"I know. Please, please, forgive me?"

He propped up on his elbow. "I read Psalm 130 in *The Message* last night: 'If You, God, kept records on wrongdoings, who would stand a chance? As it turns out, forgiveness is Your habit.' If God makes a habit of forgiving me, and He gave me you, of course I can forgive you, sweetheart." He pulled her down beside him, kissing her tears.

"And, Nick . . . I don't do this."

"What?"

She sat up, blushing and clutching the rumpled bed sheet around her. "I've never thrown my clothes off or fallen asleep before I got them back on." She looked down at him. "You make me crazy."

Nick laughed. "Should I take this as a compliment?" She giggled and pushed him. He grabbed her and drew her down again. "I've never felt like this before, either," he whispered.

"You haven't? I thought you had hot, steamy sex all the time—in your former life."

Nick nuzzled her rumpled hair. "Yeah, that part, Barb, but it felt empty. I've never had *this*—this completion, this satisfaction, fulfillment, joy, whatever. This is communion. It's a holy thing." He drew her tenderly to him, kissing her, and then he lifted his head to one side and chuckled.

"What are you laughing about?"

"I hear Cinderella stirring, babe."

"Oh, where are my clothes?" Barb jumped out of bed.

"Last I saw your T-shirt, it was on the bathroom floor. Your shorts are beside the bed." Laughing as he heard Alice Marie call for her, he added, "I'm not jealous at all, Mommy." Nick pulled his shirt on over his head, and she rushed out. A moment later, fully dressed, he stood at the child's doorway. "Feeling better, Cinderella?"

"All better, see? Mommy kissed it."

"Mommy's kisses make lots of things better." Barb threw a pillow at him. "Let's watch a movie with Mommy and me."

By the time Barb had Alice Marie out of the bathroom and picking out a movie, Nick was coming from the kitchen with a big bowl of kettle corn. Barb started the DVD, and the three of them cuddled together on the couch. Nick had his arm around the two of them, his hand on Barb's shoulder. Before long, the door opened, and the boys rushed in.

"We caught lots of fish, but Mr. Jimmy took them home to clean," Robbie said breathlessly.

"Hi, Ella, Ella, Cinderella," Alan sang, rubbing her head.

"Here comes Ella, here comes Ella. She's her daddy's Cinderella,"

Robbie sang."

The tot laughed and swung around on Nick's lap, facing him. "I *am* Daddy's Cinderella!" she said proudly.

Nick laughed and hugged her. "Yes, you are, baby. You're Daddy's Cinderella. You boys go wash—get those worms off. Robbie, take our bathroom." He turned Cinderella around so she could see the screen. Keeping one arm around her and putting his other around Barb, he drew his wife close and kissed her hair. "Mommy's hair is kind of messed up. Looks bedroomy," he whispered. Barb blushed and tried to hand-comb her hair. "I love it when you blush, baby."

"I have blushed more in the past few months than I have in my entire life, Nick Jo Costas!"

He laughed and nibbled softly on the side of her neck.

Robbie came in with the phone in his hand. "Can I go over to Angela's house to watch a movie? Her dad will come get me."

"What are you going to watch?" Nick asked.

"*Lord of the Rings III*," he replied. "He said it'd be 11:30 before I get home. Please? School starts next week."

Nick looked at Barb. When she agreed, he said, "Okay, kid."

Robbie rushed off to get ready. When he came back, he looked at them mischievously. "Gosh, Nick, it's gotten a lot warmer in the house! Want me to turn up the AC?"

Nick grinned. "You'd better shut up, you little smart a—" Barb cleared her throat. "Aleck! Here." He thrust the bowl of popcorn at Robbie. "Did you guys eat?"

"We ate Subway, and I put some sandwiches in the fridge for you guys." Hearing a horn honk, he dashed off, calling back over his shoulder, "'Night, guys."

Nick let Alan pick out the bedtime story books, since his sister had chosen the movie. He and Barb stretched out beside the two kids on the boy's double bed while Barb read story after story. When Alice Marie begged for her own story, he firmly said, "No, that's all the stories for tonight. Time for bed." She tightened her arms around his neck as he stood up to carry her to her room. She giggled when he leaned down to kiss her brother, and she dangled down from her hold around his neck. "Kiss your brother goodnight."

"'Night, Ella. 'Night, Daddy Nick," Alan said.

Barb sat on the edge of her boy's bed, praying with him. She ran her fingers through his hair, kissed him, and told him goodnight. She heard her daughter beg for just one more dance, and she heard Nick waltzing her around the room singing Stephen Curtis Chapman's song "Cinderella"—their song—as he danced with his Cinderella. Barb entered the room as he tucked her in bed. She watched them and then knelt to kiss her daughter and say prayers.

Nick came out of the shower, water glistening on his dark hair. As Barb came into the bedroom, he rubbed his head with a hand towel and glanced at the kids' rooms.

"Both asleep," she whispered.

He crossed the room, shut the door, and turned her around, gently pinning her against it. He kissed the hollow of her throat and down her neck. "Mmm, I love your long, elegant neck. I believe we have some unfinished business from this afternoon?"

"I'll shower real quick."

At midnight, Nick woke up, realizing he hadn't heard Robbie come in. He checked the boy's room and found it empty, so he went to the family room and snapped on a light. Picking up a Bible, he began to read. About an hour later, Robbie crept in. "Aren't you over an hour late, Robbie?"

"Yes, sir. We talked after the movie. It was late, and I didn't want to wake you guys. I told them Tolkien was a Christian and the story is a story about a story. What do you call that?"

"An allegory."

"Yeah. I explained that Strider was Jesus, who leads the saints into warfare. They'd seen some stupid play and asked if His bride was Mary

Magdalene. Can you believe that? How stupid can you get? I told them Jesus never married."

"Jesus does have a bride. Look here, I was reading this." Nick flipped to Ephesians 5:25. "I really messed up today with your mother. I didn't love her—not the way God expects me to, the way Christ loves His church. Listen to what Paul writes":

Husbands, love your wives, just as Christ loved the church and gave Himself up for her, to make her holy, cleansing her by the washing of the water through the word, and to present her to Himself as a radiant church, without stain or wrinkle or any other blemish, but holy and blameless. In this same way, husbands ought to love their wives, as their own bodies. He who loves his wife loves himself. After all, people have never hated their own bodies, but they feed and care for them, just as Christ does the church—for we are members of His body.

Nick continued, "Down here, in verse 31, Paul reminds us that husband and wife are united and become one flesh, and verse 33 tells us men to love our wives as we love ourselves. That's the New International Version." He looked Robbie full in the face. "This afternoon, I didn't do that. She said some mean things, and I got defensive. I didn't try to explain or help her understand so she'd be cleansed. I didn't feed her the word of God or cherish her. I didn't tell her how I felt. All I thought about was myself. Christ loved His church so much He died for us, and all poor Nick could do was pity poor Nick, you know? She forgave me, though. Come on, let's get to bed. I've got work in the morning."

As Nick started to rise, Robbie asked if they could pray. "I invited Angela's family to church."

Nick sat back down. Robbie took his hand and laced their fingers together. Nick bowed his head, and they prayed quietly. "You did good, kid, to witness to them. But, for future reference, I'd rather wake up to a phone call than sit up worrying."

"Okay, Nick. 'Night." Robbie stood up to walk away and then turned back and awkwardly hugged him.

Nick drew him into an embrace. And, though he tried to slip quietly into bed, Barb stirred. "Is Robbie home?"

"He's home. I can't believe this family. I'm holding hands and hugging the boy. I wouldn't have been caught dead doing that a year ago."

"Well, I, for one, am not about to question your gender orientation."

Nick laughed out loud and propped himself up to kiss her neck.

"Go to sleep. It's too late to start anything more. Haven't you had enough?"

"It's almost 2:00 a.m., baby," he teased.

"Shut up, Nick!"

"Listen to *her*! See what marrying a heathen does to a nice Christian girl?"

"Go to sleep!" she retorted.

Chuckling, Nick gathered her into his arms, and they slept.

CHAPTER 14

Nick's Baby

NICK WAS ALONE in the family room. The younger kids were in bed, and Robbie was spending the night with a friend when Barb got home.

"I'm sorry I'm so late. Quarterlies are due tomorrow and payroll today. Thanks for watching them two nights in a row." After checking on the children, she stood in front of Nick. He looked up, and she straddled his lap, facing him. She leaned into his chest as his arms circled her. He rubbed her legs where her jeans stretched tightly.

"Uh, Nick, we've never talked about kids, you know?"

"Seems to me we talk about kids all the time."

"No, I mean . . . would you like to have a child?"

"We have three wonderful children. I couldn't love these kids any more than I do." He began nuzzling her neck.

Barb shuddered, took a deep breath, and began again. "I mean, a baby—*our* baby. Do you want one of your own?"

"Sweetie, I'm quite content. You've already had three children. It's your body you're talking about."

"Would you be upset if we had a baby?"

"Upset? No. I've just never given it any thought."

"We've been . . . active, you know? And we married in such a hurry. We didn't think much about . . . precautions."

"Barb?"

"I'm pregnant, Nick. Is that okay?"

He leaned her back, his hands supporting her. His brown eyes sparkled. "You're asking me if that's okay?" He crushed her to himself, laughing and kissing her over and over.

"I went to the doctor today."

"You did? Is everything . . . you're fine, right?"

"I'm fine. I wanted to be sure. I'm glad I had that period when we had our weekend away together. I wouldn't want to have a baby nine months after we married. What would people say?"

"Who cares what people say, Barb? You know, and I know, and God knows." Nick drew her into a hug.

"You *are* happy, aren't you?"

"Oh, honey . . ." Resting his forehead on Barb's, Nick searched for words. Unable to find them, he reached over and shut off the light. They sat wordlessly, contented in the dark, with Nick's arms surrounding her as he rubbed her back.

* * *

Crossing the family room the next afternoon, before Barb and the kids arrived home, Nick answered the doorbell. "I'm Elizabeth Miller, from the Department of Health and Human Services. We had a call about this home, and we are required by law to investigate. May I come in?"

"*This* house? Who'd call, and about what?"

"We are required to protect the anonymity of our reporters. I cannot give you that information. Is this the home of Barbara Westfall and her three children?" Puzzled, Nick said it was and asked if she had identification. Irritation tightened Ms. Miller's mouth as she rummaged through her purse to find her card. "May I come in now?"

"Barb isn't here."

"I can begin with you. You are Nickolas Costa, I presume?"

Nick pushed open the door. "Nick. It's Nick Costas." He spotted

Barb pulling into the driveway, so he continued to hold the door open after the social worker entered the house. The car doors flung open, and the children swarmed him.

"Daddy, Daddy, I made a picture in school. It's me and you, dancing with your Cinderella."

Laughing, Nick reached down to Ella's outstretched arms. Resting on his arm, she hugged him and kissed him soundly.

"Barb, this is Ms. Miller, from the Department of Health and Human Resources. She has come about an investigation."

"Mrs. Westfall—" the social worker began.

"Mrs. Costas," Nick corrected. "We married in July."

"Oh, you are married. Legally married?"

Barb stared at her. "Is there such a thing as an illegal marriage? What is this about?"

"We had a report. By law, we are required to investigate."

"Investigate what?" Robbie demanded. "What's she talking about, Nick?"

"Beats me. Come on in, guys. I'm sure we can get to the bottom of this."

"Who would do such a thing?" Barb demanded.

"She can't say, honey."

"I consider this an invasion of our family's privacy, and I insist you leave!"

"Mrs. Westfall, the law requires—"

"Costas. It's Mrs. Costas," Nick corrected again.

"If we can get a few questions answered, I'm sure we can get this done."

"What sort of questions?" Barb asked.

"When were you married? Do you have proof of the marriage? How long has Mr. Costas been living here? How are the children adjusting to his presence in the home? Are you a legal resident of the United States, Mr. Costas?"

"I was born in California. My mother was born there. I was a legal ward of that state for twelve years. I joined the United States Marines and received an honorable discharge. Barb and I married July 20. Prior to that time, I lived in an apartment in Ridgeview Estates. Would you care to be seated?"

"No, she would not care to be seated. She doesn't plan to stay long," Barb retorted. "My children love Nick. Furthermore, he has legal custodial guardianship."

"That may have to be revisited."

"Just when did God die and leave you in charge of my life, Ms. Miller? You need to leave."

Nick put his arm around Barb. "This is just a misunderstanding. We can get it cleared up. Robbie, would you take the little ones to the back, please?"

"Yes, sir. Come on, guys." Robbie herded the wide-eyed children to the back of the house.

"Robbie, I'd like to have a word with you, privately, before I leave," Ms. Miller called after him. "So, Mr. Costas, you say you are a US citizen?"

"He already made that clear." Barb was fuming.

Wondering if steam would come out of her ears, Nick placed a restraining hand gently on her arm and shook his head at her.

"Are you aware how much money the children receive from their father's benefits, Mr. Costas?"

Nick shrugged. "No, not really. Barb manages all the children's funds."

Ms. Miller made a note. "And are you employed? How much do you make?" Barb gasped. Nick calmly gave a five-figure number. "Would that be per year, Mr. Costas?"

The corners of Nick's mouth twitched. "No, ma'am, that would be per month."

"Per month?" Ms. Miller parroted in astonishment. "Where do you work? Aren't you a gardener?"

"I work for O'Malley Productions."

"What do you do? I have a report you were working in a yard at 1611 Elm Street last week." Obviously, Nick's information strained Ms. Miller's imagination.

Nick looked puzzled, and then he remembered. "Oh, that. We have a family in our church—the man had a heart attack, so I cut their grass. At my job, I'm a producer for extraordinarily gifted musicians. Are you familiar with the music industry, Ms. Miller?" When she shook her head, he continued, "We create beautiful music. The O'Malleys do traditional bluegrass and contemporary gospel. We cut CDs, and I mix them and market them. We make music videos as well. I sign contracts with major retail outlets, and we also sell from our website. We publish songs we've copyrighted, so if others wish to use them, they pay royalties. That's the tip of the iceberg, but an overview."

"I see. Would you have documentation, Mr. Costas? Of your citizenship? Also, may I call your employer?"

Nick reached into his back pocket, drawing his driver's license and a copy of his birth certificate out of his wallet. Noticing Robbie hovering in the hall, he asked, "Do me a favor? Would you go back to my printer and copy these for the lady?" Robbie shrugged, holding out his hand. "Thanks, buddy." Then he gave her Ian's phone number. "I'll have my accountant fax you over a copy of my income tax returns."

"Your . . .?"

"My accountant, if I may have your fax number? Barb, don't you want to sit, honey?"

She nodded curtly, her arms folded across her chest.

"Do you use any of your substantial income on behalf of the children, Mr. Costas?"

Nick laughed. "If you count trading in my Porsche for that bus in the driveway that I need to transport my family, yes, I do. And I manage to fork over a few dollars for food and utilities and other odds and ends, like clothes, shoes, computers, wireless networking . . . oh, and cell phones, so we can stay in touch. Let's see, Barb, do you need a new dress?"

"This is *not* funny, Nick, and don't you make a joke out of it." She spun to face the social worker. "And you can tell Pat Westfall she would've seen us get married if she'd come to the wedding. She was invited. She wouldn't even come to her grandchild's second birthday party. She should see how happy these children are. I can't believe this crock. Now, are you through?"

"No, Mrs. Westf . . ." at a warning look from Nick, Ms. Miller amended. "Costas. Are you aware your husband has been married three times, and that he was court-ordered to go through an anger management program?"

"Uh, three? I knew about the anger management program."

"The first marriage was annulled by my foster father. We were underage kids. That would be an illegal marriage, Barb," Nick explained.

"I don't see that it's any of your business anyway, Ms. Miller."

"My 'business,' as you put it, is the protection of children. Now, a word with the boy?"

"He's a minor. If I do not give permission, you may not."

"Barb, we have nothing to hide. Robbie is a well-spoken young man. He'll do fine."

"Thank you for your cooperation, Mr. Costas."

Nick put his arm around Robbie, who was standing in the doorway, and whispered, "Just be honest. It'll be okay."

"This sucks, Nick."

"Sometimes she rescues kids for real, Robbie." Robbie rolled his eyes. "Barb, Ms. Miller wants to have a word alone with Robbie."

Barb kept her arms tightly crossed, her eyes shooting daggers.

"Come on, Barb. Call us if you need us, Ms. Miller." Nick steered Barb to the back of the house, where she paced back and forth until Robbie came back and said the woman was gone.

Barb burst into tears. "I have never been so humiliated in all my life! Nick, how could you take that? And why do you have your birth certificate in your wallet, for heaven's sake?"

"Wise Hispanics carry proof of citizenship because of all the illegals in our country. I've needed it more times than I can count."

"You aren't Hispanic, Nick. You're American!"

"Spoken like a gringo, Robbie. This whole hemisphere is American—North America, Central America, and South America—but not all Americans are from the United States. I'm not ashamed to be Latino, kid. It's who I am."

"But you're white, Nick!"

He laughed. "I didn't say I don't have a lot of gringo in there, but you see these?" He pointed to his eyes. "It's a dead giveaway! Shh, sweetheart, it's okay." Nick tried to put his arms around Barb, but she jerked away.

"But, you don't even speak Spanish," Robbie exclaimed. Looking straight at the boy, Nick let loose a volley of rapid-fire Spanish. He turned to Barb and spoke softly, gently, with the lyrical, musical sound of his voice surrounding her until it filled the room and rolled under the door. Robbie's mouth dropped open, and Barb's eyes got wide.

"What did you say, Nick?" Robbie asked.

"I had a few choice words for you, you little sh—" Barb cleared her throat, interrupting him. "Turd-bird, who knows nothing about anything. No, I told your mother she is exquisitely beautiful, that I love her beyond my poor words . . . and a few other things I'm sure she wouldn't want me to translate."

"Hush, Nick! She had no right. I'm calling Lyn Fuller to have him draw up papers. I can't believe you were so nice to her."

Robbie muttered an unkind word under his breath. Nick silenced him with a look. "I could've used a Ms. Miller in my corner a few times when I was a kid. She's doing her job, Robbie."

"I told her you were the best thing that's happened to this family in a long time, and we all love you!"

"Thanks, Robbie. Now, let's see about some food for this family."

"I couldn't eat a bite!" Barb protested, twisting her hands and blinking back tears.

"Well, you'd better, babe. You've got to feed the kid."

Robbie's eyes got large. "Mom?"

"Come on, Robbie." Nick dragged him out of the house. "Let's go get KFC tonight. Your mom doesn't feel like cooking." Pulling him out the door and grabbing him in a headlock, Nick teased, "I'd better do this while I can. You'll be bigger than me soon."

"Nick," Robbie laughed as soon as he stood up, "is Mom expecting?"

"I guess I shouldn't have let the cat out of the bag."

"Oh, man! This is way cool, you know, because Mom was so sad at the time Cinderella was a baby. God's giving her another baby she'll be totally happy about, but it's going to send Nonna over the edge! I know she sent the social worker here, Nick, and I hate her. I'll never go see her again."

"Hate is a strong word, Robbie. God will help you forgive her. You're all she has left of your dad. You look so much like him. Maybe your mother and I could've done better with keeping them informed. I'm sorry about that."

"I told her you were proud of Dad, and that you promised never to take him away from us, but she wouldn't listen. I heard her and Gramps talking about contacting a lawyer. They can't take us away, can they?"

"Over my dead body, kid. We've had the papers drawn up, and we'll talk to our lawyer in the morning. Don't sweat."

* * *

Nick came into the studio late the next day and found Ian bouncing off the walls. "Just who is this Miller woman, and what stunt is she trying to pull?" Ian wanted to know. Nick ran through previous night's visit from DHHR and then called the accountant to have his returns faxed.

"This is such supreme stupidity! We have kids running the streets, beaten up, molested, and abused, and she's wasting my tax dollars investigating you and Barb? Let me tell you, she got an earful from me when she called!"

"Thanks, Ian. Can we get to work?"

Later, the attorney called. He'd talked to the judge after their emergency meeting earlier, and the judge wanted to see Robbie in his chambers at four. Nick rode over to the ball field and explained to the coach that he needed Robbie for a little legal work. On the way to the courthouse, Nick explained. "He's somebody's dad, Robbie, maybe even a grandfather. Don't worry about what to say. Mr. Fuller will be in there with you."

"Can't you be with me, too?"

"That probably won't happen, kid, but I'll sit right outside and pray."

After Robbie had been in the judge's office a few minutes, the attorney brought Nick in.

"This young man thinks you are some sort of a superhero, Mr. Costas, so I wanted to meet you myself. Mr. Simpson, at the school, speaks highly of you as well," the judge added.

"Thank you, your Honor. God watches after fools and children. I'm no superhero, but I love these kids like crazy."

Robbie put his arm around Nick, hugging him hard and hanging on to his waist.

"That's evident, Mr. Costas—quite evident. And this boy sure loves you. Now, Fuller, I wish I could have you draw up a cease and desist order. If I could get those names, I'd tell you to sue them for libel. I can dismiss the charges, however. I'll call the social worker in the morning and give her a heads-up."

Robbie practically skipped out of the courthouse. Dancing a jig and flipping open his cell phone, he called his mother.

"What have you learned in all this, Robbie?" Nick asked when he hung up.

"Huh?"

"We faced some pretty practical life lessons about fear and bigotry and rushing to judgment. You demonstrated remarkable loyalty and courage. Thank you."

"All I did was tell the truth."

"Sometimes that's hard to do."

"It's a lot easier than forgiving Nonna. I read those Scriptures you gave me last night." Nick put his arms around the boy's shoulder as they walked to the car. "Mom's got the little kids. Let's go home, Nick!"

When they walked in, the spaghetti was almost ready. Barb put the spoon down and walked over to Robbie, hugging him briefly.

"Spaghetti smells scrumptious, Mom. I'm starved!"

"What else is new, Robbie? You did a good job, son. Mr. Fuller was real proud of you." She kissed him on the cheek and stepped into Nick's arms, not saying a word as he rubbed her back gently.

"I told you it was no cakewalk being married to me, babe."

She pulled his head close and whispered, "Maybe, but I like the icing!"

"Now, that's not fair. How long must we wait until these kids go to bed? I can translate that Spanish for you—but you might blush," he whispered in her ear.

She kissed his cheek, smiling. "Help me get this supper on the table, you nut."

"Shall I translate now?" he asked her. Robbie giggled, and a look of horror came over Barb's face.

"Nick, for heaven's sake! Be quiet, for once in your life."

Nick soothingly, softly, spoke words of love in Spanish.

"What did you say, Nick?" asked Alan.

"It's a secret for your mother."

"I like secrets," Alice Marie piped.

"Me, too, Cinderella. Me, too." Nick leaned down and kissed the child's shiny cheek.

CHAPTER 15

A New Home

NICK HERDED THE BOYS into the kitchen and called Barb. Cookies and milk waited on the table. "What's up, Nick?" Robbie inquired. Cinderella was asleep, and the boys were ready for bed. He looked at his mom, who shrugged.

"I am praying about something I need to talk to you guys about." He glanced at Barb. "Alan, Robbie, I promised you I wouldn't take your father away from you. I can't replace him, and I won't try. He's a hero, who laid down his life for his friends, and Jesus says there is no greater love. But, we face a small complication. Your dad and mom bought this home. You've lived here . . . how long, Barb?"

"We moved in after Robbie was born."

Nick sighed. "Your mom already has Robbie in the dining room so that everyone can have a bedroom. And now, it seems we need another bedroom."

Barb put her hand on Alan's. "We're going to have a baby, Alan," she explained.

Robbie grinned and gave Alan a high-five.

Nick cleared his throat. "We need to think. I've talked to Tim. He can add on to this house, if we decide to. But do you guys want to look at some houses on the market? We could build one, so we could also look at land." He fell silent, considering their faces.

"Would we leave Elkins, Daddy Nick?" Alan asked. "I want to stay in my school."

"No, doofus, Nick and Mom work here," Robbie said.

"Robbie," Barb warned. "The question boils down to if we want to stay here and add on, or look around, right?" Nick nodded.

"If we looked, we wouldn't definitely have to move, would we?" Alan asked.

"No, buddy. We see what's out there and make a better choice. What do you think?" He cut a glance at Robbie, who remembered Nick including him in decision-making, and it made him feel important. He nodded at Nick, who encouraged him with a smile.

"Well, Mom, it wouldn't hurt, would it? Wouldn't that be a good idea?" Robbie asked.

"Yes, it's a good idea. Shall I set up an appointment with a realtor, Nick?" Barb smiled at him. Everyone agreed, so she called Sue Parker, a friend from church. They set a time for Friday evening.

"I really don't know, Sue. Let me put Nick on the line." She handed him the phone. Nick took it to the deck and talked to the realtor out of earshot.

* * *

On Friday, the boys climbed noisily into the Suburban. Nick fastened Cinderella in her car seat, and they drove to the realtor's office. "Robbie, why don't you set up the third seat, and you and Alan can hop in there and let Mrs. Parker sit in the back seat." Nick held out his hand to the realtor. "Nick Costas, ma'am. I've seen you at church. You know Robbie and Alan."

"Yes." She leaned into the car, smiling at Cinderella. "And I've been with Alice Marie in the nursery many times. Hi, Alice."

"I'm my daddy's Cinderella, but you can call me Ella," the child responded.

Barb laughed and slipped her arm around Nick. "We may have to change the birth certificate, Nick. You gave her a name that will stick."

"I have two Alices in my life, but only one Cinderella." The child beamed at him, and he dropped a kiss on her cheek. Looking into the back, he praised Robbie. "Good job, man, you handled that 'help' very well." He winked at him, knowing Alan's assistance was in the way more than truly helpful. Robbie grinned and gave Nick a thumbs-up. "Okay, Alan, sit down and belt up. Let's get this show on the road," Nick said.

Once on their way, Sue asked Nick if he wanted to start with the Wilson property. Glancing in the rearview mirror, he replied, "Let's save that one for last." He winked at her. Barb looked puzzled as she shuffled through the papers and didn't find the printout.

The boys ran excitedly through several properties, and Barb admired the kitchens. Cinderella fell asleep on her daddy's shoulder, but he carried her without complaint when they were too far from the car to leave her.

"I can't thank you enough, Sue. You've given us a lot to think about," Barb said as she sorted through the property descriptions in her hands. She had jotted notes on several of them.

"Now we'll go to the Wilson property," Nick said, glancing in the rearview mirror and winking at Sue again.

"I don't have a paper on that one, Nick," Barb pointed out.

Wordlessly, Nick steered the vehicle north, out of town. "You'd have to change schools for this one, Alan, but it's Jamie's school." He pulled into a wooded lane and drove about a half-mile, stopping on a hill. The redwood and stone structure spread out before them had two stories, with wings on both sides, and a spacious manicured lot. "I like not seeing the neighbors, but nice families live nearby—one of the boys from your softball team, Robbie. Of course, you boys will have to use a lawn tractor to mow it."

"Oh, yeah, I thought I'd been out this way before. Remember Brandon's back-to-school party last summer, Mom?"

Barb was quiet as Sue and the others got out of the car. Cinderella was awake by this time, and she raced after her brothers. The realtor took the children through the garage. Nick's eyes twinkled. "Pretty out here, isn't it?" Seeing Barb hesitate, Nick stopped. "What is it, honey? Are you afraid out here?"

"Nick, we can't afford this. It's entirely out of our price range. I won't have you getting in over your head for my . . . for this family," she said firmly.

Nick leaned back on the truck and drew her into his arms. "Barb, have you ever seen me make stupid financial decisions?" She shook her head. "I believe in being debt-free, right?" She agreed. "I talked to the bank and my accountant, and I assure you I can afford this, baby. But I love you for your concern. You want to go see it?" Hearing the children's excited screams, she took his hand. They walked up the front stairs, and Nick opened the door with a key.

"You haven't bought this already, have you?"

He hesitated. Holding the door, he put his other arm around her. "Of course not, we make decisions as a family. I'd never do that to you, or the boys." He pushed the door open to reveal a stone foyer and a double staircase to the second story. Barb heard the kids' feet pounding along the corridor as Nick drew her to the side and opened a heavy door to the master suite on the east side. "Our bedroom, if we decide on this one."

Barb gasped.

"Come see the bathroom," Nick urged. "Tim told me the Jacuzzi is worth the price of the house. He, Ian, and Jimmy rave about theirs— *and* what it does for their marriage."

Barb stood in the beautiful tiled bathroom and stared at the Jacuzzi and the double shower. She turned and wandered back into the bedroom. "This is huge. We could put a crib here easily."

Nick turned her to a double door that opened into a private sunroom. "And when the baby's bigger, we could make this into a nursery."

Tears spilled down Barb's cheeks. "Oh, Nick, this is too much."

Nick drew her into his arms, kissing her tears. He put his mouth over hers and tasted her sweetness.

"Mom, Nick, where are you guys?" Robbie backed up, clapping his hand over Alan's eyes, but he stared at them from the hall.

Nick pulled his face away and glanced at Robbie with a huge grin. "You like this place, big guy?"

"This is super cool! Mom, you've gotta see. We've got a ton of bedrooms. Alan and I picked ours out. Come on, Mom." Robbie grabbed her hand and pulled her to the stairs.

Upstairs, Barb discovered five more bedrooms. Alan and Robbie chose bedrooms with a bath between them on the west wing. Directly at the top of the stairs was a bedroom that also shared a bath with another bedroom. Cinderella wouldn't be too far from them. At the end of the west wing, Barb found another bedroom with its own bathroom.

"Come on, sweetheart, let's look at the kitchen," Nick prodded. Sue beamed as they clambered down the stairs. Cinderella reached for Nick, and he carried her. Ignoring the large living room across from the master suite for the time, he steered Barb into a modern kitchen. He watched her eyes widen as she took in the magnificent center island, the wide expanse of counters, and the brand-new modern appliances. Nick placed a finger on her lips to cut off her protests and said, "Wait, Barb—wait till you hear."

"Do you want to tell her now, Nick, or should we show her outside?" Sue asked after the boys had burst out the French doors from the family room.

"There's a pool!" they screamed, giving each other high-fives. Barb looked at Nick, a serious frown pulling at her face.

"You'd better tell her, Sue, or she won't take another step."

"It isn't fair to get these kids all excited, Nick. I mean . . ." Her voice trailed.

"This is the best part, Barb," Sue said. "The owners are billionaires,

and they're semi-retiring. They settled in Vail after selling major hold-
ings in West Virginia. I told them about you guys, and about Bob. This
guy is some sort of a philanthropist and a real patriot. He told me he'd
get back to me, and he called yesterday. He talked to Nick and Nick's
accountant, and he's selling you this house for less than two of the
properties you looked at today."

Nick handed Cinderella to Sue as Barb swayed ominously. "Hey,
don't faint on me, babe."

"How could God be this good, Nick?" She wept. "It's huge, and the
pool. Can we afford to maintain it?"

"Okay, Eeyore!" Nick chuckled, holding Barb firmly around the
waist. "We have a reasonable mortgage, free gas, and the exterior is
virtually maintenance-free. Now, do you want to see the backyard?"
Sue, who had walked with Barb through the dark valley after Bob's
death, almost danced with joy as they stepped into the yard. Barb
started weeping in earnest then, burying her face in Nick's chest. "Is
this too much of a surprise for a pregnant lady? Are you all right?"

The boys screeched to a halt in front of them. "What's wrong,
Mom, don't you like it?" Robbie asked. "Oh, I bet we can't afford
anything like this. It's okay, Mom, we're a family. God answered our
prayers and gave us a family. That's the most important thing. Isn't it,
Nick?"

"If I can get your mother to calm down, I'll explain, boys." Barb
sniffed, looking at him with a tentative smile. "I'm totally not used to
pregnant women!" She giggled and hugged his waist, clinging to his
support. He eased her into one of the lawn chairs gathered on the stone
patio. "Sit, boys. I wouldn't excite you about something we couldn't
have. You should know me better." Nick explained the unusual circum-
stances.

"Mom, you said we should never ask for charity! Wouldn't that be
charity?" Robbie asked. Nick was at a loss to respond, but Barb had
herself together enough to explain they hadn't begged or even asked for

anything, and God would bless the giver. "So, we can move here? When?" Robbie tried to contain his excitement. "School's already started, but I'll help on a weekend. We can get a U-Haul."

Nick laughed. "There is no way I'll let your mother handle a U-Haul move, boys. We'll hire a mover, but the owner wants to know if we want the furniture. They took most of the bedroom furniture, obviously, but the rest is available. Oh, gosh, she's crying again." Nick rose, sat on his haunches beside Barb's chair, and took her into his arms.

"Miss Sue is crying, too, Nick. Are you going to hug *her*?" Alan asked. "It must be a girl thing, Robbie," he told his big brother seriously.

Sue laughed, ran her fingers through the boy's hair, and said, "You're right, Alan. It's a girl thing."

Cinderella pulled on Nick's pant leg. "Daddy, is Mommy all right?"

Nick sat on the stone patio, gathered her into his arms, and laughed. "Mommy is fine, Cinderella. But tell Daddy, would you like to live here?"

She looked at him with her earnest blue eyes. "Can you bring my Cinderella room?" He nodded. "Can I get the room at the stairs?"

"She wants the room at the top of the stairs, Daddy Nick," Alan explained. "We told her you and Mommy would be right downstairs, real close."

She nodded and reached her arms around his neck.

"Daddy would be real close to his Cinderella, and we'd put a little box in your room so you could talk to us, and we could hear you the minute you cry. And Daddy would run up those stairs so fast and hold you safe and dance with his Cinderella. How would that be?"

"Good, Daddy, I'd like that."

They dropped Sue off at the real estate office and headed home.

* * *

"**W**hat's going on? Why is the whole O'Malley clan here?" Barb asked once they were back at home.

"I don't know, Barb," Nick replied. But his eyes danced. When they walked into the house, everyone started to talk at once. Missy jumped up and down. She and Julie joined hands and danced in a circle, laughing.

Alice smiled with her eyes but calmly said, "We have dinner for you. We can hardly wait to hear all about the house. Isn't God good, Barbara?"

Barb started to cry again, and Nick drew her into his arms. "Now you've gone and started the waterworks again, Alice. She's going to dehydrate if she doesn't stop."

Barb giggled and lifted her face for his kiss. "God has turned my mourning into dancing. He has put off my sackcloth. I don't have words to thank Him enough. Have you seen that place, Missy?"

Missy and Julie nodded. "What took you so long to make up your mind, girl?"

"He dragged us to three or four other places before he let Sue show us this one. Oh, here she comes now. Wonder what she wants?"

"She probably has some papers for us to sign." Nick crossed over to the door and opened it.

Sue, who was dressed professionally, was almost prancing. "You really won't believe what God has done. I told Mr. Wilson about your tour. He was moved by Robbie's comments when he said he didn't need this house, the most important thing he had was family. Then I told him the charity discussion. Mr. Wilson has prayed about the whole deal, and after hearing all that, he wants to sign the deed over to you guys. You own the house free and clear, Barb!"

Barb stood up and clasped her hands in front of her. She gaped at Sue. "Nick, what did she say? What does that mean?" She turned to him.

"Sit down, honey," he replied gently and guided her to the couch as excited hubbub swirled around them. Alice calmly set dishes on the table, along with chicken, scalloped potatoes, and salad. The smells drew the ever-hungry boys to the table.

Sue pulled Nick out onto the front stoop. "If you could come by the office tomorrow, say around two? I'll have your attorney do the title search and work up a deed." She reached for his hand to shake and added, "It's been a pleasure, Nick. Robbie's right—you're a wonderful family, and that *is* the most important thing. I had my reservations. I heard stuff. But these kids, and Barbara—they're blessed to have you."

"Thanks, Sue. They teach me how to love and do the family thing. I've never had a family before."

"I'd say Father God is truly making you a father after His own heart, Nick."

* * *

That night, as she lay in Nick's arms, Barb said, "I don't understand. Why me? Why is this happening to me?"

"I always said you'd given enough for your country, Barb. I couldn't give you enough for your sacrifice. Apparently, Mr. Wilson agrees with me."

"Oh, Nick, you've given me much more than a house. You gave these kids love, a family, a father, understanding, guidance. You give me passion I never knew existed—but not tonight, I'm too tired."

Nick laughed delightedly. "I can contain myself for one night. We have many more to look forward to. Do you want to buy a bigger bed for that huge bedroom? I do love you, Barb, and I can't thank you enough for loving me, for giving me this family—my family. A house is just a house. You've given me a home." Barb turned to face him and receive his kiss, and she found she wasn't too tired after all.

CHAPTER 16

Run Away

NICK WAS DRIVING beside Kroger's when his phone rang. He pulled into the lot and glanced at the screen. It was Barb. She probably wanted him to pick up something at the store. He smiled and brought up the call, but all he could hear was her sobs. "What is it, honey?" She was gasping for breath. "Hang on. I'm almost home. Are you okay?"

"NO!" She broke into renewed wails.

Nick thought he heard "home" and "quick," but he couldn't understand a word she choked out. Throwing the phone onto the seat, he wheeled the Suburban around and broke into traffic, leaving a flurry of furiously honking vehicles behind him as he sped toward the house. He pulled into the driveway, threw the truck into park, and left the door open when he ran.

Barb flung herself at him. "We can't find her! Ella's gone. She ran away. And it's my fault."

Nick drew her into his arms. "Shh, baby. We'll find her. She's just a little girl. She can't go too far."

Robbie stood, anxiously wringing his hands, and Alan had tears on his cheeks. Robbie's voice broke. "We've turned the house upside down."

Nick's eyes swept the family room, noting that everything in the front closet was thrown around the room.

"I went up and down the street and asked all the neighbors. No one has seen her," Alan added in a tremulous voice.

"We need to call the police!" Barb cried.

"She's here, and we know the One Who knows where she is. We'll find her," Nick said.

"You aren't listening to me! No one knows where she is. I want my baby."

Nick tightened his arms around her. "God knows where she is, and He's watching after her. Come on, guys, let's pray."

"Someone grabbed her. I know it. I made her run away, and now she's been kidnapped."

"Honey, I fixed the gate, so she couldn't get out. Did anyone see her leave the front door?"

"She couldn't have, Nick. We were all in the living room," Robbie said.

Nick gestured to Alan and Robbie, and they gathered close to their mother, placing their hands on her while Nick calmly prayed. "She's in here, Barb. She's in this house." He gently let himself out of her arms and walked to the Cinderella bedroom. Clothes had been strewn everywhere. the closet was empty, and the place was in chaos. The bedspread had been stripped from the bed and the comforter and sheets flung across the floor. He sat down on the bare bed, his head down.

Robbie came in and lowered himself beside Nick. "Miss Julie dropped us off. She and Mom talked a bit in the driveway, and Mom walked in and found Ella jumping up and down on Dad's picture screaming, 'You are *not* my daddy,' over and over. Alan and I had gone to our rooms, and we ran back when we heard Mom yelling at her—she kinda lost it, Nick. She tried to pick up the photo. Ella grabbed for it, and it tore. It was downhill from there. Ella ran off, screaming that she was going to run away."

Nick sighed. "Where did that come from?"

"When we were in Pittsburg, Ella talked about her daddy—you. Nonna got angry and told her you were not her daddy—her daddy was in the pictures on the mantel, and she mustn't ever forget that. You would never be her daddy, Nonna said."

Nick rubbed his face, stood, and walked to the doorframe. He put his hand up and leaned on it and blew out a breath. He straightened and asked, "Where have you looked?"

"Everywhere, Nick. We've taken this house apart, and we've looked under every bush outside."

"Where are you, Cinderella?" Nick whispered. "Daddy needs you to come out." Alan hovered in the hall. Nick put his arm around the boy's shoulder. "She's here. I know she is. I feel her. We'll find her. Let's be real quiet. Show us where she is, God." He could hear Barb's moaning cries in the living room, and they tore at his heart. He walked slowly across the hall to their bedroom.

"Where is my Cinderella?" he said aloud. "I want to dance with my Cinderella, and I can't find her anywhere." He listened. Bringing his finger to his lips, he looked at the boys and crept toward the closet. He leaned his head on the door and smiled, motioning to them to indicate she was in there. He waved them off and whispered, "Go tell your mother she's in here, and pull the door shut, will you?"

Alan ran down the hall and whispered, "Nick thinks she's in the closet in your room, Mom."

"I looked in there," Barb said.

"I think he heard her."

Barb rushed to their bedroom door, and Robbie caught her arm. "Let him talk to her."

Nodding mutely and blinded by tears, Barb stumbled back to the family room and sank onto the couch. "My poor, poor baby. I shouldn't have yelled at her. But, why would she do a thing like that? She's never been destructive." The brothers exchanged a glance. "What?" she demanded, swinging her head back and forth between them. "You boys tell me."

Robbie hung his head. "I think she's just confused, Mom." He signaled to Alan. "Let's start cleaning this mess up." They began with the
front hall closet, hanging up coats and putting boots back on the floor.

Barb walked back to their bedroom and heard Ella and Nick talking
quietly, but she couldn't make out the words. She leaned her head on
the door, and fresh tears welled up and ran down her face.

Robbie came beside her and turned her. "Help us in here. She won't
be able to sleep in her own room if we don't straighten this mess. He'll
settle her down."

Nick had opened the door to the closet. When his eyes adjusted to
the dim light, he saw Ella's little legs. She stood in a pair of his shoes,
wrapped up in one of his shirts. He knelt and opened his arms. Ella
pressed her tear-streaked face against his chest. He kept his arms
around her and waited, then he stood and carried her out of the closet.
"Mommy's mad at me, Daddy."

"She was frightened when she couldn't find you, Ella. We get mad
at each other sometimes in a family, but Daddy's learning that we don't
run away or hide from people who love us. Mommy loves you."

"I broked the picture."

"Why did you break the picture, baby?" Nick walked over to the
bed, set her on it, and sat beside her.

"He's not my daddy. You are my daddy. I don't care what Nonna
says." She looked up at him and placed her little hands on each side of
his face. "You are my daddy. You are. Aren't you my daddy?" New
tears welled up in her blue eyes and spilled over to trickle down her
cheeks.

Dear God, help me. Nick leaned against the pillows and pulled her
beside him. He brushed his lips in her hair, holding her close. "Do you
remember when Daddy didn't live here, Ella?" She nodded. "And
remember when Daddy and Mommy made promises at the church? You
wore a beautiful little blue dress and looked so pretty—remember? We

got married, and then Daddy moved to your house, right?" She looked at him, a tiny frown puckering between her eyebrows. He smiled. "Do you remember when you used to call me 'Unca Nick?' Hmm?"

"But, you are my daddy."

Nick blew a long breath. *Okay, God, give me some words here.* "Everybody has a mommy and a daddy, right?"

"Yes," she said in a small voice.

"Who lived in your house before I came to live with you?"

"Mommy, and Robbie, and Alan."

"Where was your daddy?"

"Where were you, Daddy?"

Nick smiled at her. "Once upon a time, the handsome man in those pictures lived in this house with Mommy and the boys. He left you with Mommy and went to heaven."

"With Jesus?

"Uh-huh. He lives with Jesus. But Jesus knew Mommy was very sad and lonely, and Cinderella needed a daddy on earth, so He sent me to be your daddy. You grew in your mommy's tummy and lived here in this house for almost two years before I came. But when I came, you grew in my heart. I chose you to be my little girl, and you chose me to be your daddy. You are a very blessed little girl, Ella. You've had two daddies."

"Will you go to heaven, too?"

"Someday, but not for a long, long time. Not until Prince Charming comes and carries you off to his castle, and you have lots of princes and princesses of your very own."

Ella lay quietly beside him. "I don't want you to leave, Daddy."

"I won't leave. I promise."

"But Nonna said you aren't my daddy. She wants to make you go away."

"That's not Nonna's decision, Ella. She can't take you away from Mommy and me."

"And the mean lady won't make you go away?"

"Ms. Miller isn't a mean lady, Ella. She is a good lady. Her job is to take care of kids. Some mommies and daddies aren't nice to their kids. They even hurt them. She helps those poor kids find a safe place to live."

"Why did she come here, Daddy?"

"Well, somebody was afraid Daddy wasn't good to you, so she came to make sure you were happy. Now, she knows you are happy, and she is happy you live with Daddy. She's a nice lady, Ella."

Ella pulled out from under Nick's arm and threw her leg over his lap, leaning against him. She sighed. "Two daddies?"

"That's right. Two daddies who love you very, very much." He held her back. "Your first daddy was Nonna's little boy, all grown up, and she misses him very much. It's hard for her that you chose another daddy."

"Will I see my other daddy in heaven?"

"You sure will."

"Who'll be my daddy in heaven?"

Nick smiled. "Let's let Jesus figure that one out, okay? But, I figure we can share. He crossed his legs and tucked her head under his chin. "Nonna only had one baby, your first daddy. His name is Robert Westfall."

"That's Robbie's name."

"Yep. He's Robbie and Alan's daddy, too, and Robbie was named after him." Ella sighed. Nick held her quietly until he felt her little body stop trembling. "Mommy feels very sad. She couldn't find you any-where. She looked, and she looked. She took all your clothes out of your closet and threw them on the floor."

"She looked in your closet, but I hided."

"Poor Mommy was so scared when she couldn't find her baby."

"I'm not a baby!"

"Her big girl, I mean. But you know, you, Robbie, and Alan will always be Mommy's babies. That's how mommies are. And Nonna misses her baby so much."

"I'm sorry I broked the picture." Ella sniffed.

Nick slid off the bed and held out his arms. "Can you tell Mommy?" She nodded. Carrying her out of the room, Nick looked across the hall and saw that the Cinderella bedroom was perfect once again. He smelled cooking, and they followed the enticing fragrance into the kitchen.

From the safety of Nick's arms, Ella whispered, "I'm sorry I broked the picture, Mommy."

"Oh, baby, Mommy can live without the picture, but I can't live without you. I'm sorry I yelled at you."

"Let's forgive up, Mommy."

Nick leaned forward and deposited her into Barb's arms. "That's a good idea, Ella. You forgive Mommy and Mommy forgives you." He winked at Barb, who hugged her little girl and rocked her back and forth.

Nick turned down the stove and went into the living room, where he found two sober boys sweeping up glass and carefully putting the photo pieces together.

"I think we can tape it up," Robbie said.

"I can take it to a photo restoration place in Morgantown, boys. We'll make a new one. In fact, we'll make four: one for Mommy, one for each of you boys, and one for Ella."

"Man, the poor kid. What did you say to her?" Robbie asked.

"I told her she was blessed to have two daddies who love her very much. One lives in heaven, and one lives here."

Tears sprung to Robbie's eyes. "That's two more than you had, huh, Nick?"

Nick felt a wrenching in his gut, but he smiled. "God has restored all that the enemy stole. He's given me you boys."

Alan wiggled himself under Nick's arm. "I'm glad, Daddy Nick."

"Me, too, kid. Me, too. What's Mom got cooking?"

Robbie giggled. "I don't think she knows."

When they arrived in the kitchen, Ella stood on a chair against the counter, carefully stirring instant pudding. Barb pulled tater tots out of the oven. She had stacked hamburgers on a platter, surrounded by tomato slices and lettuce. Nick reached for a bowl for the potatoes, Alan got mayo and ketchup out of the fridge, and Robbie set the table.

"You guys did a good job of getting this house put back together," Nick said as he pulled out Barb's chair and tucked Ella in her high chair.

Barb put her hand on his arm when he sat beside her. "That was the easy part. We wrecked it, and we could fix it, but you put our home together, Nick. Thank you."

He shrugged. "Alan, will you say the blessing?"

CHAPTER 17

Nonna

"ROBBIE, TELEPHONE," Nick called. "It's your grandmother." Robbie made a face and reached for the phone. "Hi, Nonna. . . . No, ma'am, I need to cut our own grass. We're putting our house on the market and moving. Maybe you ought to talk to Mom about it, Nonna. . . . No, ma'am, we decided as a family. . . . She's out with some friends. Bye."

"Wasn't that fudging a bit, Robbie? We got the grass done this morning. Why won't you help your grandmother?"

"*You* are asking me? She's the one who sent Ms. Miller out here! I hate her. Look at what she put poor little Ella through last night!"

"We've talked about this. We need to forgive her. I lay awake a long time praying for her last night. God knows, it must be the toughest thing in the world to lose a child. Your dad was her only child, Robbie." Nick patted the boy on the shoulder, adding, "We've got to reach out to them, and this is a good way to do it. Your mom told me your grandfather is fishing with a friend today." He took a deep breath. "Let's pray, shall we?"

Robbie sighed, threw himself on the couch, and said irritably, "I know what Jesus would say."

"We could ask Him to help you do it graciously." Nick ruffled his hair.

Robbie eventually called his grandmother, and a few minutes later Nick dropped him off at Nonna's. Almost immediately, the cell phone rang. "You gotta get here, quick! Something's wrong with Nonna. She's blue, and I don't think she's breathing," Robbie reported in a panic.

"Call 911 and give them the address. I'll be right there." Nick hardly stopped before he was out of the truck and up the steps. A terrified Robbie held the door. Nick dropped to his knees and began to press Mrs. Westfall's chest. She made a gurgling noise, and color returned to her face.

"Thank you, Jesus!" Robbie exclaimed.

Nick glanced up. "I hear the siren, Robbie. I can't stop here. Open the door and wave them in."

The paramedics rushed in with a handheld defibrillator. They worked on her a few minutes and lifted her onto a gurney, telling Nick to follow them to the ER. He motioned to Robbie and flipped open his phone as they walked to his Suburban.

"Hi, baby, we're leaving your mother-in-law's house. She's had a heart attack, and the ambulance is taking her to the ER. We'll meet you there. I dropped Robbie off at her place to cut the grass, so I was close when he found her. . . . Barb, Mrs. Westfall had a heart attack. You need to go to the hospital. I know Gramps is off fishing. . . . Honey, go to the hospital. I know you're having a day out with your girlfriends, but this is an emergency, and you need to leave *now*. I'll meet you there." He flipped the phone shut. "She's in shock, Robbie. She couldn't seem to take it in."

Robbie was crying. "What if you hadn't made me go? What if nobody'd found her? She'd be dead!"

Nick reached over and patted him. "But you *were* obedient, and we *did* get to her. God is in this. Let's trust Him."

"She doesn't know Jesus. She's gotta live, or she won't be with Dad."

Nick carefully turned the vehicle toward the hospital, praying as he drove, asking God to preserve Nonna's life until she could come to know Him. He parked and put his arm around Robbie's shoulder as they walked into the ER. He walked to the receiving desk and tried to relate the information he knew, watching for Barb to arrive. When she came hurrying in, he motioned to her. "You need to answer these questions. Robbie grabbed her purse to see if her Medicare card is in there. That was really smart thinking, kid," he praised as he steered Robbie over to a chair.

Barb finished up at registration and walked over to them. "She's critical. I need to go outside and call Gramps. Pray!"

Robbie bowed his head. Suddenly, he jerked up. "I didn't cause this, did I? She didn't know we're selling the house. It really shocked her."

"No, buddy, news didn't do that. We'll find heart blockages, most likely, and she'll have bypass surgery and be better than ever. Maybe this ticking time bomb has been affecting her moods for a while."

An ER doctor walked up to Nick. "I understand you're the man who saved her life. Are you a relative?"

"No, sir. But her daughter-in-law is outside calling Mr. Westfall."

"She has you to thank. Good job on CPR. The EMTs said you did everything right."

"They were able to do a lot more with that defibrillator. Here's Barb now. Did you reach him?"

"No, he must be out of range. How is she, Doctor?" The doctor filled them in on her condition, confirming Nick's guess that a helicopter would fly her to Charleston. "What should we do? I can't reach Gramps."

"How long will he be gone?" Learning that the fishing outing was a day trip, Nick suggested he could remain at Nonna and Gramps's house until Gramps got home, while she kept trying to reach him and gathered their own family at home.

"I want to stay with you," Robbie said. Nick nodded, and the two of them returned to the Westfall house.

Barb called them about an hour later. "I finally got him. He's on his way. He wants to go to Charleston immediately, but he can't drive at night."

"I'll take him. I'll drop Robbie off." Nick held a warning finger up to the boy. "There's no sense for you to be up all night."

"But, you can't drive home by yourself!" Robbie protested.

"I won't drive home tonight. I'll stay with him. He doesn't need to face this alone."

Robbie looked at Nick, tears swimming in his eyes. "You're showing me what it means to turn the other cheek. Has Mom called Great Aunt Nell? She's his sister." Nick rang Barb again. She had called Gramps's sister, who lived in Charleston, and Nonna's brother. They would meet him at the hospital. "See, I told you. You need me to help you stay awake for the trip home. I'm going with you."

"All right. We're in this together, kid."

When Gramps arrived, Robbie filled him in on how Nick had saved Nonna's life, but Nick cautioned him about over-exuberance, giving credit to the EMTs. On the trip, Gramps came to appreciate the incredibly kind man who had married his daughter-in-law and obviously loved his grandchildren. He apologized for not getting to know him sooner. Nick refused to leave Mr. Westfall until they'd located his family at the hospital and he was settled in their care.

"Be sure to keep in touch, Robert. Let us know what we can do. We can get things in the house ready for when she comes home, and if you need us here, we'll come back." Nick put his arm around the elderly man. "She *will* come home. Would you like us to pray with you before we go?"

The family held hands around a circle, and Nick was gratified to hear Mr. Westfall's sister speak to God intimately, as a believer. She stood beside Nick and squeezed his hand. They exchanged a private smile. Nick patted Mr. Westfall's shoulder. He was surprised when the older man pulled him into a hug.

While they were driving, Robbie mused aloud, "Isn't God amazing? I mean, how was He going to get through to them? Did you hear Aunt Nell pray? She's a Christian. God has a wide-open door into their lives. Nonna can't make him think badly about you now!" They stopped to eat on the way, but Robbie fell asleep long before they arrived home.

Barb opened the door and helped Nick get the teen inside. When he fell on his bed, she gently removed his shoes. He barely acknowledged her presence when she praised him.

"Have you been up all this time?" Nick asked.

"How could I sleep with my two favorite men on the road in the middle of the night?"

"You worry too much." Nick stretched, pulling his shirt over his head as he walked down the hall to their room. Barb admired his rippling muscles. Accustomed to his scars, she hardly noticed them anymore. She chided herself, knowing how exhausted he must be. Nick filled her in on the conversation he'd had with Gramps on the drive and on the events in Charleston. "Did you know his sister's a Christian?"

"I thought she might be, from things I'd heard, but I honestly don't know her well. That's good. She can pick up where you and Robbie left off." She put her arms around him and leaned on his bare chest. "I love you, Nick Jo Costas. You never cease to amaze me."

"How so?" He crossed over to his dresser to rummage for his pajamas.

Barb sank on the bed and tried not to watch her husband changing clothes. "Robbie told me how much he learned today, watching you. He said he's heard a ton of people talk about WWJD, but he saw it today."

Nick walked into the bathroom to brush his teeth, and Barb followed, leaning on the counter. "What's WWJD?" he asked.

Amazed, Barb explained the phrase. "You never hesitated—you

returned good for evil, and you went the second mile. Some of us memorized all kinds of things, but you show us how to live them."

"You just do what seems right. What else could I do, leave the old man to fend for himself when his wife is facing heart surgery?"

"Or not save the life of a mean old lady who hates you?"

Nick shrugged. Barb took him into her arms and kissed him thoroughly.

"It's not that your charms fail to move me, wife, but I'm really tired, and I've got to sleep, much as I hate to admit that." Nick stretched out on the bed. "It's even past two a.m."

She giggled and turned off the light but snuggled up to him. They fell asleep entwined in each other's arms and legs.

* * *

The next morning, Barb kissed Nick awake gently. "Hey, sweetie, we've missed Sunday School. Do you want to go to church?"

Nick sat up and rubbed his eyes. "Sure. I can catch a nap later. We need to spread the word to pray for the Westfalls."

"The O'Malleys will pass on the news, if you want to sleep in."

"I'm up. Let's give God the praise for what He's done and what He's going to do. Maybe we should let the lad sleep in, though."

"You sound like Ian. I'll go see how he is. Alan and Cinderella are ready to go."

They decided to leave Robbie home. Nick, Barb, and the other children piled in the Suburban. Nick glanced over at Barb. "You look lovely today in your new blue dress, Mrs. Costas. Did you buy it with the girls yesterday?"

Barb colored slightly. "Yes, I did. I'm glad you like it."

He grinned. "I like what's in it even better!" She did blush then, and he laughed at her. "Isn't Mommy pretty, Alan?"

"Yes, sir, she's pretty. I like her dress, too."

"Do you like *my* dress, Daddy?"

Nick looked in the rearview mirror. "Oh, yes, Cinderella. You look especially beautiful in pink."

She beamed. "Thank you, Daddy."

Barb walked into church knowing she was blessed abundantly, above all she could ask or even think. Nick slipped his arm around her waist and squeezed her softly. Ella had missed him the night before, so she wanted to sit on his lap in church. Before service began, Missy asked the latest news, and Barb filled her in. "Can you believe all the things God has done already?"

"What the devil meant for evil, God will use for good, to save many people alive," Missy whispered. She gave Barb a quick hug and hurried over to her family as the first strains of music began to fill the sanctuary.

Nick held Ella in his arms as they stood to sing. He looked over at Barb and Alan. Barb slipped her arm around Nick's waist and leaned her head on his shoulder. "I love you," she whispered.

"I love you, too. I thank God for you all day, every day."

Tears sprung to her eyes. "I thank Him for you, too."

Barb went to bed early that night, but Nick played UNO with Alan, talked to Robbie about their day on Saturday, and read stories to Ella. The children couldn't seem to get enough of him since he'd been gone all day and night on Saturday. Nick reveled in their affection. He laughed and joked with the boys and held Ella in his lap until she fell asleep. When he slipped into bed beside Barb, he propped himself on his elbow and watched the gentle rise and fall of her chest. Love for her took his breath away. He thought of the miracle of his baby growing within her, and he lay down beside her and cupped his hand around her breast.

She stirred, moaning. "Nick?"

"I certainly hope so. At least, I hope you don't have any other men in your bed."

"Hmm, I like having you in my bed, Nick."

"I like being in your bed, babe." He gently rubbed her breast. She moaned again. "Is that a 'welcome, Nick, moan,' or a 'go away and leave me alone groan,' Barb?" She turned in his arms and made sure he knew the difference.

CHAPTER 18

Nonna Comes Home

WITHIN A WEEK, Nonna was home. Her pride restrained genuine warmth, but she invited the family to her house to thank Nick for saving her life. It was a start.

Nick followed Gramps into the kitchen to help prepare some drinks, and they planned to get together for Bible study within the week. Nick heard Nonna say, "Come give your grandmother a kiss, Alice Marie," and he heard pain in her voice. When he went into the living room, Ella ran to him, wrapping her arms around his leg and holding tightly.

"Will you excuse us for just a moment, Mrs. Westfall?" Nick asked. He glanced at Barb, who was chewing on her lip. Robbie looked sad, and Alan looked confused. At Nonna's dismissive nod, Nick carried Cinderella out into the yard. "Nonna's been really sick, Cinderella. She needs some of your good sugar to help her feel better. Can you give her some hugs and kisses for Daddy?"

The little girl's blue eyes filled with tears, and she tightened her hold around his neck. "She doesn't like you, Daddy. I want to stay with you."

Nick sighed and set her down, squatting in front of her. "Nonna needs to get to know Daddy, Ella. Remember, her little boy was Robbie and Alan's father, and he went to live with Jesus. Nonna misses him very much, and it's hard for her that I live in his house, with you kids."

He took a deep breath. How could he explain this to a child?

"But she was mean to you, Daddy."

"No, baby, she was afraid of me. She needs to get to know me, and we're going to make sure that happens. If you hurt her feelings, it will be hard for her to like me. You need to show Nonna that you can love us both. Can you do that?"

Robbie slipped out the door. "She's in there crying, Nick. I feel awful for not forgiving her. She feels bad about the way she's been to you."

Nick pulled Ella into his arms. "Do you hear what Robbie said?"

She nodded against his chest and sniffed.

"Jesus forgave us all the bad things we did. I've done bad things. Robbie has done bad things. Jesus paid for all the bad things we've done, so we could live in heaven with Him. He has paid for all the bad things Nonna has done, too, and you can show her how much Jesus loves her by forgiving her."

"Mommy says I have to forgive because Jesus forgived us."

"Mommy is a smart lady. She knows if we don't forgive, it makes us mean inside."

"Like Nonna, when she didn't forgive you?"

Nick sighed. "When you have Jesus in your heart, He helps you to forgive. That's why we must love Nonna and forgive her, so she will see Jesus in us."

Robbie squatted beside his sister. "I didn't forgive Nonna, Ella, and I felt bad because I didn't show her how much God loves her. Jesus wants her to ask Him into her heart, so she can live with us in heaven."

"She won't make you go away, will she, Daddy?"

"No, Ella. Daddy will never leave you. Nonna made a big mistake. She didn't know Daddy." He hugged her and stood. "Now, can you go in there and give her a big hug for Daddy?"

"Oh, I get it. I'll let this little light of mine shine."

Nick grinned. "You sure will. Now, Daddy will pray for you,

okay?" Ella squeezed her eyes closed. "Lord Jesus, help us to show Nonna Your love and forgiveness so she can live with us in heaven and we can be a family right now." Nick set Alice Marie down and took her little hand in his. "Ready?"

She nodded. "Come on, Robbie," she said. "Let's go make Nonna feel better."

Robbie took a deep breath, put his hand on her head, looked at Nick and said, "Let's do it, Ella!"

When they went back into the room, Nick gently put his hand on Ella's back and pushed her toward her grandmother. Ella stepped away and walked by herself to Nonna's chair. "I'm sorry you were sick, Nonna."

The elderly lady put her hand on the child's shoulder. "I made some mistakes, Alice Marie. I'm sorry." Her voice broke.

"Daddy says you need some sugar to feel better." She tiptoed up and kissed her grandmother's cheek. "I love you, Nonna, but I'm daddy's Cinderella, and I don't ever want to leave Daddy, okay?"

Tears filled Nonna's eyes as she nodded. Alan walked over to the chair and patted his grandmother awkwardly. "We're glad you're okay and that you came home, Nonna."

Barb gently slipped some tissues into Nonna's hand. Nonna patted Barb's hand and whispered. "I've made such a mess of things, haven't I?"

"You're alive, and we have a new beginning."

Gramps cleared his throat. "I ran to the grocery today and got some ice cream and cookies. Does anybody want some?"

"I'll help you, Gramps," Robbie said as he followed him into the kitchen.

Nonna was visibly tired, so after they finished their snack, they left, promising to bring dinner by the next night. As they pulled out of the driveway, Barb drew a ragged breath. "That was a pretty good beginning, don't you think?"

Nick caught Ella's eye in the rearview mirror. "Thank you, baby, for giving Nonna sugar. That was the best medicine she could have."

Ella beamed. "She was nice to you today, Daddy."

"I told you, she just needs to get to know me better. She will always be your grandmother, and she needs you kids now more than ever. Right, Robbie?"

Robbie drew a deep breath. "Right, Nick. I'm glad we have another chance to show her God's love. I'll do better this time."

"After you guys get ready for bed, we'll gather in the family room and pray."

The kids were in their rooms when Nick followed Barb down the hall. She checked one last time on Ella, and he was propped up in their bed when Barb came into their room. He watched her peel off her jeans and shirt.

"What are you looking at, Nick?"

"You. I'm watching you."

"Well, quit that!"

"You might as well tell me not to watch a sunset or not to look at a rainbow. I love to look at you—especially when you have no clothes on." He got out of bed and walked over to her, gently placing his hand on her rounding tummy.

"I'm beginning to show, aren't I?"

Nick grinned at her. "You are, with my baby." He took her in his arms. "I can't tell you how that makes me feel."

Barb circled her arms around his neck. "Guess we'd better enjoy this while we can. Soon, we'll have someone coming between us."

Nick leaned his forehead on hers. "Somehow, I don't think I'll mind."

* * *

They got together with the children's grandparents, Robert and Pat Westfall, regularly—once every other week or so—and Nick and

Robert met weekly for Bible study. Nick came to love the old man. Within two months, Robert had surrendered his life to Christ. He asked Nick about attending church, but Nick realized their exuberant place of worship would be too much for the Westfalls.

The next time they went to breakfast, Nick invited Julie's mother, Agnes, and Jimmy's mentor's widow, Lenore, to join them. They chatted about the dinners they'd had when Nick had lived in the apartment nearby. They told Robert how Nick had put up shelves for them and still came by to make repairs. They recommended the Presbyterian church they attended.

"I'd like to get my wife, Pat, to go to church," Robert said.

"We'll work on that, but first we must meet her. How can we do that, Agnes?" Lenore asked.

"We could have a housewarming party for Nick and Barb. Have you seen their new house, Robert? I'm sure Nick has told you what God has done for them." Agnes got excited at the prospect.

"Now, Agnes, you can't call it a housewarming. No gifts! We could make it a collection for the mission, but Barb and I *cannot* receive any more," Nick said.

Since Robert hadn't heard about the new house, Agnes and Lenore happily filled him in.

"That's amazing, Nick. Why didn't you tell me?"

"It was hard for you when we left the home Bob bought. It's a sore subject with Nonna, and I didn't want to bring it up."

Robert put his hand over Nick's. "You are a good man, Nick. Barb is happy, the children love you, and I know Bob would like you, too. I'm sure he's pleased."

Nick looked up at the older man. "Thank you, Robert. I appreciate your blessing more than words could say."

With a pat on Nick's hand, Barb's father-in-law stood. "I'd best get home. But let me know what you ladies come up with."

* * *

Within two weeks, Nonna and Gramps were driving up to the new house. "I can't believe they can afford this place!" she exclaimed.

"I told you how God gave them this house, free and clear."

"You are beginning to sound like them, Robert!" she snapped.

They went into the party, which was billed on the invitations as "A Celebration of God's Generosity," and they found a house and yard full of friendly people. Robert moved comfortably into the group, and Lenore and Agnes made sure Pat was not left out. Before they left that evening, they'd invited the Westfalls to their church.

Eventually, Pat joined her husband in his faith walk, although her surrender took more than a year, and much prayer and fellowship on the part of Agnes and Lenore.

CHAPTER 19

Rosa

BARB GROANED as she got out of bed. Nick's eyes popped open, and he jumped up. "Is it time?"

"Nick, would you chill? I have two more weeks." She groaned again.

"What's wrong? Can I do anything?" He moved around to her side of the bed.

"You can stop hovering!" she snapped. Seeing his bewildered and crestfallen face, she reached out and placed her hand gently on his cheek. "I'm sorry I'm so crabby, honey. It's almost the end of the road."

"I've never been around pregnant women until I watched Julie and Missy, but you get to me. I love you so much."

Barb leaned her head against his chest. "You've been wonderful. With every other pregnancy, I worked until I went into labor." Shuffling her feet near the edge of the bed, Barb couldn't come up with her shoes. She heaved a huge sigh. "Could you find my shoes?"

Nick rummaged around. When he found them, he gently slid them onto her feet. "How can your feet be swollen at this time in the morning? You haven't even been on them. You need to take it easy, put your feet up."

"With a three-year-old here? Nick, be reasonable."

"That's it. I'm not listening to you anymore. I'm getting some help in this house today."

"Nick, first you let me stay home, and now you want to hire help? What am I supposed to do all day? How am I supposed to make a living?"

"You can keep your night job, being with me."

"Ain't much of that happening these days, either, is there? And then, after the birth—I never missed that part of marriage so much before. I always had my mind preoccupied with the baby, but now I am fantasizing about my husband and when we can be in the sack again without this baby in the way. It's kind of . . . frustrating."

Nick laughed and drew her into a hug. "We'll store up a whole lot of loving, baby." She laughed, too, as she reached for his hand. Nick drew her to her feet. "At least your fantasies are about me. Guess that makes them holy fantasies."

At that, Barb laughed out loud. "You are incorrigible!" Holding him tightly around the waist, she whispered, "I love you. I'm happy and proud to be having your baby. You're an amazing father." Nick stood silent, and when Barb leaned back to peer into his face, she saw tears. "It's true. God taught you about a father's love by making you into one."

"I have a glimpse into His heart because mine is filled with you and these kids. I want to meet their needs. I want to soothe them when they hurt. I want to guide them in the way they should go, so they don't make mistakes."

"That is His heart. You have a glimpse of His perfect love for His children. Now, let's cut the theology and let me get to the bathroom before I pee all over these beautiful floors." A few minutes later, Barb came out, brushing her teeth. Taking the toothbrush out of her mouth, she said, "I still can't believe this amazing place is ours, you know?"

Nick began to make up the bed. Coming out of the bathroom again, Barb crossed over to the crib in the corner. It was a bit too frilly for her taste, but the day Nick had found out they were having a girl, he'd insisted on a canopy crib, which he'd decked out in yellow ruffles. "You have my nest all ready, Nick. Have you given more thoughts to names? You love Missy. We could name her Missy."

"Just not another Alice, please! I'm not sure. I want to see what she looks like first. I hear Cinderella. Go into the kitchen and sit. I'll cook."

"Will you quit? How do you think I did this with Ella? It was all by myself with two boys."

"God knows. But as Alice says, 'That was then, this is now.' I'm here, and you're the only pregnant wife I'll have, so I intend to take care of you. Were you this big with Ella?"

"I am rather a house, aren't I? Actually, I'm a few pounds lighter with this one."

"Really? Coming, sweetie," he called up to Cinderella, but soon she popped her head in the door. "Look who's here, Mommy. It's Daddy's Cinderella." The child ran to him and jumped into his arms.

Pretending to stagger backward, his arms encircling her, Nick cried out. "Oh, and she's gotten so big! She must have grown overnight! I believe she's three years old."

Ella laughed. "Daddy, I'm hungry!"

"So am I. Let's go eat." Carrying her into the kitchen, he set her on a barstool at the counter and turned to help Barb into one beside her. Barb looked at him warningly. "All right, babe—I won't hover. At least, I'll try not to."

"Hey, Mom. What're you fixing, Nick?"

"Good morning to you, too, Robbie. What do you want? Eggs, waffles?"

"I want bacon, Daddy Nick," Alan piped up from the hallway. Nick popped his head out of the refrigerator and threw him a pound of bacon. Alan got out the frying pan while Robbie cracked eggs into a bowl and scrambled them.

"When did you guys get to be such cooks?" Barb wanted to know.

"Nick has taught us lots of things, Mom," Robbie responded.

"Nick, you got the pan out for the eggs?" Seeing he had not, Robbie reached into the cabinet, got the frying pan, and poured olive oil into it.

"Olive oil for eggs, Robbie?" Barb questioned.

"Nick buys the expensive kind. It's very light. You have his eggs all the time, and you never noticed. Olive oil is the healthiest oil in the world, you know."

Barb bit her lip to stifle her amusement and glanced at Nick. He winked at her. After turning down the flame under the bacon, Nick came around the counter and perched beside her, propping his foot on his stool. "Maybe we should let these master chefs prepare our breakfast, Mom." With only minimal supervision, the boys did, and with great fanfare, they delivered the plates and sat down.

"I can't believe it—a counter long enough to seat six! Thank you, Jesus, for this amazing house." Barb continued to pray, blessing the food and the hands that had cooked it. She reached around behind her, pressing her hands to the small of her back. Nick noticed and began to rub small gentle circles. "Mmm, that feels nice."

"I'll call in and go with you to see Dr. Florence this morning," Nick suggested. Seeing the look in her eye, he added, "I'm not hovering. Lots of men do that. Ask Tim, ask Jimmy, ask Ian."

"Ian was a hopeless drunk when Alice had those kids."

"Yeah, but he says they were better fathers than he was. Look, this is my time. I never expected to be a father. Then you gave me these kids, and now I'm going to have a baby! Would you let me, please? Barb, you don't have to do this alone this time. Stop being so independent."

"Are you mad at Mom, Daddy Nick? She's pregnant."

"That's quite obvious, young man!" Everybody joined in the laughter as Barb balled up her napkin and threw it at them.

"My appointment is at nine, so we'd better get this show on the road. Alice planned to help you with Ella at the studio, so tell her . . . What? Shall we take her with us?" Barb moved uncomfortably on her stool. "I need to get down." She let Nick help her.

Ella protested that she wanted to go play with Willow like Mommy promised.

"If Alan wants to play with Jamie, they could use you at the soundboard, Robbie, since I'm not going in," Nick suggested. Robbie's eyes widened, and Barb swore he stood an inch taller. Yet, he contained his excitement, merely nodding his consent.

Soon, Nick and Barb dropped off the family, and they went to the doctor's office. Barb was three centimeters dilated and having contractions, so Dr. Florence sent them straight to the hospital. Once they were settled in the birthing room, Nick called Julie. "Be sure to ask if any of our kids want to be here, and I'll call with updates." Nick looked over at Barb, who reached for his hand.

"I can't believe how calm you are, after all that hovering for all these months," she said.

"I do feel calm. Peaceful, you know. Are you doing okay? Want me to rub your back?" Barb winced and allowed Nick to help her roll on her side. "You wanted to come alone, without me. Will you admit I was right?"

"You were right, okay? You were right. Feel better now?" Barb caught her breath and then remembered to breathe. Nick calmly continued the pressure on her back. "That feels so good."

"If you say so, but I don't know how anything could feel good right now. You women are amazing. I wouldn't do this for love or money. I guess if it were up to men, we wouldn't have a next generation."

Barb smiled. "That's what they all say." They chatted for a bit, but after a time she whimpered softly. "Nick, I hate to complain, but this is happening fast. Could you call the nurse?"

Nick pulled the call button and relayed Barb's comments. By the time the nurse arrived, Nick could hardly time the contractions. The nurse checked her and went out to the nurse's station to call the office.

Dr. Florence came in a few minutes later. "I hear you are not letting the grass grow, Barb. Let's see, what's going on? You okay, Dad? This is your first, isn't it?"

"I am fine—it's her picnic. All I feel is excited." He leaned down and brushed his lips over Barb's, soothing the hair of her brow. "You want some ice chips, baby?"

Barb felt the chair drop into the birthing position. She sucked in her breath. "I don't think . . . we have time for that."

"Breathe, Barb. You need to push soon . . . like, now," Dr. Florence instructed her.

Nick felt God's presence move into the room, and he began to pray. Soon, Dr. Florence handed him a squealing girl. "Let's put this gal on her mommy's tummy, Dad." Awestruck, but still surrounded by that amazing peace, Nick did as he was told, surrounding his daughter with his hands.

"Hi, baby," Barb crooned, smiling at her daughter and placing her hands around Nick's.

All too soon, the nurse took the baby girl across the room to be cleaned and weighed but quickly returned her to Barb and settled the baby on her breast.

"Good job, Mom. And you did well, too, Dad," Dr. Florence said.

After Barb nursed her, Nick sat with the baby in the rocker, singing quietly and rubbing his cheek against her softness. Barb watched him, knowing he was unaware of the tears that dripped off his face. "Oh, Nick, I wouldn't have missed this for the world, seeing you with her like this. I'm so glad God gave us this child!"

"I didn't think I could love you any more than I already did, Barb, but how can I thank you for this miracle?" Cradling the baby's head tenderly, Nick brought her up to his shoulder, rubbing her tiny back. "God, You are awesome." Gently, he lowered her, holding her out and looking into her face. "Her eyes will be dark, Barb, and she'll be darker than me. My mother was quite dark. Is that all right?"

Barb smiled. "She can play with her little Indian friend, Nick. I'm glad she and Jeri are close in age. They'll grow up together. Have you called the kids?"

"Her name is Rosa. Is that good, Barb? Rosa?"

"That's perfect, Nick. Rosa, my little Latina. Call the kids and tell them." Noticing his hesitation, she added, "You can let go of her, honey. Put her in the bassinette."

Nick reluctantly laid Rosa down and reached for the room phone. "Alice? . . . Yes, she's fine. Tell the kids they can come see Rosa anytime." He laughed. "Yeah, she didn't mess around, did she? She looks wonderful, beautiful. . . . Oh, the baby. She's beautiful, too." By the time Nick hung up, both his women were asleep. Pushing back in his chair, he drifted off in the middle of worshipping God.

Missy rushed in, camera in hand. Barb stirred, smiling. "Did you see her?"

Missy was already staring down in the bassinette. "Nick, that is your baby!"

"I certainly hope so! She *is* a little Latina, isn't she?"

"Oh, she's beautiful! When they have that darker skin, they don't look so blotchy, you know? Barb, I can't believe you did this to us. We didn't even have the camera. Tim's parking the car. How much can you stand? The whole rowdy gang wants to come see."

Barb sat up and winced. Nick hurried over to raise her bed and rearrange her pillows. "She came so fast!" Barb exclaimed. "I've never had such an easy birth. She's tiny. She only weighs six pounds. She just slipped right out of there, easy as pie."

Nick rolled his eyes. Tim entered the room, grinning from ear to ear, and he joined his wife at the bassinette. Lifting the camera, he began clicking off shots. Rosa stirred, protesting.

"Look, Tim, she doesn't like those bright flashes! Jeri was oblivious when she was born." Missy reached down and lifted Rosa to her shoulder. "Hi, precious baby. Welcome to the world, sweet Rosa. Ooh, you don't smell like a rose." Missy lowered her and stripped her, cleaning her bottom and quickly replacing her diaper. "I got the honors—

first poop. Now you have to make me godmother! Come on, sweetheart, let's get you to Mommy. Shh, she's right here. Where did you come up with the name? It's perfect. She looks like a Rosa."

"Nick said her name is Rosa when he held her. We couldn't think of one, and he said we'd know her name when we saw her, and we did." Barb reached for the baby to nurse her, and Tim shifted uncomfortably, but she reassured him. "It's fine, Tim. If you don't mind, I don't. You've been around nursing mothers before." Missy helped her drape a cloth strategically and giggled as Rosa smacked greedily.

"Don't you love it, Mom? I love it when they latch on and drink from me. It's such a miracle." Missy sighed, and Tim put his arm around her shoulders. They would never have another, but they were grateful to God for the miracle of their Jeri. "Wow, look what you've got! From Mike, I'll bet you," Missy exclaimed as a huge bouquet festooned with balloons crowded through the doorway. She read the card: "Love and prayers, Mike and Clare." She looked up, "Have you called them yet? I'll call when we leave. Need help?" Missy went around the bed to help Barb move Rosa to her other breast.

Nick looked at Tim. "God made an amazing creature when He made woman. I never knew what carrying a baby did to a woman's body, or the wonder of a new life. You told me when you had your babies, Missy, how God moved right into the room. I thought I could see Him. It was that strong."

Missy nodded, tears crowding her eyes as she gazed in wonder at the baby tugging at her mother's breast. She began to sing, praising God with one worship song after another. She heard her father's voice join her, and she turned to embrace him. "Look, Mom. Isn't she a beauty?"

Alice moved over to the bedside, where Missy had been efficiently covering Barb. Lifting the baby to her shoulder, she patted her until she burped. "Hey, little girl, didn't you hear where you came from that babies are supposed to take time coming into this world?" Rosa made little whimpers, as if in response, and everyone laughed. "Look, Ian, isn't she beautiful?"

"May I hold her, Barb?" After her immediate reassurance, Ian cradled the newborn in his arms and walked her toward the window. She scrunched her face and turned her eyes from the bright light. He stepped back into the shadow and began singing to her.

"Ian loves babies. He's happiest when he has one in his arms," Alice informed them.

Ian looked over the baby and met her eyes. "Maybe second-happiest, next to having you there, me sweet brown Indian girl." But he made no move to surrender the baby, brushing his lips in her downy, dark hair. "She's going to be darker than you, Nick."

"My mother was quite dark. Ian, you're the only grandfather she'll have."

"That's a proud honor that I embrace, and Gram always has room in her heart for another."

Alice beamed. "With Jimmy's three and Missy's two, this makes number six!" She reached down to pick up a thermal container. "I brought you food, Barb, and enough for you, too, Nick." She began unpacking a pot of stew. "Didn't they bring you lunch?" She handed Barb a plate from the picnic basket and then served one for Nick.

Missy laughed. "Mom's answer to every situation: food. That smells good. I guess I'd better tear myself away and go relieve Julie. Of course, the kids are staying with us tonight, Barb. Let us know when you want them home tomorrow. I'll call Mike and Clare." She bent down and kissed Barb on the cheek, then went over to Nick and gave him a big hug. "Isn't God good? Uncle Timmy, are you ready to go?" He smiled and offered her his hand.

"She was rather busy during lunchtime, Alice, and we were asleep when they tried to bring food in later," Nick said.

"Thanks, Alice. This is good. I didn't realize how starved I was," Barb added.

"Ian, you can put Rosa down," Alice said. "Maybe we should leave this family alone. Do you want anything, Barb? I didn't get out to your house, but I brought in a gown of Julie's. Do you want me to help you change?"

Ian set the baby down and went into the hall while Alice helped Barb change. Patting Nick's arm, she said, "Now, you be sure to tell us. She won't ask for anything, you know."

"Thanks, Alice. This was very thoughtful. Thank Julie, too. I'd love to see my babies, and I need a toothbrush," the new mother said.

"Done. But now you must nap, while she's asleep." Alice leaned over and kissed her. "Have you called your mother?" Barb hesitated. "I'll talk to her, sweetie, don't you fret." Barb's mother was polite to Nick, but not warm, and Bob's mother still struggled with all the changes in Barb's life.

"Could you get me some water, please?" Barb requested. Nick brought a glass and helped his wife with the straw. She laid her head back. "Isn't God good to give Rosa loving grandparents? What a wonderful family!"

"Is it all right that she sleeps so much?" Nick asked, looking over at Rosa.

"She's new. She'll be waking you up plenty in a few days. I love you."

He leaned down and took Barb in his arms. "I don't have the words." He shifted into Spanish, covering her with words of love that filled the room. She buried her fingers into his dark hair, pulling him into her breast. He breathed in the sweet scent. "I think I understand the Mary worship thing," he murmured. "Will you rest now? Get a little sleep? 'She just slipped right on out of there,' Lord knows, woman!" Barb laughed at him as he kissed her eyes and her nose and tenderly took her lips.

Nick found a Gideon Bible in the drawer and read while his wife rested. Hearing the boys in the hall later, he walked to the door. "This is a hospital, boys. Settle."

Immediately, they sobered up. "Cinderella's with Miss Julie. We ran up the stairs," Alan announced. "Can we see our sister?" Nick led them over to the bassinette. "Gosh, she's tiny. Ella was a lot bigger than that! She's cute, though, isn't she, Robbie?"

Robbie looked at Rosa with awe. "Oh, wow, Nick. I always thought all babies were alike, but she really looks like you!" Julie came in the door with Ella in her arms. Ella grabbed for Nick, who took her while Julie fussed over the baby and immediately began to change her.

"Gross! I hate that black stuff, it stinks," Robbie exclaimed.

Julie explained to the boys how God cleaned out a new baby, as she lifted Rosa to her shoulder. "Oh, Jimmy," she said to her husband. "Look at her!" She brushed her lips on Rosa's tiny head.

"She is beautiful, but let's don't get carried away, Jules."

"Don't you want another, honey?"

Jimmy rolled his eyes at Nick. "Do you believe women? Would you ever want to do that again?"

Nick laughed and shook his head.

"Thanks for the gown, Julie," Barb said. "I did have a bag packed, but Dr. Florence wouldn't let me go home for it."

"It's a good thing, girl! Alice sent you toothbrushes, a hairbrush, and some deodorant. Missy always had her babies fast in the hospital, too. But she labored at home."

"I started having back pain about midnight."

"You lied to me, Barb," Nick said.

"I thought it was Braxton Hicks. She wasn't due until the fifteenth." Julie carried the baby over to her Mommy, who reached out for her. Ella watched from Nick's arms, straining to see, fascinated as Rosa latched on.

"Rosa's getting milk from Mommy," she announced.

"Did you nurse any of the others, Barb?" Julie wondered.

"As long as I could. But once maternity leave was up, they had to go to a bottle. Nick wants me to stay home with Rosa and Ella. Here, boys, let Miss Julie help you hold her." As the boys had turns, Ella peered into her sister's face. "Do you want to hold her, too, Ella?" She nodded solemnly, and Jimmy sat her in a chair, piling pillows around her. She sat quietly with her arms around Rosa until he lifted her up again.

"It's Uncle Jimmy's turn, Ella. She's lost her real name, you know, Barb," he pointed out.

"I told Nick we're going to have to change the birth certificate to 'Ella.' She'll never be 'Alice Marie' in school."

"I'm my Daddy's Cinderella! My name is Ella Marie," she announced.

Nick caught Barb's eye. "Maybe we do need to contact Mr. Fuller about that," he suggested.

Barb nodded, her eyes shimmering. "Daddy had to hurry up and get here to name both his girls."

Nick drew Ella into his lap, and she cuddled into his chest. "I love you, Daddy, and I love baby Rosa, too. She's going to live at our house. Our new house God gave us. Thank you, Jesus, for our house and our baby! Amen."

"Amen," everyone echoed.

Jimmy smiled down at the baby in his arms, whispering, "Hello there, you beautiful creature." He moved quietly around the room, singing to her as she stared up into his face, pursing her tiny mouth. "Lord knows, Nick, how could anything this beautiful look like you?"

"You guys need to get out of here and let Mommy rest. We'll bring Rosa home tomorrow," Nick said.

"I'll go with Willow, Daddy. We'll make gingerbreads men. Miss Alice promised. I'll save you one. Not Rosa. She drinks Mommy milk."

Jimmy made a noise in his throat. "Why do all the women in this family talk so much?!" Julie laughed and gathered the children up, and Jimmy surrendered the baby to Nick.

"Come on, Ella, let's go. Boys, back to the farm. See you later, guys. Let us know if you need anything—besides peace and quiet," Julie said.

Robbie and Alan kissed their mother and followed Julie into the hallway.

"Quiet in the hospital, boys," Nick cautioned.

"Yes, sir," they replied. "See you tomorrow."

Nick took a deep breath and gazed down at his new daughter. "When I began to realize I was a stepfather, I understood the phrase 'a broken heart.' How can a heart be so full that it breaks wide open? Missy could make that into a song. Am I prejudiced, or is she the most beautiful baby in the world?" He lifted his eyes to meet his wife's.

"She is a beautiful baby, but would you put her down and help me to the bathroom?" Chuckling, Nick complied.

* * *

The next morning, Tim brought in a baby seat for the car. "I'll go install this, so you can bring her home. Nick, give me your keys."

"Thanks, Tim. We were going to get one next week."

"But Rosa didn't wait, did she? When are they going to release her? She looks all dressed in that outfit Missy brought yesterday. Did Julie send you any clothes, Barb?"

"We are getting discharged now," Barb replied. "She sent me a nice robe to go home in."

"Should I pull the car up front, and you can wheel her down, Nick?" Tim asked.

Tim left and pulled their vehicle under the canopy. While Nick helped Barb into the car, the nurse handed Tim the baby, and he settled her in her seat. "Drive safely with that precious cargo, Dad." Tim clapped Nick on the back and flashed him a grin. "Call us when you're ready for the crew. We can keep them, so Barb can rest up from the trip. It's not far, but it'll wear her out."

Nick got both his girls home. Despite Tim's warning, he was surprised how tired Barb was. Rosa was fussy, so after Barb fed her, he walked with her on his shoulder and sang to her. Barb was sleeping by the time he eased his daughter into her crib. She looked tiny in the big bed. Thinking he would shut his eyes a moment, Nick fell asleep beside Barb. Later, hearing car doors slam, he realized his family was arriving.

Barb stirred. "The kids are home," she said.

"I fell asleep, too. It's four o'clock. Are you ready?"

"Ready or not, here they come." Rosa let out a wail, and Nick picked her up.

Ella came bursting through the door and climbed up on the bed. "Hi, Baby Rosa. She's hungry, Mommy. Feed her." Ella leaned down and gently kissed the baby. "You hungry, Rosa?" she asked.

Julie, watching from the doorway, said, "What a little mother she is, like my Maryanne!" She moved down the hall, carrying food to the kitchen.

Missy peered in. "I am glad Jeri will have a little dark playmate. Won't they have fun together? You've got tons of food. The church folks have been dropping stuff off at our house. I'll mark it and put it in the refrigerator for you." She moved down the hall after Julie, and Barb heard them chattering in the kitchen.

"Come on in, boys," Barb invited her sons. Shyly, they moved into the bedroom, eyeing their baby sister at her mother's breast. She handed the baby up to Nick as she tried to cover up. Nick rubbed Rosa's back until she burped, then asked the boys if they wanted to hold her. Crowding up against the high headboard, Alan lifted his arms. Nick settled Rosa, carefully piling pillows around her and her brother.

After a few minutes, Alan asked his brother, "You want a turn, Robbie?"

Robbie came over and carefully lifted Rosa, supporting her head. He crossed over to the rocker and sat with her. "I've been practicing with Jeri. Missy's been giving me lessons. Rosa and Jeri sure are little, aren't they? Jeri's getting bigger, though—and you will, too, Rosa."

Robbie smiled down at her. "I'm glad, Nick. I told you God knew what He was doing."

Nick looked at Robbie with affection brimming in his eyes. "You were right, kid."

"Yep, she's good for Mom, and she's good for you, too. God sure knows what He's doing." Robbie lifted Rosa to Nick.

Missy crossed the room. "Barb, you're all set. Do you need anything else?" After Barb thanked her, she added, "Come on, Nick, I'll show you what's in the refrigerator, and we'll be off." She dropped a kiss on Rosa's cheek after Nick settled her into Barb's arms.

Julie came into the bedroom while the others were in the kitchen. "Want me to hold her while you pee, Mom?" Barb looked up with gratitude and eased off the bed. "Are you okay by yourself?"

"I'm fine, thanks. She might be ready to go down, but she's been fussy."

"Coming home is a change," Julie reassured her. "It's a new place, isn't it, you doll?" she crooned, swaying the baby as she held her. "Are your nipples doing okay? I got in such trouble after Willow was born, but she wouldn't stop crying! I wouldn't have made it without Alice."

"A little sore. I wonder if I should move around. Nick will fuss at me, but it's such a nice day. Maybe you could help me get out to the patio?"

Nick did fuss, but Missy and Julie assured him that moving was healthier than staying in bed, so he accepted the walk. He opened the pack-and-play and set it up in the shade outside. Alan and Robbie had their suits on and had already gotten into the pool.

"Can I swim, too, Daddy?" Ella asked. Nick looked at Barb.

"That would be good. Wear her out a bit. I'll be fine."

Barb rested comfortably on a lounge chair, so Nick offered Ella his hand, and they went inside to change. Missy and Julie let themselves out, marveling at all God had done in their friends' lives.

* * *

The next morning, Barb sat up in bed and looked down at Nick, saying, "Honey?" Nick threw back the covers to head for the crib. "She's not awake yet. Is Mr. Fuller coming today about Ella's papers?" Nick mumbled that he was. "I had a dream. Bob was here, in this house."

Nick sat up. "We don't *have* to change her name."

"No, listen. He didn't say anything. He walked into the family room, and he looked back to see if I was coming. You were in the big chair with Ella, and the two of you were laughing. He smiled and walked over to you, putting a hand on each of your heads, as if in a blessing, then he disappeared. I woke up, and it felt like he was in this room. I heard him say, 'Her name has always been Ella, Barb.' We're doing the right thing. And I know he's happy for us." Barb slid down, putting her arms around him.

"This is a bit weird—my wife having two husbands in her bedroom."

"Only one in the flesh."

"I didn't hear Rosa in the night." But Barb told him she had been up and back down. "Did Bob say anything about *her*?"

"He didn't seem to notice her. I think God wanted us to have confirmation about Ella—Ella Marie. It's a beautiful name. Remember when she said it? 'My name is Ella Marie,' like she knew. Can you go back to sleep? I'm sorry I woke you."

Nick's lips brushed her hair. "I don't know, but I can enjoy lying here with you, like this. Fuller wanted to come early, though, on his way to the office. I'll get us some coffee in a bit—tea for you, Mommy." Barb rested her hand on his chest, feeling it gently rise and fall.

CHAPTER 20

The Dream

NICK CLIMBED THE STAIRS. His little legs were heavy—really heavy—and he was hungry. He pushed open the door to the dank apartment, not noticing the fetid odors. He was used to the smell of body-waste, sweat, and drugs.

"Mama? I'm hungry, Mama," Nick cried, but no one answered. He looked through the two-room apartment, but no one was there. He opened the cabinets, but they were empty. The refrigerator held a sour aroma, but no food. Finally, Nick found a couple of stale crackers in a drawer. He went to the stained mattress in the corner and crawled on it. In the early morning, Mama came in, her boyfriend behind her, and they were arguing and cursing. The sounds were as normal as the smells.

"Mama? I'm so hungry, Mama." Nick reached for his mother, who staggered as she dropped to the floor to reach for him.

"Shut up, brat," a big man said. "You always want something. Get out of my way." The big man grabbed Nick by the arm and threw him against the wall.

Nick cried out in pain as his arm dangled beside his small body. He heard his mother scream. And someone yelled outside the door. "I'm calling the cops! Someday, he's going to kill the poor kid."

"It's none of your business. Leave them alone," a male voice yelled.

"No, Pedro, this time is too much. I'm calling them. Give me the phone."

"You want him to kill us, too?"

Mama shoved her boyfriend with all the strength in her tiny body. Fortunately, he was so far gone he stumbled, laughed, and fell into a heap. Nick heard sirens and running footsteps on the narrow stairway. Someone knocked at the door, announcing a police presence, and two men in blue uniforms pushed it open in response to Mama's cries. Their eyes swept the room, and the first one pulled his gun out when Mama's boyfriend struggled to rise.

"He hurt my baby. I think he broke his arm," Mama cried.

One of the policemen cursed profusely. "I'll never get used to the stink of these holes. Jesús, I can't talk to these people."

The officer called Jesús squatted down beside Mama, whose head lolled weakly on her neck. "She's pretty much gone. You got him covered?" he said, referring to the large man who was too stoned to stand up but dangerous nonetheless.

"Yeah. Get her in the car and help me cuff him, then we'll take care of the kid. I'm calling for backup." The first officer thumbed his walkie-talkie on his belt.

In Spanish, Jesús told Mama he was taking her to a hospital and asked her if she could walk. She tried to rise, and his hand caught her under the elbow. "Say goodbye to your boy, ma'am. You won't see him for a long time." Mama tumbled to her knees and crawled over to where Nick lay against the wall.

"Nickie, Mama's so sorry. Did he hurt you? I know he hurt you. Nickie—"

"Get her out of here and help me with this dude. He's a monster."

"We've got to go now, ma'am. Come on. We'll get you some help," Jesús instructed her.

Mama kissed Nick over and over. "I'm sorry, Nickie. You're a good boy, Nickie. I love you."

The policeman lifted her up and walked her downstairs while Nick sobbed broken-heartedly. Two other men in blue arrived, cuffing Mama's boyfriend and leading him out. The officer who had taken Mama, Jesús, returned and squatted down beside Nick. "Hey, little man, will you go with me?" he asked in Spanish. "We'll take you to the hospital to fix that arm. Okay?"

Nick emphatically refused. The woman from across the hall, who had called the police, stood in the doorway and told the officer the boy was hungry. She'd heard him crying alone in the apartment all night long.

"Stay with him a minute, okay?" he asked her, and he ran down the stairs and back. "Hey, kiddo, you like peanut butter? I got a peanut butter and jelly here and some donuts. Sound good?" He gently extended the food offering to the boy.

Nick stared at him and shrank away, but he finally yielded to his hunger and reached out a tentative hand. He smelled the food, and the officer reassured him. When he put it in his mouth, he smiled and frantically stuffed the whole sandwich into his cheeks.

"Hey, buddy, don't choke. We'll get you more. You like donuts?" Nick smiled, nodding his head vigorously. The policeman stood up, wondering how he could get this frightened child in so much pain to the hospital. "Maybe we should call an ambulance," he suggested to the other officer. "They could give the kid a shot or something. He's scared and hurting."

The other officer called, but when the EMTs arrived, Nick clung to Jesús and wouldn't let anyone else touch him. The cop turned the child's face into his chest and spoke soothingly to him while the medical personnel gave him a shot. Although the little fellow was drooping, he whimpered quietly and looked at Jesús with terrified chocolate eyes.

"Do you want to ride in a siren, Nickie?" Jesús asked the boy. Nick shook his head no, so he added. "What if I ride with you? Come on. It'll be fun." Nick held up his good arm, and Jesús lifted him gently and carried him to the ambulance. The EMTs helped Nick climb in as Jesús balanced the boy in his arms. Cradling Nick to his chest, the policeman felt him drop off to sleep.

* * *

Sometime in the middle of the night, Barb woke up, hearing a broken-hearted cry. "Don't leave me, Mama! Please don't leave me!"

She sat up abruptly, ready to run to Rosa, but she found Nick sobbing beside her. She scooted down in the bed and took him in her arms. "Nick, I'm here. It's me. It's Barb. I'll never leave you. Can you wake up?" Nick reached for her, drawing her into a fierce hug that squeezed her breath. She shifted to breathe, then loosened her arm and swept the stray lock of black curl off his forehead. "It's me, Nick. Are you okay? Were you dreaming?"

Nick shuddered. "Yeah. I was a little boy. It was the night they took Mama." He pushed himself out of bed and went into the bathroom. Washing his face with a cold cloth, he tried to orient himself. He returned and sat on the bed. Barb took his hand. "I'm sorry I woke you. What time is it?"

"It's four. You wanna try to go back to sleep?"

"Yeah, I guess so." Nick reached over and turned off the light. He curved himself around Barb, spooning her against his body. Her long legs stretched back and tangled with his. He breathed in the familiar scent of her hair and felt his heart rate return to normal. "You say you never blushed until I came into your life. I never cried after that night, and now I cry all the time. I cry when you love me, I cry when the kids crawl in my lap, I even cry in my dreams."

"Sounds like you had a lot of tears stored up. It's better they came out, sweetheart."

He sighed, pulling her closer. "Maybe you're right. I can't stop them anyway. Ian cries, and I've seen Tim and Jimmy cry, too."

"Tim sure cried a lot when Missy was in the hospital, and when Jeri was born."

"Can you go back to sleep?"

"I will, if you promise you'll wake me if you need me."

"Rosa looks like my mother, Barb." Nick sighed.

"Maybe that's why you dreamed about her."

"Maybe. God knows I love you, *amada*."

"I love you, too. God's bringing you healing so one day you'll minister to others. You told Missy she belongs to more people than her family, remember? You've given so much to me and to our family, and we must treat you like Tim and share you with all the people out there who need you."

"Um, I don't know about that."

She smiled and patted his hand curved around her waist. "Oh, I think so, Nick. I do. I'm excited to see what God is doing in your life."

CHAPTER 21

Nick's Boy

NICK LOOKED UP from the paper when Barb came in from the sunroom, temporarily used as a nursery for Rosa. "She's such a good baby!" she proclaimed.

"Is she? I haven't been around babies much. Which one wasn't a good baby?"

"Robbie was the worst, but I was a new mom, too. Guess you learn on the first, but he was colicky and had us up a lot. Bob wasn't home when Alan was born. I held him and Ella all the time, but Rosa never fusses unless she is hungry or wants a change. Sometimes I go check, because I haven't heard from her—especially since we put her in the sunroom. I find her with her eyes wide open, arching her back and looking around. She's sweet-natured, and now she sleeps six straight hours. I feel like a new woman!" She came across the room and sat on Nick's lap. "Are the kids asleep, honey?"

"Sound asleep." He pulled Barb down and kissed her hair. "I hope Robbie is having a great time at youth camp." Barb nodded. "Let's take a swim. It's a beautiful night, the moon is full, and you're beautiful."

"I'll get my suit on. It's wet, so it will be freezing to put on—brrr."

Nick followed her to the bathroom, where she got her suit off the towel rack. "Now, why would you need a suit? It's only me and you." Barb looked at him, her eyes wide. Nick leaned against the doorframe and looked at her. She blushed scarlet. He laughed delightedly. "I can promise you one thing, Mrs. Costas: if you struggle into that wet, cold suit, I'll have it off two minutes after we hit the pool. He pulled a terrycloth robe off the hanger. "Here, put this on." Barb started to shrug into it, and he patiently set it aside, stripped her clothes gently, dropped them on the floor, and offered her the robe once more. She shivered, but not from the cold. "Ready?" he smiled.

Her eyes demurely cast down, Barb took his hand, and they quietly tiptoed through the sunroom, leaving the door to the patio open in case Rosa woke up. Nick floated on his back and drew Barb into his arms on top of him. His arms around her, they gently floated. "I can't believe I'm doing this. I've never skinny-dipped in my life."

"This is hardly daring, wife. It's our own backyard, and I am your husband. We won't get arrested for indecent exposure."

She giggled. "No, I guess not, but it feels daring to me. You have me doing things I never thought of doing!"

"So, this is daring?" Nick drew her up beside him and covered her mouth with his own. "You are beautiful," he murmured. Barb's breath caught in her throat as he began to caress her, kissing down her neck.

"Are we going to swim, or what?" she asked huskily.

Nick laughed. "Given a choice, I opt for 'or what.' But in honor of your sensibilities . . ." He pushed against the side of the pool with his feet and began long, powerful strokes down to the end of the pool and back. Barb loved to watch him swim effortlessly. His arms hardly moved the water. "Are you going to swim, Barb?"

"I love to watch you."

"And I love to watch you."

Barb shoved off, her long legs glistening in the water. The full moon shimmered on the face of the pool. Nick surged to catch up, and they swam side by side, until they decided it was time for "or what."

* * *

The next week, the O'Malley crew surged into the house. Todd jumped up and down, and Willow screamed. Alice and Ian shushed them and herded the children outside. "Thanks for letting us descend on you like this, Barb," Julie said. "You okay? You look tired. Is Rosa still keeping you up?"

"No." Barb sighed. "She's slept six or seven hours for a month now. I felt terrific until recently, but I have been so tired the last couple of days, and I feel . . . I don't know, queasy. Maybe I'm coming down with the flu or something." Missy and Julie exchanged glances.

Nick came in, carrying a big casserole. He dropped a kiss on Barb's cheek and opened the container, letting the fragrance waft into the room. "I've got Ella, babe," he called and hurried out to the patio.

Barb threw her hand up to her face and ran for the half bath under the stairs. She returned, looking pale, and tried to smile. "I must have the flu." Her friends exchanged glances again, and she demanded: "What?"

"Uh, Barb, you could be pregnant," Missy said.

"Rosa's only six months old. I haven't even had a period yet. I have to have one infertile period, right?"

Julie regarded her carefully. "Well . . . usually, that's the case. But I've heard of women getting pregnant without having a period."

Barb slumped into a stool and leaned her head on the counter. "Oh. What will Nick say?"

"Well, you didn't do this by yourself. I mean, if you are."

Barb stopped her with a warning look as Nick came in the door.

"I forgot to set the oven. I showed Alice how to make chili relleno this afternoon. Smells good, doesn't it?" He didn't notice Barb's weak smile.

He'd barely left the room when she fled once more to the bathroom. "You guys go swim, I'll be out in a minute." Barb quickly moved to the bedroom and called to make an appointment.

* * *

The next week, Nick came in excited. They had wound up the next album. "I've got the finished product right here. You want to hear it?" Barb settled Rosa in the swing, Robbie and Alan piled on the sofa, and Robbie pulled Ella onto his lap. The family sat down to hear the latest release, a collection of bluegrass love songs—some old tunes, but also originals, including Ian's "In Your Arms," Missy's "Lost in Your Eyes," and the newest, Jimmy's "Always, Only You," which he'd written for Julie. Barb sat beside Nick, who had his arm around her.

"Isn't it awesome? What beautiful music! I'm grateful God let me be a part of this company." Everyone raved, but Barb was noticeably quiet. Nick shoved off the couch. "What's for supper? Do you want to warm up the chili?"

Barb pushed herself up with an effort. "No, I have baked chicken and mashed potatoes. I'll fix a salad."

Nick looked at her carefully. "You sit, Barb. I'll do it." Soon, he had Alan washing the lettuce and Robbie cutting tomatoes while he diced carrots. After supper, he helped her settle the children to play. "Okay, sweetheart, what gives?"

Barb's eyes misted over. "I went to the doctor today."

Alarm filled Nick's eyes. "And?" He gathered her in his arms. "What?" She didn't answer. He held her back, looking into her face. "You're scaring me. What's wrong?"

"It's . . . well . . . I'm pregnant again."

Astonishment swept across his face. "But you haven't had a period. I thought . . . I mean, I was going to set up an appointment for a vasectomy. Are you sure?"

She sighed. "It's too late for that. It appears that horse is out of the barn. Oh, Nick, I'm sorry!"

"What's to be sorry about? It's not like we didn't both do this. It's hard on you. Are you okay?"

"Yeah. Dr. Florence says it's a little soon, and I'm not as young as I used to be, but—"

"Well, as long as you're good, what's the problem, Barb? Don't you want another baby? Another baby, wow!" he enthused.

"You sure you don't mind?"

"Mind? Why would I mind? Children are a blessing. That's what everybody around us tells me. And it's what God says. We'll get you more help. You tell me what you need, because I'm new at the family thing, but I'll do whatever you say."

"Oh, Nick, can we afford this?"

Nick gathered her into his arms and kissed her tears. "I thought God was in charge, here. You think He'll give us a baby and let us starve? We have good insurance, no mortgage, and a decent income. Our living expenses are less than they were."

"Are you really okay with this?"

"Barb, don't be silly. I can't believe God trusts me with another, but this is good news, isn't it? You did well with Rosa."

She finally met his eyes. "I love you, Nick, and I thank you for the privilege of being a full-time mom. I've enjoyed Rosa—although it makes me sad how much I missed with the others." She leaned her forehead on his chest.

"Mommy, Rosa poopied," Ella cried from upstairs.

"You sit, Barb. I'll get this."

"Two in diapers, Nick. I've never had two in diapers."

"Well, there you go. It'll be a first." Nick dashed into the nursery, grabbed a diaper, and headed up the stairs.

When he got back downstairs, with Rosa happy and clean in his arms, Barb was on the phone. "You were right, Julie. I just told him. He seems better with it than I am. . . . No, it's fine. Come on over. We'll be closing the pool all too soon."

Nick called up to the kids, and everyone started to run around and get into suits. Nick challenged them to a race, but he lost because he had to get Rosa in her swim diaper. He handed the baby to Barb, ran to the poolside, and cannonballed in to screams and both boys' attempts to dunk him. He overpowered them, dunking one with one hand and one with another. Ella jumped up and down on the steps and threw herself in with her little swimsuit preserver.

Pulling himself out of the pool, Nick shook like a wet dog, spraying water all over. When everyone gathered on the patio, he was full of mischief. Jamie immediately jumped in the deep end with Robbie and Alan. Nick turned to the adults and swept his arm in a grand gesture. "Welcome to the Costas's clothing-optional pool—not that clothing options are available until the wee small hours of the night."

"Nick!" Barb fumed, her face flaming.

His eyes were round with innocence. "What, honey? Did I say something wrong?"

Jimmy and Missy cracked up. "Lord knows, Barb. No wonder you're pregnant!" Laughing, Missy spun around and wagged her finger at Nick. "And it's entirely your fault. You took this innocent and lured her into your scandalous activities."

Nick laughed delightedly, joining in the general merriment. He hollered to the boys that it was fine—they really didn't need to know. "I certainly hope it's my fault, Missy." He took Barb, who was holding Rosa, into his arms and kissed her soundly. Rosa began to cry and reached for him. "Where's Ella?" he raised his voice.

"I've got her, Daddy Nick," Alan cried.

"Wait, Jeri. You wait for Mommy," Missy fussed. But Tim already had her. He swirled her around in the pool, and Missy's baby laughed.

Barb sat on the steps with the mommies, gently lowering and raising Rosa between her legs as she held onto her arm. "He embarrasses me to tears sometimes. I don't know what to do with him!"

Alice smiled and patted her on the leg. "Enjoy him, Barb. I've never seen Nick this happy. Listen to him laugh."

Nick swam underwater and popped up in front of Rosa, who laughed and reached for him. He took her in his arms and brought her up out of the pool and onto his lap. He sat beside Barb.

"How are you, babe?" he asked. "Are you mad at me?"

"I'm good, Nick." Her eyes shimmered with love. "I'll never get used to you."

"That keeps things exciting, doesn't it? Isn't it a good thing?"

Barb leaned over and kissed his cheek. "Yes, it certainly does! It's a good thing, I guess."

Nick took Rosa into the water, and she splashed her hands, spraying water in his face. He shook the droplets off his shimmering black hair, making a game that caused her to belly-laugh and him to repeat the performance, over and over.

"Look at those gorgeous silken ringlets that baby has," Missy observed. "Poor little Jeri with her thick, straight hair. Another Indian girl to braid, Mom."

Alice's lips curved into her gentle, serene smile. "I love my Indian girls, Missy, and your father does, too. Do you remember how patiently he braided your hair?"

"I do. And when I was in the third grade, it was practically to my waist. You cut it to below my shoulders, and Grampa was furious. Tim, you want me to take Jeri?" Tim handed their baby to Missy and swam out to the deep end to join the fun with the boys. "Todd swims like a fish since he had lessons, but he makes me nervous out there alone."

"Nick insisted on lessons for Ella, even with the fence around the pool. I'm glad Willow and Todd joined her. It made it more fun for all of them and worth what he paid the teacher to come out here. And we mothers are certainly more relaxed."

* * *

Barb's pregnancy progressed with some difficulty. Her body hadn't fully returned to normal after Rosa, so she began to show early. She was as large in the sixth month as she'd been when Rosa was born. Dr. Florence began to discuss a possible C-section, because it appeared the boy would be a large baby.

"You're telling me! I already waddle. I feel like he's between my knees," Barb complained.

The doctor asked Nick to come to his office while Barb dressed after her sonogram. "This pregnancy has been hard on Barb, Nick. I want to talk to her about a tubal ligation. She doesn't need any more pregnancies, but we need you to sign off on that."

"Doc, I can't stand to see her go through this. I planned to get a vasectomy."

"I expect we'll have her opened up to get the boy. We can take care of it easily while we're in there."

To help her deal with some of her discomfort, Alice insisted Barb wear support hose, and Nick required her to rest every afternoon. Nick wanted to hire a nanny and checked on Hispanic legal immigrants through a nanny service, but Missy and Julie knew some women who would be excellent candidates for a full-time housekeeper/nanny. He hired Sally Hicks, Angela's aunt. By eight months, getting up was a struggle for Barb, though she tried to be game.

"How's she doing, Nick?" Jimmy asked when Nick returned to the studio after he'd dropped Barb off at home after an appointment.

"She tries not to complain, but she's miserable."

"You've hardly taken a day off since we started this company. Go home, lad, and be with her." Ian turned him around and pushed him out the door. "Don't come back until that wee wain is born."

Nick made calls from home, designed labels, and made additions to the O'Malley Productions website. He created an option to pay for lyrics and music for a download fee, which turned into a money-maker. But mostly, he chased Rosa. Ella was happily in preschool. With Nick home and the housekeeper around, Barb spent most of the day on the couch.

CHAPTER 22

Michael James Costas

NICK CAME DOWNSTAIRS one evening after putting the girls to bed and found Barb in tears. He knelt in front of her, praying quietly. She leaned against his shoulder. "I think something's wrong," she whispered.

"What is it? Are you in labor?"

"I don't know. No, it doesn't feel like that, but . . ." She gasped. "I don't know what's going on. It hurts." They watched heaving motions roll across her belly. She put her head on Nick's chest and cried.

"All right. We are going to the hospital." Barb tried to protest, but Nick climbed the stairs two at a time, telling Robbie he was in charge of the house. Flipping his phone open, he called Alice. Barb was calm but weeping. Since Nick hadn't seen her cry during the entire labor with Rosa, he tried to stem his rising panic.

Barb was holding onto her belly and gasping by the time Nick wheeled her into the hospital. After a sonogram and several hours of monitoring her in the emergency room, they learned that the baby had shifted, and now he was lying breech. Once he got settled, the movements ceased, but Barb became anxious because she couldn't feel him at all.

The ER nurse laughed. "He's fine. All these monitors say he's doing well, but he's sorry he tried to find more room because he's got less now." After talking with Dr. Florence by phone, they allowed Barb to go home, but she was to follow up in the doctor's office the next morning.

The doctor confirmed that their son had moved into a breech position. "We have no choice now. I'll schedule a C-section for two weeks," he said.

Nick heard Barb up one night the next week and followed her into the family room. Placing his hand on her belly, he began timing contractions. "We need to get you to the hospital. This baby isn't waiting until next week."

"I'm such a pain in the neck!"

"You're my pain, and I love you. I'm calling Sally to come back and stay with the kids. I'll get your suitcase."

When Dr. Florence came into the hospital, he took Barb to surgery immediately. Alarms began to sound. Nick stared intently at the monitors. "Barb, we're putting something in this IV for your blood pressure," Dr. Florence explained, signaling to the nurse.

"Let's get this baby out of there, doc!" someone cried out. Nick notched up his prayers.

"I've got my hands on him." Dr. Florence lifted out the baby, and Nick was relieved to see him pink and lusty.

Nick squeezed Barb's hand. "Another beautiful baby, Mommy. You've given me another beautiful baby."

She smiled sleepily at him. "He's a loud one, isn't he? Go with him."

Nick brushed his lips across hers and followed their son to the nursery. When he came out of the operating room, Jimmy and Mike rose. Grinning, he waved to them, leading the way to the nursery. Soon, the three of them crowded in front of the window, admiring the screaming red-faced boy.

"Where did this monster man-child come from, Nick? Mike teased. "Where did he get his size?"

"You never know how big I would've gotten, Mike, if my mom had eaten when she was pregnant, and I had eaten regularly as a boy. My boy's never going to be hungry!" Nick's eyes flashed with bitterness.

Mike put his arm around Nick's shoulders. "Nick, none of your children will ever want for anything, because they have a fine father."

Nick looked at him gratefully. "Because they have this incredible mother and this wonderful family—and a heavenly Father Who picks up this poor stumbling guy and sets him on the right track, over and over."

Jimmy said nothing but also slipped an arm around Nick, hugging him briefly. He cleared his throat and was able to ask, "Have you guys chosen a name for this fine, strapping boy?"

"His name is Michael James Costas." The men were silenced by the significance of that name for both of them, and they turned to watch the baby—their namesake.

Nick stuck his head in the nursery and was rewarded, as a nurse gowned him and led him to a rocking chair. Another nurse settled his son into his arms. Holding him close, Nick sang softly to him, and the baby stared up to make eye contact as his little body relaxed.

"Like I said, that is one lucky baby to have such a fine father," Mike said, watching through the glass.

"Nick teaches me to pray about even the smallest decisions. He wouldn't even take a honeymoon because he put Barb's kids' emotional comfort first. Blessed," Jimmy confirmed. "All those kids are blessed."

"Amen. 'Blessed' is the word," Mike agreed.

* * *

Barb thought no baby in the world could be easier than Rosa, but Michael was a large baby—he filled himself up and didn't need to eat for three or four hours, so she got more sleep. Of course, since Nick insisted on keeping Sally full time, the new mother could nap during the day. In no time she felt stronger, although self-conscious about her weight gain. One night, she walked into their bedroom where Nick was sitting in the easy chair, his feet propped up on a hassock, reading through a contract. He glanced up: "Hey, honey, are you ready to go to bed? I can go into the living room." He started to rise.

"No," she replied irritably. "I don't want you to go to the stupid living room."

Taken aback, he said, "I thought you might want to go to sleep."

"He'll need to eat again before I go to sleep. No sense in going to sleep and having to wake up again." She did change into pajamas, glancing covertly at him as he resumed his reading. "What are you reading?"

"I'm going over this contract. The artist substituted her own contract for our standard one. Something bothers me. I'll send it to Ian's copyright attorney in Nashville." Barb walked over to the chair and stood beside him. "What's up, Barb? Something wrong? You sound upset."

"Why don't you come to bed with me? I miss you. You never hold me." Nick wordlessly held his arms up, and she snuggled into his lap, sighing with contentment. He idly ran his fingers down her long slender neck, and she all but purred. He shifted uncomfortably in the chair. Feeling him against her leg, she giggled, "Are you sure you want to wait until after my follow-up appointment?"

Nick grunted. "I didn't say I *want* to. I said I was *going* to. You've never realized the powerful effect you have on me. That's why I'm not coming to bed with you and holding you. I don't trust myself. Don't you know that?"

"Oh. Well, I'm sure it will be fine."

"No, Barb, it won't be fine. I want you so badly. I don't want to hurt you. You had a hard pregnancy, and you've had surgery. For heaven's sake, give your body a rest."

"I don't want you to have to go somewhere else to have your . . . needs met."

"Pardon me? Barb, I take offense at that. Why would you say that?

Do you think—no, wait. I want to say this right."

"I know how you are. You have such passion. I want to meet your needs."

Nick's strong arms turned her swiftly toward him. "You already do, sweetheart. Surely you know that."

"But now . . ." Her voice trailed off. "I heard a teaching on marriage. The woman said wives must fulfill our responsibilities, so our husbands don't look elsewhere."

"You're saying—no, wait. God, help me say this right, the way I'm learning. I hear you saying—or maybe you're not saying, but what I hear is—I'm some dumb animal, a stallion with no self-control that is looking for release somewhere."

Barb blushed and started to reply, but Nick put his finger on her lips. "Don't you know you are the only one who can satisfy me? I don't want anyone else. I want you, I belong to you. You're a part of me, and I'm a part of you." He paused and smiled. "And that's the answer I've been seeking. I wondered how being married to you for two years could bring healing for a lifetime, and that's it. I belong to you. I have never belonged to anyone before, ever. But I belong to *you*," Nick repeated in wonder.

Barb's eyes spilled over. "I've gained so much weight, and I'm too old for you. I want you to be happy. You make me happy. I was afraid you're repulsed because I'm fat."

Nick pulled her into his arms, crushing her against his chest and kissing her hair. "You are beautiful. God gave you to me. I still can't believe that, but I'm terribly grateful. Honey, your body nourished my children. You've given me two beautiful children! That is all I see when I look at you, and I'll wait for us to enjoy one another for all the years ahead of us. And where did this 'too old' stuff come from? Have I ever mentioned anything about your age? Has anyone else? Because I will take it up with them." Nick's eyes flashed with anger.

"No, no one has. I guess it's just the enemy, trying to rob me of what God's given us."

"You are perfect, *mi amor*. Perfect for me, and the perfect mother for my children, the way you are. You are my woman. Don't you know that? Now shut up and kiss me." He drew her to himself and settled his mouth over hers. He broke away, shifting again under her. "Although you *are* making this quite difficult for me."

"Another week? I don't know if I can take this." She tried to put a little space between them while remaining on his lap. "Thank you for loving me. Are you sure—"

Nick interrupted her question with another thorough kiss. "That, *amada*, is but a down payment." His fingers traced the curve of her neck. "You have the most beautiful neck. Have I ever told you that? So graceful. I get turned on just looking at your neck."

"When you do that, I get turned on, too," she replied.

"Now, do you see why I have to stay away from you?" He smiled, snuggling her into his lap. "I'm sorry you didn't know that. I should've told you. You women have to have everything spelled out in words."

"Time and touch. Women need our man's time and touch. I need your touch as well as your words. I have never been to the places where you take me. Your passion overwhelms me."

"I told Mike once I never was attracted to fair-skinned women, and then you came along. Now I can't get enough of you. Do you want me to change?"

"Don't ever change! I love you exactly the way you are. I like the way you make me feel."

He laughed. "Good, because I couldn't change what you do to me, woman. And it is you, I might add. I did fine after my divorce, living alone in the apartment. But one day, I took your hand and suddenly I wasn't fine anymore. When we played in the hose with the kids later that day, your wet T-shirt drove me crazy. I wanted you, Barb. I could never want anyone else now."

"You make me feel like a woman. Beyond anything I've ever experienced before."

"Hold that thought, baby. As Jamie says: 'catch ya later on that.' Believe me, I will catch you later, and we'll make this six weeks a distant memory."

"That sounds like a plan." Barb got up reluctantly, hearing Michael. Nick heard her crooning softly and watched her come into their bedroom with him in her arms, settling in the rocker to nurse him.

Nick reached up and dimmed the light. "He doesn't usually wake up too much this time of night. He's a good baby, isn't he?"

"He's a perfect baby. You have given me two replicas of yourself, and I love them. I'm so glad we have them both. Whoever would have thought I'd have two dark-eyed babies?"

"Whoever would have thought you'd marry me? Must have been God, Who does all things well! I'll go make the rounds upstairs, and we can go to sleep when Michael does." Nick held Barb close to him that night, although it took him a long time to go to sleep, and he really needed a cold shower.

CHAPTER 23

Barb's Insecurities

NICK WAS EATING a sandwich in the kitchen of the O'Malleys' home when his phone rang. He glanced at the caller's name and smiled. It was Barb. She'd been to the doctor that morning. "Hi, babe, how'd it go?"

He could hear the smile in her voice. "Fine. We have the all clear."

Looking around to make sure Ian and Jimmy hadn't come in from the adjoining studio, Nick lowered his voice. "So, tonight's the night?"

"Finally."

"I've missed you."

"I know, me, too. Want anything special for dinner?"

"You."

"Nick!"

"The kids will most likely take forever to go down tonight."

She sighed. "It's the price we pay for having two babies."

"I love my babies, *amada*."

"See you tonight."

On the way home, Nick stopped by the florist and bought two dozen long-stemmed roses—a mixture of pink and yellow—for Rosa and Michael, the babies Barb had given him. He hummed on the drive and ran up the stairs into his home. Smelling dinner, he headed down the hall to the large kitchen and family dining room, looking for his wife.

Barb had opened the steamer to check the vegetables, and her hair curled in the steam. She smiled over her shoulder. After Nick laid the bouquet on the counter, he came up behind her and slipped his arms around her waist, nuzzling her neck. She turned and put her arms around his neck, lifting her lips for his kiss. When they broke apart, he presented the flowers, and she went to the cupboard for a vase.

"Why isn't the table set? Do I need to get on the kids?"

"No. Missy's dropping the girls off in a minute, the boys should be getting home from practice any minute, and Michael is asleep."

"How much time do we have?"

"Not enough. They are all on the way." Barb was arranging the roses. "These are beautiful, but too extravagant. You shouldn't have done this."

Nick hushed her with another delicious kiss, and they heard the door bang.

"Hi, Mom, we're home," Robbie called. "I'll come and help as soon as I put my stuff down." They heard the two boys run up the stairs.

Soon, the door opened again, and Missy called, "Here are your girls. I left Todd and Jeri in the car, so I gotta run. We enjoyed them."

"Thanks, Missy," Barb called back.

The girls came bursting into the kitchen, demanding to be hugged and spilling over with excited chatter about their afternoon with Todd and Willow.

"God knows, I had no idea little girls could talk so much!" Nick smiled at Ella and Rosa. "You girls need to wash your hands, and let's help Mommy get supper on the table. It smells wonderful in here. What did you make?"

"Your chili relleno recipe, but I'm sure it's not as good as yours."

"I thought it made you sick."

"Only when I'm pregnant."

"Hopefully that won't happen again. But I wouldn't trade the two we have."

After interminable hours for the impatient couple, the house was finally quiet. Nick came into the bedroom from the sunroom they'd made into a nursery. Barb was propped up in bed, her freshly shampooed hair curling around her head. "Are you too tired?" Nick wondered.

She lifted her arms. "I've missed you."

Nick climbed into bed beside her and pulled her down. "I like this blue gown," he said as his hungry hands began roaming her body. She shuddered. When he began reaching for her soft maternal belly, her hands covered it. He stopped. "What is this? Are you hiding from me?"

"I'm fat," she complained. "I promise I'll get back to the gym."

He gently took her hands and held them up on the pillow, one on each side of her head. "Look at me. Do you see the love I have for you?" His eyes caressed her, and she trembled. "I will show you." He began to kiss down the long neck he loved, delighting in her response. "I will let go of your hands if you use them to touch me."

She did, and he resumed his path of kisses down her body. When he came to her torso, she stiffened. "*Cara mia*, listen to your husband. Let me tell you what I see. What I feel." His hands gently stroked her belly. "I see your sacrifice. I see the gift of your body, which has given me two beautiful children—one petite Latina and a strapping *chico*. My body took pleasure only. Yours gave nine months twice to cherish them, to grow them, and to pain in birthing them. I love you more. I adore you." Barb sighed. "Do you hear me, beloved? I will show you my love." And he did, thoroughly convincing her.

* * *

Several days later, Barb turned into the driveway and saw Nick's Suburban. "We got home after Nick, boys. I wonder why he's early today."

"I bet they finished up the album and took off early to celebrate!" Robbie said. "I'll carry Ella inside. She's down for the count."

"I can get Rosa," Alan offered.

"Thanks, guys. Take Rosa's seat and put it in her crib. I'll get Michael. Did we get everything you need for school?"

"I don't need anything else," Alan confirmed. "Thanks for the new clothes."

"I have to get a math calculator, but that's it. Yeah, thanks, Mom," Robbie said, as they unbuckled their seatbelts and quietly gathered the girls.

Barb freed the infant seat from the car and smiled at her beautiful baby. "Hush, now, little one. You go on to sleep."

"His eyes are rolling like they do. He will go to sleep," Alan gave his sage opinion.

"You boys can come back for your clothes," Barb said. "We got a lot done. Thanks."

Barb shifted the infant seat into one hand and held the door for the boys. Robbie headed upstairs with Ella, and Alan followed to put Rosa in her bed in Ella's room. Barb set the sleeping baby's car seat in the crib. After collecting the groceries, she headed down the hall to the kitchen to put them away.

Nick rose from the couch in the adjoining family room with his usual lithe grace. His black jeans clung to his narrow hips, and a black tee hugged his muscular torso. Barb sucked in her breath: *Dear God, he's gorgeous!* His welcoming smile flashed across his tanned face as he crossed over to her. Estaban's guitar music filled the room. No wonder he hadn't heard them come in. She dumped the bags on the counter as the notes hit a rapid downbeat.

Nick's left arm curved over his head, and he clicked his fingers, snapping the rhythm sharply. His right hand went to his firm belly. He danced over to Barb, grabbed her by the waist, and spun her out. His chocolate eyes never left her face, and she shivered. *What does he see in a small-town girl like me? No, not girl—older woman. How can this beautiful man be in love with me?* Tears sprung to her eyes, and Nick hesitated in his move to claim her lips.

"What's this, *mi amor*? It's a little late for the postpartum thing, isn't it? Did the boys give you trouble? Is everything all right?"

"They were golden. We did our back-to-school shopping."

"The girls?"

"Asleep. The boys are putting them in their beds, and I put Michael in the crib. Sorry to be so late. I fed them already."

Nick drew her to him and ground his body into hers. She gasped and tried to pull away. He laughed at her and tucked her closer as the romantic music swirled around them. "Why does my beloved wife have tears?"

Barb put her head on his shoulder. "Because you're so gorgeous!"

Once again, his lethal smile flashed. "I believe that's my line, baby." His slender hands framed her face, and he kissed her deeply. When Barb came up for air, she tried to turn away. Nick's hand slid down, cupped her bottom, and pulled her close. "Barb?" His other hand tucked under her chin and held her until she met his eyes. Tears still lingered there. "What is it?"

"I'm fat. You, on the other hand, are young and devastatingly good-looking."

His hand stayed cupped around her backside as he pulled her tight against him. She felt his body pulsing against her. She blushed, and he chuckled. "See what you do to your husband, *amada*?" They swayed to the music, his arms still holding her against him.

Barb heard footsteps back away from the kitchen. Robbie whispered frantically, "Don't go in there!"

Alan's whisper, "Why?" faded as his brother pulled him down the hall.

Nick shook his head with a smile, pulled away, and grabbed some bags. "Guess we'd better put these away." He took out a bag of frozen peas, and mischief filled his dancing eyes. He pressed it close to his body, under his belt. "Maybe this will help, until a more appropriate time."

Barb laughed and picked up another bag of canned goods. Moving to the pantry door, she banged it. "If we make enough noise, they'll know the coast is clear." Sure enough, Robbie hesitantly stuck his head in and grinned at her. She blushed furiously and quickly stacked cans on the shelf as Nick unloaded the frozen foods.

"Your mom tells me you've been school shopping." Nick spoke over his shoulder, still not ready to turn around. Barb glanced at his bulging seams and smothered a giggle. He frowned at her, but his eyes danced with amusement. Alan hovered behind his brother. "Have you brought everything in, boys?"

"Yes, sir," Alan replied.

"Put your new clothes in the laundry so I can wash them," Barb directed.

Three male voices protested. "Why do you have to wash new clothes?" Robbie asked.

"You don't know who has handled those clothes between here and China, or India, or El Salvador—wherever those clothes came from."

"It's a female thing, guys. Go. Someday I must take you to my grandfather's country. Those sewing factories look like operating rooms. My people are very clean! But I don't know about China. Go on, boys. Do as your mother says. Make her happy with more work." They laughed and turned around.

"Hey, Nick, after we do that, will you take us over to Jamie's? He's got a new Xbox game and wants us to spend the night," Robbie threw back as he moved to obey.

Nick stole a meaningful look at Barb. "Sure, guys, get a move on." As they rushed upstairs, he moved quickly across the kitchen and turned Barb around. "Then maybe I can have some time to convince you how much I love you." He gave her a light kiss and an intense look. "For now . . ." He grabbed her keys off the counter and met the boys at the front door.

Barb sucked in a shuddering breath and calmed herself by climbing the stairs to put the first load of clothes in the washer. By the time she was downstairs, Nick was pushing the door open and heading straight to her. "What is the nonsense in your head? I love you so much. I never thought a good, godly woman would love me. 'Charm is deceptive, and beauty evaporates, but a woman who has the fear of the Lord should be praised. Reward her for what she has done, and let her achievements praise her at the city gates.' I sing your praises. I can't believe you love me, with my past, all my mistakes, and the baggage I bring. I'm the one who should cry, *amada,* and sometimes I do. I weep that you love me. But, I know you do."

He drew Barb into his arms and kissed her deeply until they were both breathless. He pulled her T-shirt over her head and backed her toward their bedroom. As she stumbled backward, she grabbed his shirt. He ducked his head, and she pulled it off. She pulled on his belt buckle as he unsnapped her jeans.

"Those girls better stay asleep," she murmured into his mouth as it closed over hers and they tumbled onto the bed.

* * *

The next week, Barb sat on the steps of the pool with the mommies. She gently lowered and raised Michael between her legs, holding him by one arm. Nick had just pushed away from the pool's edge after making comments about what milk did to a woman's body. "Whatever am I going to do with him!" Barb said.

"We share the problem of mischievous men," Alice informed her. "I never know what Ian's going to say. Enjoy Nick. He's a different man. Listen to him." Screaming and collective laughter filled the air as Nick and Jimmy chased the boys in the deep end.

"I do, but I hope he doesn't regret marrying me."

The three women gaped at her in astonishment. "How can you say that, Barb?"

"Because I'm so much older, Missy. I never would've married him if I'd known his age, but by the time I found out we were practically down the aisle."

"He doesn't appear to mind," Julie said. "Besides, Nick was born old. He never had a mother—not a real one. He raised himself on the streets of L.A. He's been through enough pain and suffering to make him way older than he is in years."

"You're right," Barb responded. "A few nights after Rosa was born, he had a dream about the night the police took his mother, and he told me some things about his childhood. He doesn't have many memories of his mother. He always seemed older than me, with my innocent little life and my comfortable family. He's lived several lifetimes, and he's only thirty-seven."

"I don't ever want to hear you say that again. You're God's gift to Nick, and he'd be the first one to tell you so," Alice fussed.

Nick swam underwater and popped up in front of Michael, who laughed and reached for him. He took the baby into the water. Michael splashed his daddy, and Nick shook the droplets off his own shimmering black hair.

"He's such a good father," Barb observed. "I wonder how he does it. He had no one to show him, but he studies his Bible, and prays, and does what God says. If he can do it, anyone can."

"I heard he adopted Ella." Missy looked at Barb for confirmation.

"It was Pat Westfall's suggestion. Can you believe it?" Barb told them about the phone call the night before the lawyer came by last year. "She told him Ella would be with Rosa all through school, and they should have the same last name. She realized Nick is the only father Ella knows. Maybe he'll get tired of me, but he'll never leave those kids. He's stuck with this family."

"You stop that kind of talk right now, or I'll take you over my knee," Alice said.

Julie and Missy laughed at the vision of tiny Alice taking long, lanky Barb over her knee. But Missy sobered. "Don't' think she wouldn't. I stay out of her way when she's on the warpath. Been there, done that—it's not pretty."

Alice laughed and put her arm around Missy, hugging her hard. "I only do it when my girlie-girls talk nonsense."

The sun moved from under a cloud and touched the surface of the pool. Laughter and splashes filled the air.

"You're right. Nick gets furious when he hears me say something like that. I've been a bit emotional lately, after Michael. And losing the baby weight is much harder this time."

"You aren't trying to take care of kids with a husband overseas. How old was Alan when you went on your deployment? You came home scrawny as a chicken."

"He was six months—Michael's age. I can't imagine. How did I do that? Poor Bob had to take care of a four-year-old and an infant. He was good with them, but Nick is amazing. You'd never know the kids aren't his. They adore him."

"He's never tried to replace Bob," Missy pointed out. "When Robbie is in the studio, I hear them talking about his father."

"Robbie appreciated that right off. He said lots of people avoided talking about his dad, but Nick never did. Nick insists on keeping the photos on the mantle—our family photos and Bob's photo in uniform. Last Christmas, he had Bob's Medal of Honor framed for the boys. Nick never knew a father, and God's made him a father after His own heart."

"The only father he's known is Father God," Missy said.

"He thinks of your dad and Mike as father figures. He says he's watched Tim and Jimmy to see how to be a father. But mostly he 'does unto others.' He lives the Word like no one I've ever known," Barb said. "Sometimes I think when you come to Christ later in life, you appreciate Him more. I've taken a lot for granted in my walk with the Lord."

"You came home from Iraq changed, Barb."

"We experienced a revival there. You can't face death daily and not cling to God. We used to baptize soldiers in the sand. We dug a pit and pumped water into it. It was a mess, but the happiest faces you ever saw! I remember one kid who got killed the next week. I had to write his folks, and I sent the picture of him coming up out of the water, sand streaking down his uniform. They wrote me back. It meant the world to them to know he'd be waiting in heaven."

"I remember when you and Bob started coming to our church after you got back, and Pat and Robert thought you'd fallen off the deep end." Julie laughed. "Mom says they go to church with her and Lenore now. It sounds like a real conversion, if Pat told Nick to adopt Ella."

"She didn't talk to me about it. She spoke directly to him. She and Robert are going on some mission trip next week. They're building houses for Habitat in the southern part of the state, where the floods were. They're happier than I've ever known them. Not so self-absorbed. God has done a work."

"Just think—if Nick and Robbie hadn't gotten there when they did . . ." Missy's voice faded.

"Nick said Robbie was so upset because if Nonna didn't live through the heart attack she wouldn't be with Bob. They prayed on the way to the hospital. Come on, let's get some food out here. Everyone has to be starved!" Barb rose and turned toward the kitchen, and the other ladies followed behind her.

"Where're you going?" Nick called out.

"We're going to bring some supper out."

"We'll have our dessert later," Nick and Tim chorused together. They laughed and gave each other a high-five.

"No," Jamie shouted. "Gram's got brownies. Bring out the brownies, too, Gram, please?"

"We'll bring out the brownies, Jamie, but I'll save the icing for later," Barb said.

225

Nick laughed hard, sputtering water. He threw his arms in the air to sink in the pool.

"Every grown-up here gets that joke," Missy said. Barb nodded and chuckled. "As if he'd ever stop loving you!" Missy hugged her friend.

When they returned with the food, Nick held Michael in his left arm as he lay on the chaise. Barb leaned over and threw toys into a plastic bin. He grinned and grabbed her arm as she walked by. He pulled her toward him. "You gave me an idea, beautiful. I think I'll put that lovely bottom on a couple of pillows tonight," he said softly.

Barb's face flooded brilliant red, and she protested, "Nick!"

He tugged her down beside him. "Shh! The whole yard will hear our private conversation."

"What am I going to do with you?" she murmured into his shoulder.

He made a few suggestions, and she rose. He laughed. "I love you. Can I help it if you're so beautiful?"

CHAPTER 24

Taylor Wilson

MICHAEL WAS MONTHS OLD, and Barb was slowly getting back to normal. One morning, while Ella was in preschool and Michael was asleep, she cuddled with Rosa on the couch and read her favorite book. When the phone rang, she hollered back to the kitchen, asking Sally to answer.

"Barb, a man named Taylor Wilson would like to speak to you. Do you want to take the call?"

"Oh, yes!" Barb said to Sally before she turned back to Rosa. "I'm sorry, sweetie, Mommy has to take this call. Can you be patient?" Rosa nodded and flipped the pages while her mother grabbed the phone on the end table.

"Barbara Costas?"

"Yes, it is. Mr. Wilson, how may I help you?"

"I'm in town for a day or so doing some consulting work for the firm that bought my business. I'd love the opportunity to meet you and your husband, if that would be convenient."

"Oh, Mr. Wilson, my husband and I and our children would love the privilege of thanking you in person for this beautiful home. Your kindness has overwhelmed us."

"I got your lovely letter. What's a good time? May I take you out to dinner?"

"It would be much more convenient if you could join us here, if you don't mind. We have all these children. It would be much easier for me."

"I hesitate to impose, but I want to make it easy for you, so you set the time and place."

"I'm here full-time now. Nick wanted me to stay home with the children. Thanks to you, we can afford that. When will you be available?"

"I should wind up about four today. Should I bring something?"

"No. I'd like to do this for you, and I know Nick would, too. In fact, he and Robbie will probably grill."

Barb hastened to answer when the doorbell rang at four. "Please come in. It must be awkward to ring your own doorbell." Barb was amazed to see Taylor Wilson casually dressed in jeans and a black turtleneck, with a denim jacket. He still looked impressive, tall and slender and in excellent shape. She knew he was retired, but he looked too young, although his dark brown hair had streaks of silver framing his long, narrow face. She felt awkward. Still unable to get into regular clothes, she wore loose pants and an overblouse.

Taylor smiled graciously and stepped into an obviously child-friendly home. It was clean and neat, but a baby swing was centered in the living room where Barb motioned for him to enter. "Can I get you something to drink? Coffee? A soda?"

Running feet pounded down the hall upstairs. "Is he here, Mom?"

"No, thank you," Taylor said with a warm smile. "May I meet the children?"

"I'm afraid neither of us has a choice in the matter." She turned to the stairs and raised her voice. "Yes, you may come down and say hello."

Alan and Ella bounded down the stairs. Alan stopped awkwardly. Ella ran up to the stranger and took his hand. "We love you, Mr. Wilson. We thank God for you every day, and we pray for God to bless you, too, the way you have blessed us. Daddy says you are very special to God!"

Taylor squatted down to be level with the little girl. "Thank you so much. Indeed, God has blessed me, and I appreciate your prayers."

"Would you believe she used to be shy of men?" Barb laughed. "This is Ella and Alan. Nick will be home soon with our oldest, Robbie. He's picking him up at practice." Rosa was wailing at the top of the stairs. "Ella, did you leave Rosa upstairs? Please help her down and then set the table while Mr. Wilson and I chat," Barb requested. "You can put your surprises on the table. Have a seat, Mr. Wilson." Barb sank into the large chair, more comfortable for her to disguise her baby-fat body.

Alan came back down the stairs with Rosa in his arms and took her with him into the kitchen. While the children ran into the dining area, Taylor asked Barb about her husband. She thought he meant Bob, and she briefed him on their courtship and marriage and his devotion to their family, their country, and the West Virginia National Guard. Taylor walked to the mantle and picked up Bob's photo, noticing several of him and the children.

"Nick keeps these where the children see them every day. He's proud of their heritage and wants to be sure they remember and honor their father," Barb informed Taylor.

"I want to meet Nick," Taylor said. "I've been thinking about him a great deal lately. How did you meet?"

"He works for a family in our church who are good friends of mine. Have you heard of Ian O'Malley, the musician? Nick is the producer for O'Malley Productions. When Nick began following the Lord, he volunteered with my son's scouting program at church."

"Your broker thinks very highly of him. She says he's an amazing stepfather."

"He is, and it's truly amazing because he never had a father's love. He came to know Christ working with the O'Malleys, and he's grown spiritually. He puts me to shame. I've been raised in the church, and yet he outlives me in faith. Robbie was in a world of trouble before Nick came into his life, but Nick has been such a role model. He poured love into him." She told Taylor about Nick and Robbie's drive to Charleston with Gramps after they had saved Nonna's life. "They're quite close, and Alan and Ella adore him. Hey, Rosa. Come see Mommy."

Taylor turned to see a beautiful toddler hover at the door. Her beauty took his breath. Silken black curls tumbled about her brown pixie face, and her black eyes sparkled at him, even as she peeked shyly.

"Rosa, this is Mr. Wilson. Can you say hi?"

Rosa ran to the safety of her mother's lap and whispered, "Hi," as she peeked out at him.

"So, this is Nick's baby. She's a beauty!" Taylor tried to coax Rosa to come to him, but with flashing grins, dancing eyes, and even giggles, she kept her distance as she eyed him from afar.

"Both girls, Rosa and Ella, are Daddy's girls. I found out I was pregnant with Ella after Bob died. Nick's the only Daddy Ella knows, and she began to call him 'Daddy' right after we were married. She was a little over two. She had a Cinderella birthday party for her second birthday, and Nick has called her Cinderella ever since. They dance to Stephen Curtis Chapman's song 'Cinderella.' Are you familiar with it?"

"I cry every time I hear it. It is all too true. Our daughters are in college now. Tell me about Nick. Was he raised by a single mother?"

"Nick was taken from her when he was five. He grew up in foster homes—some of them were quite abusive. He still has scars from the beatings he had as a child." After they set the table, Barb told the children they could go outside. "Would you mind taking Rosa with you? Be sure to put on your jackets."

Ella stood in front of Taylor. "Do you have any kids, Mr. Wilson?"

"I do. Two girls in college and a son in high school. I had another little boy who died when he was seven."

"But you'll see him in heaven. My first daddy is in heaven. Robbie's in high school. He's my big brother. He works with Daddy at Da O'Malley's studio."

Emboldened by her big sister, Rosa walked closer and stood close to Taylor's knee.

"Do you mean your mother has two pretty girls *and* another fine son?" Taylor asked.

"I have three brothers: Robbie, Alan, and Michael." Ella smiled. "You'll meet them all. I'm so glad you came to see us." She grabbed Rosa's hand. "Come on. You wanna play in the sandbox?" Ella began to run through the kitchen but screeched to a halt and called back, "Please excuse us, Mr. Wilson."

Taylor chuckled, and then he turned to Barb with further questions about Nick. Barb filled him in on the remarkable testimony of God's goodness in Nick's life.

Delighted cries filled the air as Nick and Robbie walked in, and the children dashed through the house to greet them. Ella and Rosa flew to Nick's embrace. With a girl in each arm, he walked into the living room. "Mr. Wilson. How nice of you to come by! Forgive me, I seem to have my hands full. This is our oldest, Robbie."

Taylor was almost eye to eye with a tall, handsome, broad young teen, closely resembling the proud warrior in the photo on the mantle. His handshake was firm and confident. His eye contact was clear and direct, and he smiled. Taylor saw no evidence of the troubled kid Barb described earlier.

"I'll take the steaks out to the kitchen and start marinating them, Mom. We brought some veggies for the salad. Would you like me to fire up the grill now?"

Barb nodded, quickly moving to a crying baby.

"You want me to get him, honey?" Nick asked.

"No. I'll have to nurse him before I come back out. Mr. Wilson hasn't had anything to drink. The coffee is set. Just push the button."

"Please, both of you, just 'Taylor.' I feel like you're talking to my father when you say Mr. Wilson." Immediately, Taylor felt self-conscious, remembering Nick didn't have a father.

Barb moved toward the bedroom, and Nick set the girls down and walked toward the patio, inviting Taylor to join him. Ella clung to his hand, and Rosa wrapped her arms and legs around his leg. He carried her along. All three of them laughed.

"Come on with us, and we'll get dinner started," Nick invited. "What is this on my leg, Alan?" He put his arm around the young boy and drew him into an easy embrace. "I have this weight on my leg. It's hard to walk like this." He pretended to limp, sending both girls into helpless giggles. "Get off my leg! My leg is not your ridey horse." He reached down and tickled the toddler until she let go. "Daddy should help light the fire."

"I can do it, Daddy Nick. Robbie's marinating the steaks, like you said." Alan carefully poured the charcoal on the grill.

"I suggest we let the chefs prepare our dinner," Nick said to Taylor. "Let me get some coffee. Do you want to sit out here? It's a bit chilly."

"I have my jacket on. I bet your family gets a lot more use out of the pool than we ever did. We never had it open this early."

"With the free gas, we have it open early and close it late," Nick said. "The kids live in it."

Robbie walked out onto the patio with sugar and cream on a tray, and then he returned with the steaks in a flat casserole dish with sauce lapping around them. "They won't have enough time in the marinade, but we can baste them as they grill," Robbie said. "It'll be a while before the charcoal's ready. Mom had the potatoes in the oven and the salad made—except for adding the veggies. Is she with Michael?"

Nick nodded. He rose with his easy grace to check on them, but Barb walked out, holding a baby in her arms. Nick reached for him, and the baby settled comfortably in his arms. "Hey, buddy. Have you been a good boy for your Mommy?"

"Rosa was a good baby, but she was tiny and needed to eat every couple of hours. This fellow was born half-grown, and he stretches out for hours at a time. This is our youngest, Mr. . . . .Taylor." Barb corrected herself, watched Nick with Michael, and turned back to Taylor. "It's hard to call a hero by his first name. You *are* aware that all of us in the WV Guard think of you as a hero? I was in Iraq myself when the huge shipment of pepperoni rolls arrived. Did you hear the Mountaineers yell all the way back home?"

They all laughed as Barb talked about the day Taylor Wilson's shipment of a taste of home arrived in the foreign desert.

"I found out about Ella after Bob died. Nick moved here about two years later, and I must confess I was terribly rude and unkind to him. When he said he'd been to Iraq three times and once to Afghanistan, I felt so small!" Barb leaned over and slipped her arm around Nick's neck. He lifted his head to kiss her cheek.

"And she's been making it up to me ever since," he said. "Sit, honey. Did you have a rest today?"

Barb sat beside him on the chaise and rolled her eyes. "Yes, Nick, I slept for two hours. Rosa woke up before I did."

"So, you see why we need Sally?"

"You spoil me rotten. How can an honest woman make a living with a husband like you?" She smiled and leaned her head against him.

His arm circled her. "You can keep your night—"

"Nick!" she cautioned. He laughed, pulled her tight against him, and kissed her cheek lightly again.

"I'll sit if you go finish up the salad. Here, let me take him," she said.

"May I?" Taylor plucked the baby from Nick's arms. "I didn't know you had a second baby, and isn't he fine? Both these children are so like their father. How old is he?"

"He's six months," Barb informed him.

Robbie came up and leaned down to snuggle with Michael. "I was excited when Rosa came because Ella was a mixed blessing for Mom, and God gave us another baby—one she thoroughly enjoyed," Robbie said. "This one gave us fits, but you're worth it now, aren't you, tiger?"

The baby responded to his big brother's affectionate kiss on his belly with a toothless grin as he tangled his chubby fingers in Robbie's hair. "God knew what He was doing. The babies have been good for Nick, haven't they, Mom?"

"When Rosa was born, Nick could hardly put her down," Barb said. "He sat in the rocker at the hospital with tears running down his cheeks and sang to her with this amazing contentment on his face. She was a surprise. They both were, but, yes, Robbie's right—they've been good for their daddy. But he was already an excellent father. I told Mr. Wilson the impact he had on your life, Robbie."

Robbie nodded. "I was headed for real trouble. I'm sorry, Mom, for what I put you through. I told you to marry him! He's an awesome stepfather, Mr. Wilson, and I wasn't an easy kid. He understood and never came on strong or heavy-handed. He made it clear he respected Dad, and he totally earned my respect. I want to be like him, and like my dad, too, of course."

Nick came out with a huge salad bowl and checked the charcoal. "The coals are about ready, Alan. Who set the table so nicely?"

Ella's head popped out of her playhouse. "I did, Daddy. Alan and I did. Did we do good?"

"You did better than good, Cinderella. You made these lovely folds on the napkins, and I see the nice cards for Mr. Wilson, too. Thank you both for helping your mom. What did we do to deserve such great kids?" Both youngsters visibly swelled at his praise. "Okay, Alan, can we get the pack-and-play set up?"

"Michael would prefer the swing, Daddy Nick. You know how he is this time of day." Nick gave Alan a high-five, and they went into the house together.

After supper, Nick and the boys cleaned up, leaving Taylor and Barb to sip their cups—coffee for him and herbal tea for her. They could hear the laughter in the kitchen.

"All right, youngsters, who has homework?" Nick asked. "You

girls, let's get you in Mommy and Daddy's tub. You boys need any help?"

"No, sir. I need to write out my spelling words and definitions. It's easy. Can I watch TV in the family room?" Alan asked.

"I have algebra, so I'll go up to my room, Nick," Robbie said.

"Come on, girls. Let's get you in the tub?" Nick suggested again.

Robbie herded Rosa and Ella to the tub. "I'll get their jammies, Nick," he said.

"I can get them."

Ella ran up the stairs and left Rosa crying after her. Robbie picked up the dark beauty and talked to her while they walked into the master bath. He assured Rosa her sister would be right back as he set the water temperature.

"The children don't seem to be jealous of each other. There's obviously enough love to go around," Taylor commented, extending a hand to assist Barb.

Nick came out to the patio and scooped Michael into his arms. "Hey, buddy. Your little nose is cold!" Nick rubbed his son's nose with his own and was rewarded with a belly laugh. "I never thought I'd have children. Isn't God good? Now I have a quiver full of them, thanks to this wonderful woman, who happens to be a terrific mother."

Listening to the happy sounds of the girls playing in the tub, Barb, Nick, and Taylor chatted easily in the living room. Nick described his work with the O'Malleys and invited Taylor to drop by the studio. "Robbie works tomorrow, from 12:20 p.m. to 3:00," Nick said. "I'll have to take him back for football practice after school. Are you familiar with their music?"

Taylor hesitated for a moment, but when Barb mentioned the album *Recovered and Free*, he immediately remembered who they were.

The girls called for Daddy, and Barb excused herself to change Michael. "Let's pray here, girls, and Daddy will take you up to bed."

Taylor listened to their sweet voices. He rejoiced he'd been able to provide this home for such a remarkable family.

Barb returned to the living room, trying to juggle Michael, who wasn't a happy camper. "He's ready to go down for the night. I'm sorry," she apologized.

"Go ahead, Barb. You've been very hospitable. I didn't realize you had a new baby, or I wouldn't have imposed like this. If you don't mind, I'll wait for Nick. I need to tell him something."

"You're an amazing example of God, and this family owes you. Only God can reward you enough for what you have done for us." Barb surprised him by leaning to place a kiss on his cheek.

Taylor stood to hug her. "The blessing is mine, Barb. I'd like my wife, Adelaide, to meet your family. She would agree that this was God's plan. This house was built with your family in His mind. Now, go put that boy to bed."

Taylor sat and leaned his head back on the couch. Soft voices drifted down the stairs, and Nick sang songs to his girls: "I'll Dance with Cinderella," and Daddy's little rosebud to the tune of "The Yellow Rose of Texas." Taylor chuckled as Nick descended the steps. "That's a unique version of 'The Yellow Rose of Texas,' but it suits," Taylor said.

Nick explained that Barb had gone to put the baby down. "But I asked if I could stay to speak to you. Can you give me another few minutes of your time?"

"You have my undivided attention."

"I'm sure Barb has told you how grateful we are. She was overwhelmed and confused by your generosity. I told her she'd given enough for her country. Obviously, you thought so, too."

"Barb and the children have all been quick to express their gratitude, although it is misdirected. I'll take the kids' cards home to Adelaide." Taylor smiled at Nick. "I've learned you can't out-give God. Ever since we gave you this house, the blessings of God have overtaken us. It's almost embarrassing. I have a message for you, but first, may I ask how you learned to be a father? Barb tells me you had no father, and God taught you how to father by making you one."

Nick shrugged. "I stumble frequently, but she and Robbie have been patient with me. I work with an incredible father, Jimmy O'Malley. And his brother-in-law, Tim Raines, is an amazing father, too. I watch them. Mostly this, though." He reached under the side table and pulled out a journal. Taylor flipped through the pages and saw Scripture after Scripture carefully inscribed from several translations about fathers and husbands. "I didn't know how to do this, so I had to ask God every minute of every day. I love these kids. I try to do what I wanted someone to do for me when I was their age. God's faithful to pick me up time after time and set me straight."

Taylor reached into his pocket and brought out a sheet of paper and his glasses. "This is confirmation," he said. "God wanted me to come tell you this. My wife told me I had to come in person to tell you, so, when I got a call about a consulting job here, we felt it was time." He put on his glasses and referred to the paper.

"As I prayed for your family—you're right," he continued. "I thought I was doing this for Barb, for all she gave for this country. But one day I distinctly felt God tell me this gift I had was for you. He said, 'Tell My beloved child I formed you in your mother's womb and walked with you through your pain and suffering.' He said this place was prepared for you. I thought He meant this house, but I see it was more: it was Robbie and Barb and these precious children. God brought you together in His timing and made you a father after His own heart. He took me to the Scripture in Genesis 18 about Abraham: 'For I have known him, in order that he may command his children and his household after him, that they may keep the way of the Lord, to do righteousness and justice . . .' Do you know the Scripture in Genesis?"

Taylor looked up and saw tears streaming down Nick's face. He rose and knelt in front of Nick to gather him in his arms the way he gathered his own son into his arms. "I didn't understand all that until I met you, Nick. God loves you. He's delighted in blessing you, and I'm honored to be a part of that."

When Nick pulled himself together, he said, "I love to praise the kids, to catch them doing good things, because I remember how hungry I was for one small word of praise. One of my foster fathers was a good guy, a plumber. It was a temporary home, but I worked with him one summer. I was only there six months, but I remember how I felt when he said: 'Good work, Nick.' So, I try to do that. That's the only good parenting I knew when I came to this family. Tonight—" Nick choked.

Taylor sat on the couch beside Nick and put his arm around his shoulder. "Tonight, God came to praise you Himself, Nick," Taylor said. "He is well-pleased with you, and this simple messenger is going to leave you in His hands. I'll call you tomorrow. Would you mind if Adelaide joined me to meet you and your family later this week?"

"We'd love it." Nick reached into his pocket, pulled out his card, and handed it to Taylor. "Thanks for coming out here. Barb hasn't gotten out much since Michael was born. She had a difficult pregnancy. I suspect she fell asleep with him. She's still tired."

The men rose, and Nick walked Taylor to the door. When Nick returned to the living room, he wept for a long time as he thanked and praised God for His goodness.

* * *

At the hotel, Taylor called his wife to tell her the amazing story of Nick Costas, a child of God and a father after His own heart. "Have you heard of the O'Malleys? Remember *Recovered and Free*? Nick's their producer. I downloaded some of their music, and it's outstanding. We need to get them out for a Marketplace Ministries Summit."

Adelaide was more familiar with their songs than he was, because she listened to contemporary Christian music stations. When she flew in to West Virginia a few days later, she fell in love with the family, like her husband had. The O'Malleys hosted a dinner for them, and they enjoyed the laughter always present at an O'Malley gathering.

While the musicians and Nick set up for an impromptu performance, Barb came over to Taylor and reached out her hand. "Taylor, I'm grateful to you again. You ministered to Nick powerfully the other night. I tell him he's a good father and a good Christian, but I see him shrug it off in disbelief. Thank you for being God with skin on. He truly felt Father God gave him praise and approval."

"Then I was a faithful messenger, because that's exactly what God the Father told me about him. What do you know about his mother, Barb?"

"Not much. I saw his birth certificate with her full name. He has some memories. He says Rosa looks like her."

"Find out what you can. I have some resources, and I wonder if we should try to locate her." Taylor saw alarm in her eyes, so he added, "I'll let you know first if I find out anything, and we can pray together about where to go from there. Okay?" Relief flooded Barb's eyes as she nodded.

Julie urged them into chairs. The concert was about to begin. Barb was surprised to see Nick sit with them instead of at the soundboard. He nodded toward Robbie. "This is a good practice run for him to go solo."

Barb looked over at her son and saw him light up like a Christmas tree. Barb and Taylor both noticed Nick unobtrusively point to one mic or another, and Robbie switched the settings. Taylor whispered to Adelaide, who saw the interaction and, smiling, whispered back: "I will guide thee with mine eye." Taylor nodded.

Once, Nick didn't give Robbie any signal. Robbie still made the switch and quickly glanced over. He was rewarded with a huge smile and a thumbs-up. Nick leaned over to Barb to ask how she was doing. "Are you ready to go home?"

"Almost. He's doing a good job, isn't he?"

Smiling, Nick put his arm around her. As she leaned into him, Michael began to stir on her lap. He stretched, opening one lazy eye.

Nick quietly gathered him up, grabbed the diaper bag, and took him to the back for a change.

Missy looked over at Barb and saw the fatigue she tried to hide. "Let's do one more, Daddy. Barb needs to go home," Missy said. "Shall we do 'In Your Arms?' Is that good?" They closed with the haunting melody that had brought Nick and Barb together.

Nick carried the baby to Barb and went to help Robbie tear down the equipment. He praised his work, pointing out the things he did well and encouraging him where he needed to improve. "Let's get your mom home, Robbie," Nick said. "She's fading fast."

Jimmy told them to go ahead, he'd finish up. Robbie carried Rosa, and Nick carried Michael and held Ella's hand as they called back their goodbyes. Both girls were asleep by the time they got home, so Robbie and Nick carried them up to the girls' shared bedroom—Ella had insisted Rosa sleep in her room when her little sister moved upstairs. Nick stopped by Alan's room, praising him for getting ready for bed so quickly and kneeling beside the boy's bed to pray with him. At Robbie's room, Nick told him again what a good job he'd done. He sat beside him on the bed, and they joined hands to pray together.

"I love you, Robbie."

"Love you, too, Nick. Thanks for all you've taught me."

Nick rubbed his head. And when he got downstairs, Barb was finishing up nursing Michael. "All down for the count. How're you doing with this one? I love to watch you nurse our babies."

"Poor Rosa had to grow up so fast." She lifted Michael up to her shoulder, but Nick took him and walked him, patting him on the back until he fell asleep.

"'Poor' Rosa is a happy little girl. Ella mothers her within an inch of her life. If Ella hadn't gone to preschool, Rosa would have been smothered!"

Barb agreed, climbing into bed. Nick had placed the baby in the crib. Michael lifted his head, but his daddy patted his back until he laid it back down.

"How much do you remember about your mother, Nick?" Barb asked when he came out of the bathroom. He got into bed, and she cuddled up to him.

"She was small and dark, like Rosa, with the same snapping black eyes," Nick said. "I remember holding her hand and climbing a long set of stairs in front of a cathedral. She told me to be quiet and then slipped into a confessional. Mostly I remember a parade of abusive men. Every man used her, hit her, and hit me, and she repeated the cycle until one night the police came after a neighbor called."

Nick closed his eyes but opened them again and said, "They arrested her, but she knelt down in front of me and kissed me. It was the last time I ever saw her. I spent a long time in the hospital. Apparently, I had several broken bones. I was petted and pampered by the nurses. She was arrested as an accessory or something."

Barb laid her head on his chest and rubbed her fingers in his dark curls. "I love you so very much, Nick." She sighed. "I like Taylor and Adelaide. Thank you again, God, for bringing them into our lives. What a blessing they are, Nick. Such kind and generous people!"

"He told me about some marketplace ministry, and he invited me to go to a meeting," Nick said. "I'll check into it. They encourage businesspeople to use their professional relationships as a vehicle to share Christ. It sounds interesting. Taylor really spoke into my life. He made me realize how much God loves me."

"I've been trying to tell you, honey."

"I should've known, because He gave me you and the kids, but I thought He wanted me to take care of you guys and that you wanted to have your way with me."

"Oh, I do, Nick. I really do."

CHAPTER 25

Sister Marie Teresa

ONE AFTERNOON, some months later, Barb answered the phone at home. Taylor had located Nick's mother. After serving time for child neglect and accessory to child endangerment and serving probation, she entered a convent, and she had been a nun for twenty-five years. Now, she was in ill-health.

"I spoke with the Mother Superior, who felt it would be a healing for her to see Nick. Do you think he'd want to go see her?"

"I know he would, and he should take Rosa."

They arranged for the Mother Superior to call Nick at six. That evening, he got irritated with Barb because he was stir-frying veggies when she insisted he answer the phone. "I'll take over. Would you catch that?" she urged him. He surrendered the spoon and walked to the phone.

"Who? . . . Yes, ma'am, this is Nick Costas." Barb only heard him agree, and she saw him shake his head and glance over at her. "Yes, ma'am. So, how much time do you think she has? . . . We'll certainly make it an object of prayer, but I'm sure my wife will agree. When can I call you back?"

Nick looked up at Barb as he hung up the phone. "You expected that call, didn't you?" Nick asked.

"Taylor called this afternoon," Barb replied." He said your mother's critical and that you need to decide quickly if you ever want to see her. What is it?"

"Cancer. I can't believe this! What do you think?"

"What's to think about? You must go. And take Rosa with you."

He leaned back against the wall. "You are quite a woman, *amada*."

"You need to bring your mother forgiveness. How healing it will be to her soul! Go, as soon as possible, Nick."

"And leave you with five children by yourself?"

"I have help, and, if you take Rosa, it'll only be four."

"Only four," he echoed. He laughed as he took her in his arms. "Is this really true? How did Taylor find her?"

"He said he has 'sources.' I think he hired a PI. He had to hire an attorney to get the records of her probation. She did community service with the Catholic Charities, and then she eventually went into the convent."

"Hey, smells good, Mom. What's for dinner?" Robbie said, tossing his books on the counter.

"Teriyaki chicken, with rice and stir-fried veggies. Call the kids to the table."

When the family gathered, Nick told them about his mother, and they prayed for her.

"Maybe God will heal her, Nick, and we can meet our grandmother!" Alan forgot Nick's mother wasn't actually related to him.

* * *

Within twenty-four hours, urged by Mother Joanna, Nick and Rosa were on their way to L.A. He called Barb when they got to the hotel. "I'm sorry, honey. It's late there, but we just got in. . . . She's asleep. She did all right. It was long and tiring, but she entertained everyone around us. We'll go over to the Mother House at nine in the morning. Mother Joanna, the Mother Superior, says she's at her best in the mornings. She knows I'm coming, but they haven't told her about Rosa. . . . I will. I love you, too. I miss you." Nick hung up the phone.

After Nick showered, he looked down at the sleeping Rosa and whispered prayers for his mother. He lay down beside the miracle his precious daughter was to him and fell asleep.

When he opened his eyes, Rosa was patting his face. "Wake up, Daddy. Are we in Calif-or-nia?"

"Yes, we are, Rosa. Are you hungry?" She nodded. "Let's go potty, and we'll go to breakfast."

"Are we having breakfast with my grandmamma?" she asked as he led her to the bathroom.

"No, Precious. She's very sick, remember? I don't think she's able to eat."

"How does she live, Daddy?"

Nick sighed and squatted down beside her. "She's going to live with Jesus very soon."

Rosa cocked her head to one side. "I'm sorry, Daddy." She moved into his arms and patted him on the back softly.

"I'm glad you came with me, Daddy's little Rosebud. I won't be so lonesome."

"Me, too. But I miss Ella, and Mommy, and Robbie, and Alan."

As they chatted, Nick dressed her and brushed her silky curls. "Now, let Daddy get dressed, and we'll go eat."

"Can I watch you shave, Daddy?"

Rosa watched him shave, and then Nick found some cartoons for her to watch while he dressed. They went down to the restaurant, and heads turned as they entered the dining room. His Rosa was indeed a beautiful child. *God, help me to raise her not to be vain and selfish!*

It was an adventure for Rosa to ride in a taxi, but the towering buildings stopped her chatter. Her eyes opened wide, and she clung to Nick's hand. They pulled up in front of the convent, climbed the stairs, and rang the bell. The nuns wore black dresses, but they weren't long, and their simple head-coverings hung softly to their shoulders. A sweet, young sister, Sister Brigit, walked them to the Mother Superior's office.

A brisk, wiry woman, who looked like any professional except for her habit, entered with a big smile on her face and stopped in her tracks. "Oh, Nick, she looks so much like your mother when she was young! I remember her curls kept slipping out of her wimple. You are good to come." She knelt in front of Rosa. "I'm Mother Joanna. Are you the Rosa your papa tells me about?" Rosa nodded solemnly. "Thank you for coming with your Papa. I know your *abuela* will be happy to see you."

Rosa moved behind Nick's leg but smiled. Nick reached down to pick her up. From the safety of his arms, she smiled shyly. "I'm Daddy's little Rosebud, and my sister is his Cinderella."

"What fortunate girls you are to have a papa who loves you so much!" Rosa agreed, and she tightened her arms around her father's neck.

"We must go while we have a window. She's alert and waiting for you," Mother Joanna said.

Nick held the door for the Mother Superior to pass through ahead of him. She led the way through the halls at a brisk pace. She pushed a door open quietly and asked, "Are you awake, Sister? Your son is here, and he brings you a beautiful surprise." She stood aside and motioned Nick into the room. "Will she let me take her, do you suppose?" She held out her arms to Rosa, who clung to Nick and looked curiously at the frail figure on the bed.

"My son, you came. I can die in peace, if you can forgive me." Sister Marie Teresa, as she was now known, looked up at Nick. Tears fell freely down her thin, sunken cheeks.

"*Mamacita*," he whispered tenderly, stroking her hair from her forehead. "Of course, I forgive you. It gives me great joy to see you living in God's house, safe and blessed. I brought your granddaughter to see you. Rosa, this is your *abuela*."

"Oh, Nickie, how beautiful she is!"

"She looks like you, Mama. Can you say hello, Rosa?" Rosa wiggled out of his arms and inched up to the bed. She climbed up carefully and leaned over to kiss her grandmother softly.

"Oh, precious girl, thank you for coming to see me!" the frail patient whispered. She reached out her hand to touch the child.

"Mommy tells me to be very careful with Michael, and I'll be careful with you, *Abuela*."

Nick explained that Michael was his son, Rosa's baby brother. He showed his mother photos of Barb, the boys, and Ella. Barb had prepared a grandmother's brag book for his mother. Rosa was quiet as they chatted in familiar Spanish about his family and his work. All too soon, exhaustion showed on her face, and Nick rose to leave. She reached out her hand, took his, and drew it to her lips.

"I prayed for you every day, Nickie. I love you. I'm sorry."

"Goodbye, *Abuela*. I love you," Rosa said softly.

"And I love you, too, Rosa. Kiss your brother for me. Remember, and tell him I will watch over you both from heaven. Be a good girl for Papa, and love him for me every day."

Nick could tell his mother was in pain, so he gathered Rosa in his arms and stepped aside to allow the nursing sister to put some medication into her IV. When Sister Brigit took him back to the Mother Superior's office, she told them Sister Marie Teresa was the most alert she'd been in weeks.

"We thought she'd leave us last week, but we told her we'd found you, and she rallied. I'm glad you got here in time. She won't be with us much longer. You made her happy—you and the child, Rosa." The older nun praised, "You did so well with your grandmother. You must be a very good big sister." She looked up at Nick. "Surely the angels were with this precious child today." She told him goodbye. "How long will you stay?"

"I'd like to stay to the end. Could I come back again?"

"If she's still with us in the morning, come back. We'll lay her to rest in our cemetery out back. Would you care to see?"

"Thank you, but Rosa's ready for lunch. Would you like a taco, Rosa?" She reached up her hand to urge him forward. "Can you say goodbye, *chica?*" Nick asked.

"*Adios, Madre,*" she said politely. Nick held her hand, and they walked to a nearby neighborhood café. Once again, his daughter was the center of attention, but she was quiet.

"Are you tired, Rosita?" he asked tenderly.

"Can we talk to Mommy?"

"I told Mommy we'd call after our visit. Let's go to the park over there."

As soon as Nick got Barb on the line, Rosa reached for the phone. "Hi, Mommy. I miss you, and Ella, and Robbie, and Alan. . . . Yes, I did. She's very tired. She wants to leave us and go to Jesus, and I just met her. She called Daddy 'Nickie,' and I think he was her little boy a long time ago. We saw lots of ladies in black dresses, but they were very nice. . . . Yes, Mommy, I will. He's very sad. . . . I love you, too."

Nick put his arm around her and held her close as he talked to Barb. "Jimmy says all little girls talk nonstop, but she was quiet around the ladies in black dresses. . . . No, she was sweet to her. She even kissed her gently on the cheek like she kisses her baby brother. We talked on the plane, and she called her '*Abuela.*' She even said '*Adios, Madre,*' to Mother Joanna." He chuckled. "Thanks for sending her with me. Mama was pleased to see her. . . . Yes, she's a huge comfort. Hug Ella for me, and the boys, and Michael."

Rosa made no move to play on the playground, a dusty wasteland where the rundown equipment was broken and rusty. "Do you want to go back to the hotel, Rosa? Maybe rest a bit?" Nick wondered. She nodded and reached for him to pick her up.

Before they arrived at the hotel, she was asleep in his arms. The smiling hotel staff, taken with her beauty, kindly opened the door for Nick so he could lay her on the bed. He picked up his Bible, read a few chapters, and then reached for his phone to call Taylor and thank him.

"I don't know if she'll be here tomorrow. The sisters said she was ready to leave earlier this week, but she hung on because they told her I was coming. She asked me to forgive her, so she could depart in peace. You must have talked to Barb. . . . Yes, she's with me, and she was such a blessing. Mother Joanna said she was surrounded by angels today."

Nick hung up, stretched out beside Rosa, and drifted off. When Rosa woke up, they walked to nearby stores to buy gifts for everyone at home. Then, in the middle of the night, Nick answered the phone. He heard Mother Joanna's voice and woke up quickly. She told him his mother had passed away, and they would plan a service, so he and Rosa could attend. The next morning, Nick took Rosa to the beach.

"Wow, Daddy, what a big lake. I can't see the end of it. Where does it end?" Nick held Rosa's hand and led her into the ocean. He laughed as she cautiously put her little foot in the lapping waves. "That tickles, Daddy." Safe in his arms, they went further out, and later they sat on the beach and made a sandcastle. "Is this a sandbox?" she asked.

* * *

The next day, Nick walked into the church, holding his daughter's tiny hand. Several of the sisters said kind words about Sister Marie Teresa, and Nick was grateful to learn about her peaceful life of service in this blessed place. Mother Joanna gave him an opportunity to speak, so he gave God the glory for the gift of new life he'd found and for Barb and her children, who taught him the love of a family. He spoke gratefully of the precious gift of reunion with his mother and thanked the sisters for their kindness.

"I will be eternally grateful to you and this place for giving her comfort and a life devoted to Christ. Even as I grieve what was so quickly gained and lost, I know we shall have a glad eternal reunion."

Rosa sat quietly in the pew while she watched her father, but she reached for him when he came back to sit beside her. He put her on his lap, and she rested her head on his chest.

"You are a good girl, Rosa," Mother Joanna told her after the service. "Your Mommy and Papa must be very proud of you."

"I miss Mommy, and Ella, and Robbie, and Alan," she replied. "But I'm glad I met *Abuela* before she moved to Jesus's house. I'll see her again someday."

The old nun smiled at her and touched her silken curls. "Yes, little one, we certainly shall." Mother Joanna gave Nick a fond hug and thanked him for coming on such short notice, adding that it was a miracle they found him in time. He thanked her, and all the sisters gathered around Rosa, clucking over her and wanting to touch her.

"Will you come back to see us, Rosita?" asked Sister Brigit. Rosa smiled shyly.

"Maybe someday we can bring the whole family out here," Nick said. "Wave to the sisters, Rosa." Nick carried his daughter to the nearby taxi stand and hailed a cab to go to the hotel.

"Papa, those ladies love Jesus, too. They just do it more quietly, I think."

Chuckling, he replied, "You are right, Rosita. They are kind of like Gram Alice and Uncle Timmy, aren't they?" Rosa sat upright, looked out the window and exclaimed about the cars and buses. "We don't have all these cars and buses and tall buildings at home, do we?" Nick said.

"Can we go home now, Papa?"

"Are you ready for the long ride on the plane? We'll go to the airport early tomorrow, so we must go to bed early tonight, okay?"

"Okay, Papa. I want to go home."

"Me, too, bambina. I want to hug Mommy and Ella."

"And Robbie and Nick. But you kiss Mommy on the lips, and she smiles."

"You don't miss a trick, do you, Rosa?"

The long plane ride home was tolerable because Nick had bought books and stickers. After they changed planes, he unpacked a new doll.

"You got me one like Ella's, but mine has dark hair, like me! Thank you, Papa."

"Thank you for coming with me on this long trip. You helped Daddy say goodbye to his Mommy." He watched her dress her baby doll carefully and smiled as she held it up to her flat chest as if she were nursing her baby, realizing how much her mother had taught her about loving a baby. When she tired, she crawled up into his lap and fell asleep.

They arrived in Pittsburgh late. Expecting to see Jimmy or Tim, Nick was surprised to see Barb and the children pull up in the Suburban under the canopy outside the baggage claim. Robbie helped him load their luggage into the car, and then they got in and pulled away.

"Isn't this a school night?" Nick asked.

"I declared a mental health day. We all missed you so much," Barb answered.

After her sleep on the plane, Rosa was wide awake. She wanted to distribute gifts, and she got a bit miffed because they were packed away.

"I made us reservations nearby," Barb said. "Maybe we could go to the zoo tomorrow."

Ella and Rosa shouted their enthusiasm and gave each other a high-five. Barb drove to the hotel, and they all piled out of the car. The boys were in their own room, but Ella wanted to be with her Daddy and Rosa, so they put them in the other double bed. Barb had already gotten a crib for Michael. The girls played quietly with their new dolls while Nick told Barb the details of their visit. Finally, they turned off the lights and heard the girls' soft breathing.

Barb curled up in Nick's arms and whispered, "I can't wait to get you home."

"You haven't been questioning my gender identity again, have you?" he teased.

"Nope. we have that settled." She smiled in the dark, slipped her hand under his T-shirt, and ran her fingers through the dark curls on his chest. Nick pulled her to him and settled his mouth over hers for a long, lingering kiss. "I'm glad you're home, Nick."

"I'm so glad to be in your arms, *amada*." Because it was much earlier for him, still on west coast time, he felt her drift off in his embrace.

* * *

Morning dawned, bright and fair. Nick and Robbie packed the car quickly after breakfast. The little girls wore their beautiful new Latina dresses as they ran around the zoo. One girl was blonde and the other dark, but both had curls framing their shiny faces. The boys went off by themselves sometimes, but most of the time they were content to hang around their parents and little sisters. Michael refused to sit in a stroller. He wanted Nick to carry him.

"I believe he's gained two pounds since I've been gone," Nick said.

Barb laughed. "He's had a growth spurt. Robbie helped me move the crib upstairs, away from our room." She blushed. "And he knew only too well why," she whispered when the children were out of hearing.

Nick laughed, put his arm around her waist, and drew her to his side. "Let's let him drive some on the way home."

"Oh, Nick, on the interstate? I don't know."

"He's a good driver, Mom. You've got to let him go."

"I guess you are right, but . . ." Nick looked at her. "You're right," she admitted.

"I'll make it worth your while tonight," he said. She shivered and smiled at him happily. He laughed and kissed her, leaning over Michael.

"Come on, guys, that is entirely too much PDA," Robbie called out. "You're robbing Alan of his innocence!" The boys laughed and grabbed their sisters by the hand.

"You'd better cut that out, or you won't drive after all, kid," Nick hollered after him.

Once Nick got the Suburban out of city traffic and on the open road, he pulled over to stop and let Robbie drive. When Robbie asked for a break, Nick said, "You did well, Robbie. Good job!"

"Thanks, Nick. It was cool. How'd you talk Mom into it?"

Nick grinned. "I have my ways." Robbie laughed and climbed into the passenger side. "Ella, Rosa missed you," Nick said. "She missed all of you. You'd think she'd be happy to have a parent all to herself, but all she could say was, 'I miss Ella, and Robbie, and Alan.' Isn't that right, Rosita?"

Rosa giggled. "I'm glad to be home, Papa."

"I missed you, too, Rosa. Thanks for the doll and the dress," Ella said.

"Yeah, thanks Daddy Nick for the ship in a bottle and the books." Alan looked up from one of his new books.

"Okay, Robbie, what's our next highway?" Nick said.

"We stay on I-79 until we turn off to Buckhannon on 33 all the way to Elkins."

"You see, Mom? He could find his way home by himself."

Barb shook her head. "Tell us about meeting your grandmother, Rosa," she said.

"She was tired, and she hurted a lot, didn't she, Papa? Sister gave her medicine to make her sleepy, but she kissed me, and I kissed her, too. She liked that. I asked Jesus to help me, and He did. I climbed right up on her bed and kissed her gently like I do with Baby Michael. Didn't I, Papa?"

"Yes, you did, Rosita, and you made her very happy."

"I kissed her hello and goodbye. She called Papa 'Nickie.' He was her little boy a long time ago."

Barb caught Nick's eye in the rear-view mirror. "I hope she didn't wear her out by talking non-stop! Did she talk like this the entire trip?"

Nick chuckled. "Pretty much, unless she was asleep. But she was quiet and gentle with her *abuela*, and Mother Joanna said she was a very good girl. I was proud of my girl. She brought great joy to her grandmother, to the sisters, and to her Papa. I was sad, but she helped me pick out presents, and we ate tacos and had lots of fun in the ocean."

As they slowed to turn on 33, Nick asked, "Anybody need to use the bathroom?" Ella and Barb both needed to stop, and Michael was ready to eat, so they pulled off. "I'm glad you brought the family," Nick said as they carried sandwiches to a picnic table.

"I wouldn't have survived if I tried to leave any one of them home. They made up their minds they were coming to get their Daddy. Or do we call you Papa now?"

"*Abuela* told me to love my papa for her every day," Rosa said. "Mommy, why don't I speak Spanic? Papa and *Abuela* speak Spanic, and Mother Joanna says I look like her, and I'm Spanic, too, amn't I?"

Barb looked over at Nick as they both smothered grins. "Honey, children speak the language they are surrounded by in their homes," she explained. "You know Emily in your class at church?" Rosa nodded. "Do you remember when her parents flew across the world to China? They brought her from a country far, far away. She was born in China, but she speaks English because it's all she hears at home. But it seems to me you have learned a lot of Spanish in a few days, and Daddy could teach you how to speak Spanish."

"Would you, Papa?" Rosa begged.

"I'm taking Spanish next semester, Rosa. We can all learn together," Robbie said. "I figure I can keep him from having secrets with Mom if I learn to speak Spanish."

Nick grinned at Barb. "We're in trouble now, Mom."

"I hope his high school Spanish class doesn't teach him some of the words you've taught me!" Barb said.

"Hey, I'm getting me a dictionary!" Robbie threatened. He laughed as his mother blushed furiously.

When they pulled in at home, Robbie grabbed the luggage, giving Alan the lighter packages. Nick got Michael while Barb helped Rosa and Ella out of their car seats. Once they got into the house, they sorted bags.

"Quick, quick now. Up to the tub," Barb said. "Daddy will be home all day tomorrow. We need to let Michael run around a bit, Nick. He's done well in the car. He likes the steering wheel you got him."

Upstairs, Ella and Rosa played in the tub. Ella dried off her little sister and helped her into her jammies. After hugs and prayers, the girls snuggled into their beds, but Barb and Nick heard them talk and giggle for a long time.

Robbie was on the phone, but Alan stayed buried in his new fantasy adventure book. Nick got on the floor, chasing Michael around the couch. The tot giggled. He crawled first one way and then turned and crawled back the other way. Finally, Barb laughed and picked him up. "That's enough. Off to bed with you!" He tried to protest, but he rubbed his eyes and lay content on Nick's shoulder as his papa rocked him to sleep.

Barb came out of the shower, her eyes dancing. Nick grinned at her on his way by to tuck in Michael in the crib upstairs. She shivered, wondering how he could send a hot flame through the core of her body with a glance and a smile. When he got out of the shower, she was coming downstairs after making her own rounds. She swiped a stray curl back from her eyes and sank on the bed. Nick caressed her with his eyes, and she smiled at him.

"It's okay to close the door?" he asked. She nodded. He crossed the room, closed the door, and turned to make his way toward her. He placed his hands on both sides of her face and leaned in for a kiss. He paused and grinned.

"What?" she asked.

"I love the way when I lean toward your lips, your mouth opens like a little bird." Barb flushed. "Do you know what that says to me?"

"Do I want to know?"

"It says 'welcome home, Nick.' You make me feel like I've come home."

"In that case, welcome home, Nick," Barb whispered, and she opened her mouth for his kiss.

Nick took her into his arms and covered her mouth hungrily with his own. He never ceased to be amazed at her response. Barb wrapped her arms about his neck and drew him down on the bed. "I feel God's love in your arms, *amada*," he whispered.

Available Now:

NICK'S HEART
(*In Your Arms* Series Book 2)

Dear reader:

Thank you for interest in and purchase of *Nick's Choice (In Your Arms Series Book 1)*. If you enjoyed this book, please be sure to obtain a copy of *Nick's Heart (In Your Arms Series Book 2)*, available now at all major book retailers (synopsis below).

Sincerely,

Van Rye Publishing, LLC

NICK'S HEART (Book 2 of the *In Your Arms* series) is a
story of inspiration:

NICK COSTAS, having coped with and overcome his rough upbringing in abusive foster homes and on the streets of L.A., having undergone a spiritual transformation, and having become a loving and passionate father of a family of seven, continues to inspire those around him but with newfound struggles. Nick now struggles to accept and perfect his newfound fame as an author and a touring speaker while also trying to build a safe haven home for boys. And he struggles to balance these new gigs with his health and with the wants and needs of his ever-changing family.

Join Nick on his journey of inspiration as he transitions from a successful music producer and a loving and spiritual father of a family of seven to an inspiration to those around him. Follow him as he inspires others through his speaking engagements and his love and passion for his wife Barb, his five children, and scripture. Follow him as he directly and indirectly guides his friends and his children through their own courtships, love lives, and marriages. And follow him as he works to build a Home for Boys as a place where struggling youths like he was can have the same opportunities for redemption and success that he experienced.

If you enjoyed the stories of personal redemption, spiritual transformation, and loving couples, parents, and families contained in Book 1 of the *In Your Arms* series (*Nick's Choice*), then you will enjoy continuing to follow Nick as he uses those stories to inspire others in Book 2 of the series (*Nick's Heart*). The story of Nick Costas, as told in this book, is here to continue inspiring and guiding you in your own personal, parental, and family life.

From the Publisher

Thank You from the Publisher

Van Rye Publishing, LLC ("VRP") sincerely thanks you for your interest in and purchase of this book.

If you enjoyed this book or found it useful, please consider taking a moment to support the author and get word out to other readers like you by leaving a rating or review of the book at its product page at your favorite online book retailer.

Thank you!

Resources from the Publisher

Van Rye Publishing, LLC ("VRP") offers the following resources to writers and to readers.

For writers who enjoyed this book or found it useful, please consider having VRP edit, format, or fully publish your own book manuscript. You can find out more, and contact the publisher directly, by visiting VRP's website: www.vanryepublishing.com.

For readers who enjoyed this book or found it useful, please consider signing up to have VRP notify you when books like this one are available at a limited-time discounted price, some as low as $0.99. You can sign up to receive such notifications by visiting the following web address: http://eepurl.com/cERow9.

For anyone who enjoyed this book or found it useful, if you have not already done so, please again consider leaving a rating or review of this book at its product page at your favorite online book retailer. These ratings and reviews are themselves extremely valuable resources for writers and for readers like you. VRP hopes you will please take a moment to share your thoughts about this book with others.

Thank you again!

About the Author

CHARLOTTE S. SNEAD holds a Bachelor of Arts in Psychology degree from Duke University and a Master of Social Work degree from the University of North Carolina. OakTara published her first three books: *His Brother's Wife*, in 2012, and *Recovered and Free* and *Invisible Wounds*, in 2014. Charlotte later received Jan-Carol Publishing's Believe and Achieve Award for her novel *A Place to Live*, the first of a scheduled five-book series. While working on the remaining books in the series, she also published her first children's book, *Deano the Dino Goes to the Doctor*, in 2018.

Charlotte married her husband, Dr. Joseph Snead, in 1962. They raised five children and a foster daughter and now proudly grandparent ten boys and one girl. One of their children and four of their grandchildren are adopted. Charlotte was the daughter of a career military officer, who served in WWII, and Dr. Snead served in Vietnam. Their son was a career military officer, so Charlotte has a special place in her heart for our military.

In keeping with Charlotte's strong belief in and celebration of the joys of marriage, family, and writing, she maintains a blog (at www.charlottesnead.com), which has the tagline "Sacred Passion—It's God's Idea." Please feel free to contact her there.

www.ingramcontent.com/pod-product-compliance
Lightning Source LLC
Chambersburg PA
CBHW071133170626
46809CB00002B/605